THE
ELEVENTH
PLAGUE

ELEV
PL

THE ENTH AGUE

JEFF HIRSCH

SCHOLASTIC PRESS
NEW YORK

Library of Congress Cataloging-in-Publication Data

Hirsch, Jeff.
The eleventh plague / Jeff Hirsch. — 1st ed.
p. cm.
Summary: Twenty years after the start of the war that caused the
Collapse, fifteen-year-old Stephen, his father, and grandfather
travel post-Collapse America scavenging, but when his grand-
father dies and his father decides to risk everything to save the
lives of two strangers, Stephen's life is turned upside down.
ISBN 978-0-545-29014-2
[1. Survival — Fiction. 2. Science fiction.] I. Title.
PZ7.H59787E1 2011
[Fic] — dc22

2010048966

10 9 8 7 6 5 4 3 2 1   11 12 13 14 15
Printed in the U.S.A.   23
First edition, September 2011

To Gretchen.
You never stop changing my world for the better.

PART ONE

ONE

I was sitting at the edge of the clearing, trying not to stare at the body on the ground in front of me. Dad had said we'd be done before dark, but it had been hours since the sun went down and he was still only waist deep in the hole, throwing shovelfuls of dirt over his shoulder.

Even though it was covered in the burlap shroud I could see how wasted Grandpa's body was. He'd always been thin, but the infection had taken another ten pounds off him before he went. His hand fell out from a tear in the burlap. Shadowed from the moonlight, it was a desert plain, the tracks of the veins like dry riverbeds winding up the crags of his knuckles. A gold Marine Corps ring sat on one finger, but it barely fit anymore.

Dad's shovel chewed through rocks and clay with an awful scrape. Finally I couldn't stand it anymore and escaped into the thicket of trees that surrounded us, stumbling through the darkness until I came to the edge of the hill we were camped on.

Far below were the slouching ruins of an old mall. Rows of cars, rusting in the moist air, sat in the parking lot, still waiting for the doors to open. Beyond the mall, the arches of a McDonald's sign hovered like a ghost.

I remembered seeing it for the first time, ten years ago. I was five and then the sign had towered in its red and gold plastic. It seemed gigantic and beautiful. One trillion served. Now fingers of vines crept up its base, slowly consuming more and more of the rusty metal.

I wondered how long it would be until they made it to the top and the whole thing finally collapsed. Ten years? Twenty? Would I be Dad's age? Grandpa's?

I took a breath of the cool air, but the image of Grandpa's hand lying there on the ground loomed in the back of my mind. How could it be so still?

Grandpa's hand only made sense in motion, rearing back, the gold ring flashing as it crashed into my cheek. He had so many rules. I could never remember them all. The simple act of setting up camp was a minefield of mistakes, and Dad and I both seemed to trip over every one. I could still feel the sting of the metal and the rasp of his calloused skin.

But that's over, I told myself. *We're on our own now.* Grandpa's fist was just another bit of wreckage we were leaving behind.

"Stephen!"

My chest tightened. It wasn't cold enough for a fire, but I didn't want to go back with nothing to do so I collected an armful of wood and brush on the way. I dropped it all between our sleeping bags, then leaned over the tinder, scraping the two pieces of my fire starter together until a spark caught. Once I had a proper campfire, I sat back on my heels to watch it burn.

"Think it's deep enough yet?"

Dad was leaning against the wall of the grave, his body slick with sweat and dirt. I nodded.

"Come on, then. Bring the ropes."

Once I helped Dad out of the hole, we knelt on either side of Grandpa's body and drew lengths of rope under his knees and back. Dad started to lift him, but I didn't move. Grandpa's hand, one finger crowned with gold, was only inches from me.

"What about his ring?"

The ends of the ropes went limp in Dad's hands. The ring glinted in the firelight. I knew he stung from it just like I did.

"There's gotta be a half ounce of solid gold there," I said. "If not more."

"Let's just do this."

"But don't we have to — ?"

"Stephen, now," Dad snapped.

We lowered Grandpa into the grave and then, before I could even pull the ropes out, Dad began filling it in again. I knew I should stop him. We could have traded Grandpa's ring for food, new clothes, even bullets. Dad knew that as well as I did.

When the grave was filled, the shovel slipped from Dad's hands and he fell to his knees, doubling over with his arms around his stomach. His body seized with small tremors.

Oh God. Don't let him be sick too.

I reached out to him. "Dad?"

When he turned, the light caught tears cutting channels through the dirt on his face. I turned toward the woods as he sobbed, giving him what privacy I could, a knot twisting tighter and tighter inside me. When he was done I laid his favorite flannel shirt over his shoulders. Dad drew it around him with a shaky breath, then searched the stars through red, swollen eyes.

"I swear," he exhaled. "That man was a purebred son of a bitch."

"Maybe we should put that on his tombstone."

Dad surprised me with a short, explosive laugh. I sat beside him, edging my body alongside the steady in and out of his breath. He draped his arm, exhausted, over my shoulder. It felt good, but still the knot in my stomach refused to unravel.

"Dad?"

"Yeah, Steve?"

"We'll be okay, won't we? Without him?" When Dad said nothing I moved out from under his arm and looked up at him.

"I mean . . . nothing's going to change. Right?"

Dad fixed his eyes past me and onto the dark trail we would start down the next morning.

"No," he said, his words rising up like ghosts, thin and pale and empty. "Nothing's ever going to change."

TWO

We clawed our way out of our sleeping bags just before sunrise, greeted each other with sleepy-eyed grumbles, and got to work.

I dealt with Dad's backpack first, making sure the waterproof bag inside was intact before loading in our first-aid kit and the few matches we had left. I did it carefully, still half expecting to hear Grandpa's voice explode behind me as he wrenched the bag out of my hand and showed me how to do it right. I paused. Breathed. *He's gone,* I told myself. I reached back in and felt for our one photograph, making sure it was still there, like I did every morning, and then moved on.

As I arranged the clothes in my pack, my hand hit the spine of one of my books. *The Lord of the Rings.* I had found it years before in a Walmart, buried underneath a pile of torn baby clothes and the dry leaves that had blown in when the walls had fallen. I'd read it start to finish six times, always waiting until after Grandpa went to sleep. He'd said the only thing books were good for was kindling.

I flipped through the book's crinkled pages and placed it at the very top of the bag so it would be the first thing my fingers touched when I reached inside. Doing this gave me a rebel thrill. I didn't have to worry about Grandpa finding it now.

When I went to water our donkey, Paolo, I found Dad staring down at something in the back of the wagon — Grandpa's hunting rifle. It was lying right where he'd left it two days earlier, when he'd become too weak to lift it anymore.

Dad reached down and ran the tips of his fingers along the rifle's scarred body.

"So . . . this is mine now."

He lifted the rifle into his arms and slid the bolt back. One silver round lay there, sleek and deadly.

"Guess so," I said.

Dad forced a little smile as he hung the rifle from his shoulder. "I'll have to figure out how to work it, then, huh?" he joked, a dim twinkle in his eye. "Come on, pal. Let's get out of here."

As Dad started down the trail, I turned for a last look at Grandpa's grave. How many such mounds had we seen as we walked from one end of the country to the other, year after year? Sometimes it was one or two at a time, scattered like things misplaced. Sometimes there were clusters of hundreds, even thousands, littering the outskirts of dead cities.

It was still hard to believe his death could have come so quickly. After all that he had survived — the war, the Collapse, the chaos that followed — to be taken by . . . what? An infection? Pneumonia? The flu? We had no idea. He was like a thousand-year-old oak, scarred and twisted, that was somehow chopped down in a day. It made me feel sick inside, but some part of me was glad. Like we had been freed.

I was about to ask if Dad wanted to make some kind of marker before we left, but he had already moved down the trail.

"Come on, P," I said, tugging on Paolo's lead and guiding him away.

The sun rose as we moved off the hill, pushing some of the chill out of the air. We passed the mall and crossed a highway. On the other side there was a church with the blackened wreck of an army truck sitting in front of it. Beside that were tracts of abandoned houses, their crumbling walls and smashed windows reminding me of row after row of skulls.

It was almost impossible to imagine the lives of the people who'd lived and worked in these places before the Collapse. The war had started five years before I was born, and over nothing, really. Dad said a couple of American students backpacking in China were caught where they shouldn't have been and mistaken for spies. He said it wouldn't have been that big a deal, except that at around the same time the oil was running out, and the Earth was getting warmer, and a hundred other things were going wrong. Dad said everyone was scared and that fear had made the world into a huge pile of dried-out tinder — all it needed was a spark. Once the fire caught it didn't take more than a couple years to reduce everything to ruins. All that survived were a few stubborn stragglers like us, holding on by our fingernails.

We made it through what was left of the town, then came to a wide run of grass, framed by trees with leaves that had begun to turn from vivid shades of orange and red to muddy brown. We shifted east, then dropped into the steady pace we'd maintain until it was time to jog south for the final leg.

"We're gonna be fine," Dad said, finally breaking the silence of the morning. "You know that, right?"

The knot from the previous night tightened in my throat. I swallowed it away and said that I did.

"The haul isn't too bad," Dad continued, glancing back at the wagon, which was filled with a few pieces of glass and some rusted scrap metal. "And hey, who knows? Remember the time we came across that stash of Star Wars stuff in — where was it? Columbus? Maybe we'll wake up tomorrow morning and find, I don't know, a helicopter. In perfect working order! Gassed up and ready to go!"

"Casey'd probably like that more than a bunch of old Star Wars toys."

"Well, who knew the little nerd preferred Battlestar Galactica?"

Casey, or General Casey as he liked to call himself, was the king of the Southern Gathering. His operation sat at the top of what was once called Florida and was where Dad and I traded whatever salvage we could find for things like clothes and medicine and bullets.

"We still got ten pairs of socks out of it," I said. "How many do you think we could get for a helicopter?"

"What? Are you kidding? We wouldn't trade it!"

"Not even for socks?"

"Hell no. We'd become freelance helicopter pilots! Imagine what people would give us to take a ride in the thing." Dad shot his fist in the air. "It'd be a gold mine, I tell ya!"

Dad laughed and so did I. It was a little forced, but I thought maybe it was like a promise, a way to remind ourselves that things would be okay again soon.

It grew warmer as the morning passed. Around noon we settled onto a dilapidated park bench and pulled out our lunch of venison jerky and hardtack. Paolo munched nearby, the metal bits of his harness tinkling gently.

Dad grew quiet. He took a few bites and then stared west, into the woods. Once I was done eating I pulled a needle and thread out of my pack and set to fixing a tear in the elbow of my sweatshirt.

"You should eat," I said, drawing the needle through the greasy fabric and pulling it tight.

"Not hungry, I guess."

A flock of birds swarmed across the sky, cawing loudly before settling on the power lines that ran like a seam down our path. I wondered if they had been able to do that before the Collapse, back when electricity had actually moved through the wires. And if not, which brave bird had been the first one to give it a shot once the lights had all gone out?

Distracted, I let the needle lance into my fingertip. I recoiled and sucked on it until the blood stopped. I heard Grandpa's raspy voice. *Pay attention to what you're doing, Stephen. It doesn't take a genius to concentrate.* I leaned back over the sleeve, trying to keep the stitches tight like Mom had taught me.

"I keep expecting to see him," Dad said. "Hear him."

I pulled the thread to a stop and looked over my shoulder at Dad.

"Was he different?" I asked. "Before?"

Dad leaned his head back and peered up into the sky.

"On the weekends he'd take me to the movies. He worked a lot so that was our time together. We'd see everything. Didn't matter what. Stupid things. It wasn't about the movie, it was about us being there. But then everything fell apart and your grandma died . . . I guess he didn't want to live through that pain again so he became what he thought he had to become to keep the rest of us alive."

Even though it was still fairly warm out, Dad shivered. He wrapped his coat and his arms tight around his body, then stared at the ground and shook his head.

"I'm so sorry, Steve," he said, a tired quiver in his voice. "I'm sorry I ever let him —"

"It's okay," I said.

I snapped the thread with my teeth and yanked on the fabric. It held. Good enough. I slipped the sweatshirt on and zipped it up. "You ready?"

Dad didn't move. He was focused on a stand of reedy trees across the way, almost as though he recognized something in the deep swirl of twigs and dry leaves. When I looked all I saw was a rough path, barely wide enough for our wagon.

"You find that helicopter?"

Dad's shoulders rose and fell and he let out a little puff of breath, the empty shape of a laugh.

"Better get going then, huh? We can start south here."

There were heavy shadows, like smears of ash, under Dad's red-rimmed eyes as he turned to me. For a second it was like he was looking at a stranger, but then he pulled his lips into a grin and slapped me on the knee.

"Reckon so, pardner," he said as he lumbered up off the bench and hung the rifle on his shoulder once again. "Reckon it's time to get on down the road."

I took Paolo's lead and gave it a pull. Dad hovered by the bench, staring back at the path west, almost hungrily, his thumb tucked under the rifle's strap.

I stayed Paolo and waited. What was he doing?

But then, in a flash, it was gone, and Dad shook his head, pulling himself away from that other path and joining me. He ruffled my hair as he passed by, and we began what would be the last leg of our yearly trip south.

"Hey! Look at that."

We were moving across a grass-covered plain. Dad was out front, facing west, shading his eyes from the glare. I stepped up next to him, but all I saw was a dark hill. It seemed out of place in the middle of the flat plain, but was otherwise unremarkable.

"What is it?" I asked.

Dad raised the rifle's scope to his eye. "Well, it ain't a helicopter," he said as he handed me the rifle. "Looks like a bomber."

"No. Really?" I lifted the rifle and peered through the scope. That's what it was, all right. About forty feet tall. Whole, it probably would have been over a hundred and fifty feet long, but it was broken up into two sections at the wing, with a long section in back and a shorter one up front. The whole thing was covered in dirt, vines, and a mantle of rust.

The remnants of a cleared stand of trees lay between us and the plane. It looked like it had been cut down only a year or so ago. I figured that must have been why we hadn't seen the plane the last time we'd come this way. How long had it been sitting there? Fifteen years? More?

I drew the scope down along the length of the plane, marveling at its size, until I came to the tail where I could make out a big white star.

"It's American," I said, lowering the rifle.

Dad nodded. "B-88," he said. "Probably heading to Atlanta. Or Memphis. I don't think it crashed, though — it's pretty intact. Looks like it tried to land and failed. Must have been forced down somehow."

I waited for him to make the next move, but he went silent after that, staring at it. Adults were always weird when it came to talking about the Collapse. Embarrassed, I thought, like kids caught breaking something that wasn't theirs.

"Well . . . we better check it out. Right?"

"Guess we better. Come on."

We got to the plane about an hour later. The two halves sat just feet from each other, like pieces of a cracked egg. The plane's wings were hunched over and crumpled. A bright bloom of flowers had grown up around them, taking root and shining purple in the sun.

I led Paolo over to where he could munch on some flowers and followed Dad to the opening. The plane had split in two just behind the cockpit, which was closed off with loads of twisted metal. To our right was the empty bomb bay. I leaned in, squinting past the wreckage. It was bright at the mouth of the steel cave, but toward the back it grew dark enough that I could only make out a jumble of broken metal covered with dirt and vines and weeds.

"I don't know," I said. "Doesn't look like there's anything here. Maybe we should —"

"It's gonna be fine," Dad said. "We'll make it quick. In and out, okay?"

"We'll need the flashlight."

Dad tugged at the end of his beard, then nodded. I pulled the light off the back of the wagon and rejoined him. There was a narrow catwalk that led alongside the bomb bay to the back of the plane. Dad stepped up onto it and shuffled crablike down its length. I crept along behind him until we came to the remains of a steel bulkhead separating the compartments. It had been mostly torn away, but we still had to crouch down low to get through it.

It was humid inside, and musty smelling. I slapped the flashlight on its side until its beam ran down the length of the plane.

The back section was lined with a series of workstations, alcoves where I imagined soldiers performing their various duties. All that was left of them were welded-in steel shelves and short partitions. All the chairs, electronics, and wiring had been ripped out long ago by people like us. Vines crept up the walls and hung from the ceiling. Every so often some rusty metal lump emerged from underneath the plants, like the face of someone drowning.

"Why would it have been going to Atlanta?" I asked, hoping to drive the eerie silence out of the air. Dad's answer didn't help.

"P Eleven."

I shivered as he said it.

"We tried to quarantine the big cities, but the people inside didn't want to be cooped up with the sick, so the government decided to burn them out."

"They bombed their own people?"

"Didn't see any other choice, I guess. If it got out . . . 'Course, in the end it didn't matter. Got out anyway."

After that first spark the war escalated fast. It was only a few months before the United States launched some of its nukes at China and its allies. P11H3 was what China came back with. Everybody just called it P11 or the Eleventh Plague. It was nothing more than a souped-up strain of the flu, but it ate through the country like wildfire, infecting and then killing nearly everyone it touched. The last reliable news anyone heard before the stations went off the air said it had killed hundreds of millions in the United States alone.

I cleared my throat to chase out the shakes. We had to stay focused on the task. The faster we got done, the faster we'd be on our way. "See anything worthwhile?" I called out.

Dad appeared in the beam of my flashlight, blocking the light out of his eyes with his hand. "Looks like it's been pretty picked over already. Let's check farther back."

We rummaged through the rubble but only found the remains of some seats and a few crumbling logbooks. There were lockers along the walls but they were rusted shut or empty. Useless. It was as though we were wandering through the remains of a dinosaur, picking through its bones.

"Last of its kind," Dad said, patting the wall. "These things went into production right before the Collapse."

The Collapse followed in the wake of P11. With so few people left alive, everything just shut down. Factories. Hospitals. The government. The military crumbled. Power stations blew one by one until the electricity went out countrywide. It was like America had been wired up to one big switch and the Eleventh Plague was the hand that reached up and clicked it all off. Millions more must have died in the darkness and neglect that followed.

"See anything?" Dad asked.

I shook my head. "Nah. Let's get out of here, okay?"

"All right, all right." Dad patted my shoulder as we started back for the bulkhead. "Hey, what's that?"

"What?"

Dad knelt down by a metal locker at my feet. It was partially hidden under the overhang of one of the workstations, right by a small crack in the plane's skin that let in a finger of sunlight. Dad pushed a cover of weeds and dirt out of the way.

"It's just an old locker," I said. "If there was anything in it, someone would have taken it already."

"Maybe they didn't see it. Come here and give me a hand."

I looked up through the bulkhead to the open air outside. We were so close. "It's rusted shut. We'll never get it open."

"We can't get careless when it comes to salvage, Stephen," Dad snapped. "Now come on. Pull on it when I do, okay? On three. One. Two. Pull!"

We threw our backs into it and, surprising both of us, the lid screeched loudly and popped off, throwing us on our butts with a heavy thud.

"Ha! See? Me and you, kid, we can do anything!" Dad pulled himself back up and leaned over the open locker, rubbing his palms together. "So, what've we got here?"

At first glance it wasn't much. Dad handed back a thick blue blanket that was worth keeping. There was a moment of excitement when he found stacks of prepackaged military rations, but they were torn up and past their prime. Worthless.

"Okay. Can we go now?"

"In a second. We —" Dad froze, his eyes going wide. "Oh my God."

I scrambled to join him. "What? What is it?"

He reached deep into the locker and struggled with something I couldn't see.

"Dad?"

His back flexed and he managed to lift whatever it was into the light.

"What is —"

It was a metal can. Not one of the little ones we used to find lining the shelves of abandoned grocery stores, but a big one. Forty-eight ounces at least. Dad turned it around so that the light shone on the label. It read, simply, in black letters: PEARS.

"Fruit," Dad said, his voice thick with awe. "Good Lord, it's canned fruit. Jesus, how long has it been?"

Two years at least. Dad had saved a can of pears for my thirteenth birthday. Since then if we had fruit, it was a runty crab apple or a nearly juiceless orange. My stomach cramped and my mouth watered at the memory of those pears and the sweet juice they sat in.

Dad set the can down between us, then scrambled into his back pocket for the can opener. He was about to crack it open when my hand shot out and snatched his wrist.

He looked up at me, his eyes looking almost crazed. "Steve —"

"We can't."

"What do you mean, we can't?"

"What would Casey give us for this?"

"Stephen," Dad laughed. "Look, I don't know, but —"

"We have *nothing* in that wagon out there. Could we get bullets? New clothes? Batteries for the flashlight?"

"But . . ." Dad scrambled for a defense, but nothing came. His eyes dropped to the can opener, considering it a moment before his hand went limp and it clattered onto the floor.

"I mean . . . we have to be smart," I said. "Right?"

Dad nodded once, looking exhausted.

"You're just like your grandfather," he said.

It hit me like a hammer in the chest. Before I knew what I was doing, I grabbed the can opener and stabbed its blade into the can, working it around. Dad tried to stop me, but before he could, I had the lid off and was tossing it aside. I dug my hand in and pulled out a fat slice of pear, holding it up into the narrow beam of light. It glistened like a jewel. Perfect and impossible.

I paused, my heart pounding.

"Go ahead," Dad urged. "Take it."

The flesh of the pear snapped in my mouth when my teeth hit it. There was an explosion of juice, so much of it and so sweet. I chewed slowly, savoring it, then dug my hand in the can and shoved a slice at Dad before taking another for myself. We devoured them, all of them, grunting with pleasure. There was still some part of me, some tiny voice in the back of my head, screaming that it was wrong, but I kept stuffing pears into my mouth until the mean, raspy voice receded.

We ate all the pears and split the juice inside, then we lay back, our bellies full and our mouths and hands sticky with sweet juice. Dad had this happy, dazed look on his face, and I was sure that he, like me, was replaying the moment over and over again in his head, committing the feel of the fruit in his mouth and its sweetness to memory.

I lifted the empty can into the flashlight beam. Its dusty sides were splattered with congealing syrup. Stray pieces of flesh clung to the insides. Empty, it was as light as air. The dazed excitement of the pears began to fade, and some dark, clammy thing took its place, creeping through me. The sweetness of the pears turned bitter. My mouth ached. In an hour or two we'd be hungry again, the memory of the fruit would fade, and we'd still need clothes, bullets, batteries, and food. Winter would still be coming. I could hear Grandpa's voice as clearly as if he was sitting right next to me.

Stupid. Wasteful.

I wished I could smash the can to pieces on the floor, tear it apart, the metal shards slicing up my hands as punishment for being so thoughtless.

"Where are you going?"

I had climbed out of the plane and was walking down to the end of one flower-covered wing. It had grown darker while we were inside. A curtain of dirty gray clouds blocked out the sun and there was a thick tingling in the air.

"Stephen?"

I picked one of the flowers off the wing's edge and rolled it around in my hand. It left a purple smear of blood on my fingertips.

"We should get moving," I said.

The rusty skin of the plane flexed as Dad leaned against it behind me.

"You ever wonder what's out there?" he asked.

When I turned around, he had his hands stuffed in his pockets and was looking over his shoulder to the west, just as casual as you please. A small range of mountains hung over the woods, gray and misty-looking in the distance.

"I always think maybe there's, like, some quiet place. Somewhere you could build a little house. Hunt. Fish." A dreamy grin drifted across his face. "Maybe even somewhere we could find other people like us."

I kicked at the dirt. "Find slavers maybe. Red Army. US Army. Bandits."

"We've stayed out of their way before."

I shot a sharp look across the space between us. Was he really talking about this? Leaving the trail? I tossed the flower into the grass and worked it into the ground with the toe of my boot.

"We should get going," I said, "and cover some more ground before dark." I tried to push past him so I could gather Paolo, but Dad stopped me, his palm flat in the center of my chest. I looked straight across at him. Now that I was fifteen, I was nearly as tall as he was.

"Listen, it's just you and me now, Steve. Maybe this is our chance."

"Our chance for what?"

"A life. A home."

Our nearly empty wagon and all the miles we still had to cover that day loomed just over Dad's shoulder. I heard Grandpa's voice, the ice-cold rasp of it, clear as day.

"This *is* our home."

I knocked Dad's hand off my chest and pushed past him, ducking back into the plane and through the bulkhead. My knees slammed into the dirt and rust, and I dug around for the flashlight and the can and its lid.

A quiet place. A home. It was a fantasy, same as the helicopter. Dad knew that as well as I did, so why would he even bring it up? What was he thinking? First it was the ring, then the pears, and now this.

I paused, feeling the bitterness of the words turning through my head. Was it true what he said? Was I like Grandpa? Part of me cringed at the thought, but who had kept us alive all these years?

"Stephen!"

What now? I hauled myself up and out of the plane to find Dad squinting off in the direction we'd come from. There was a puff of smoke rising into the air a few miles back.

"What's going — ?"

"Rifle," he commanded. "Now!"

I snatched the rifle off the wagon. Dad raised the scope to his eye and tracked it north across the horizon until he found what he was looking for.

"People coming this way. With a vehicle."

He was trying to be calm, but I knew the hitch he got in his voice when he was scared. No announcement could possibly have been worse. One of Grandpa's absolute, unbreakable rules was that if we saw other people, people we didn't know, we were to avoid them at all costs. Other people meant trouble. Other people with a working vehicle meant even more trouble.

"What do we do?" I asked, my heart pounding in my ears. "Run?"

"We're on foot. They'd be on us in a second."

"So what, then?"

In answer, Dad grabbed Paolo by his reins and drew him around to the opposite side of the plane, out of sight. He tied his lead to a jutting piece of metal and told me to get our backpacks. I grabbed them and followed Dad into the plane.

"All the way to the back," he said, pushing us past the bomb bay and again through the bulkhead. We stumbled into the last of the stripped workstations and crouched down. We were hidden but still had a straight view through the bulkhead and to the rent in the plane ahead.

"We'll wait them out," Dad said, stuffing our packs behind us. "They'll probably do just what we did — look around and head on their way."

"But what if they don't?"

"They will," he insisted.

My chest seized with nerves. I knew he was only trying to make me feel better, but he was no surer than I was.

I swallowed hard. "You're right," I said. "You're right. They will. They'll just go right on by."

But then it started to rain.

THREE

It came lightly at first, finger taps, barely noticeable, but within minutes it was a real storm. Rain slammed against the roof of the plane. Wind howled through it. We were crouched down behind the workstation, legs cramping and hearts pounding.

"Maybe they rode by us," I said.

"Would you? In this?"

There was a flash of lightning and thunder that made both of us jump, and the rain seemed to double in power in an instant. Back where we were a steady but light spray of water squeezed through the tiny cracks in the airframe, but it was a waterfall up by the opening. Water crashed down in a bright curtain and coursed down the floor of the plane, pooling at our feet and surrounding us in a cold, oily muck. I peeked over the edge of the partition, pushing a wet strand of hair out of my face. My eyes had adjusted to the dimness and I could see the entrance to the plane clearly. Nothing there.

"It's okay," Dad said. "I think they really did go —"

The waterfall split in two as the barrel of a black rifle pushed through and scanned the interior. I jerked back but Dad took my elbow, steadying me. We were about a hundred feet back and hidden. With the dark and the rain, it was a safe bet they couldn't see or hear us. Still, my hands quaked as the rifle eased forward and two men came in behind it. One man held the rifle while the other followed with what I first thought were horse's reins. As he stepped farther inside, I saw what was really at the other end.

The reins ran from the man's hand to cuffs around the wrists of a boy and a woman, and then up to thick collars on their necks. The two captives moved with the fearful slowness of people who expected to be beaten.

"Slavers." Dad spat it out, like the word itself was foul.

If there was any group we avoided the most, it was them. Some were ex-military, some were just brutal scum. We saw them skulking around the edges of the trade gatherings like a bad disease. They mostly kept to themselves, but as far as we knew, they ranged through-out the country taking whoever they could and selling them to scattered militia groups, the few surviving plantation owners down south, or even the Chinese.

The man with the reins pointed for them to go sit up against one wall, then tied the reins to the edge of the bomb bay. The woman and the boy never raised their heads to face him, never spoke, just shuffled to their places like broken animals. The slavers situated themselves in a dry spot in the bomb bay. One of the men pulled the cap off a flare and the entire plane exploded in a flash of red light. Dad and I ducked down behind the partition until the light lowered and we smelled the smoke of a small fire.

It was still dark where we were, so I took a chance and peeked around the edge of the partition. The men were gathered around their fire with a deck of cards and a bottle of liquor. Their clothes looked military to me. One was black with long dreadlocks and a thin beard.

The other was white and immense, with bull-like shoulders and a jag-ged scar that ran from his temple down his cheek, disappearing at his jaw. It glowed pale in the firelight.

Dad was up on his knees beside me. His eyes were narrowed and his lips were a tense line, but it wasn't the slavers he was watching.

The woman and the boy were illuminated by the ragged edge of the fire. It magnified the hollows of their eye sockets and the cruel thinness of their birdlike arms. The woman had scraggly hair and was wearing a short white dress that clung to her. She was so thin I could see the shadows of her ribs. The boy was smaller than me, barefoot, and wear-ing torn-up jeans and a filthy T-shirt. Across from them, the men drank and played cards, their laughter mixing with the driving rain and peals of thunder.

Dad was holding the rifle just below the edge of the partition, grip-ping it so tightly his knuckles were white as bone. His finger was on the trigger.

I grabbed his wrist. "We don't get involved," I whispered. "Grandpa said —"

"Grandpa is gone," he hissed.

I glared down into the cold muck, my arms wound tightly around my chest. We needed to stay right there, still and quiet, until the rain passed and they were all gone. The woman. The boy. We didn't know them. They weren't our responsibility.

Dad pulled the rifle back and huddled behind the partition with me. "I'm not saying we fight them," he whispered. "They're drinking. We give them time to get drunk and pass out. When they do, we untie the woman and boy on our way out and let them go. That's all."

Dad's hand fell on my shoulder, but I pushed it away.

"I know what Grandpa would say," Dad said. "But we don't have to be like him. Not if we don't want to."

I peeked around the dripping edge of the partition. The boy tried to squirm his way deeper into the crook of the woman's arm, but since her hands were tied, she couldn't comfort him. She let her head fall back against the wall. Her mouth hung open and she stared upward, blankly. The boy fell across his own knees, his spine sticking out like a range of knobby mountains.

A spark of anger flared inside me. If we had ignored the plane, or if we had just taken that can and gone, we would have been setting up camp miles from here. Dad would be cooking dinner and I'd be brushing Paolo, getting ready for the next day's hike.

"Stephen . . ."

Anger was a compact burning thing in my stomach. I prayed he knew what he was doing.

I nodded. I couldn't bring myself to speak.

After that, all we could do was wait.

FOUR

Once the men fell asleep Dad and I slipped on our packs, then unfolded ourselves from behind the panel. It helped that the rain hadn't slacked off. The constant thrumming echoed through the metal coffin of the plane, helping mask our movements.

We crept across the uneven floor, squeezed through the bulkhead, and emerged on the other side. As we moved into the firelight, the woman nearly gasped, but Dad held up his hands to show we were no harm. She glanced over at the sleeping men. For a second I thought she was going to warn them, but then she sat back and watched us through narrowed eyes. Dad slipped his hunting knife out of its sheath and handed it to me. Then he turned and leveled his rifle at the sleeping men.

As I approached, knife in hand, the boy woke with a start. His eyes were as big as lily pads. I put my finger to my lips to quiet him, then slipped the blade under his bonds and cut them. He rubbed his wrists and stared up at me blankly.

"They won't let you get away with this," the woman hissed. "They won't let you take us."

"We're not taking you," I said, sawing through the leather reins that bound them to the plane. "We're freeing you."

The woman actually laughed. It was a dreadful, breathy thing. "What do you expect us to do? Just run out into this storm? And then what?"

I glanced out the opening. The whole world was a gray mass of pounding rain and wind. She was right. They wouldn't get far. And as weak as they looked, even if the slavers never caught up to them again, they were as good as dead. I turned to Dad. His brows furrowed as he searched the muck at his feet for an answer.

"But if we had their jeep . . ."

I turned. The woman was pointing to where the black man lay sprawled out by the dwindling fire. A ring of keys was clipped to one of his belt loops.

"If you really want to help us," she said, "we need the keys."

I shook my head. If she thought we were getting any closer to those men than we already were, she was insane. I was about to signal that we should go, but by the time I did, Dad was already slipping the rifle over his shoulder and crouching down into the mud.

"Dad, no."

He waved me off. There was nothing else I could do. Any more and I'd wake them. I had to stand there and watch as Dad crept closer to the sleeping meh. The black man's chest rose and fell as he snored. The fire crackled. Dad halved the distance between them before his foot hit some debris and he pitched forward. I gasped, but he got his hand up on the wall just in time to stop himself.

Dad took a shaky breath, then another painstaking step forward. He was less than a foot away now. The fire was bright red on his face, and his wrinkled forehead glistened with sweat. Slowly, painfully, he knelt down. Thunder boomed overhead and he froze for a second, looking at the man's face, studying it for any hint of consciousness. When he saw none, he reached his hand out little by little until the tips of his fingers brushed the metal keys, then crawled up their length toward the clasp. My stomach was a knot. Dad pinched the clasp open gently and then slowly, achingly slowly, he pulled the keys away and they fell into his palm. My heart leapt.

"Put the keys down."

The man with the scar was up on his knees. An enormous gun grew out of his hand and was pointed directly at Dad's head.

"Now."

Everything was deadly still for a split second, but then Dad jerked to one side, tossing the keys at me as he did it.

"Run!" he shouted.

I scrambled to catch them but the woman sprang up behind me and pushed me down, snatching the keys out of the air. There was a *boom*, deafening in the steel walls of the plane, as the man's gun rang out. Thank God he was drunk. The bullet missed Dad by inches and slammed into the ground.

Dad scrambled toward me as the black man woke and pulled his own gun out of its holster. The slavers slid out of their places, weaving in their still-drunk state. Dad didn't say a word. He leveled the rifle and fired, its report pounding at my ears. The bullet went high, ricocheting with a wet-sounding *ping*. The men stumbled backward, surprised.

"We don't want any trouble," Dad announced.

"They're ours," the man with the scar slurred in a deep Southern accent.

Dad kept his voice level. "Not anymore."

The slaver laughed. It sounded like a landslide, boulders tumbling together. He slapped his partner in the chest and they got on their feet and came toward us.

"Get back," Dad commanded, backing up and jutting the rifle out in front of him, but the men just laughed and kept coming. They must have heard the fear that had crept into his voice. They saw us for what we were. We were no heroes.

I backed out of the plane. The woman and the boy were already gone. As I stepped outside the slavers' jeep was revving up and pulling away.

"Wait!" I screamed, but the woman didn't even look back as she took off with the boy beside her. Red taillights glowed in their wake.

Dad tumbled out of the plane and fired two more shots over the men's heads, sending them ducking inside. Then he turned and headed toward me.

"Run," he called. "Go!"

The two slavers emerged from the plane behind him.

"Dad! Look out!"

Drunk or not, the man with the scar moved fast. He was on Dad in a second, grabbing the top of his backpack and yanking him backward. Dad lost the rifle and his pack, but he whipped around and threw a punch that glanced off the man's head. It didn't do much damage but it knocked him back, into the mud. The black man came at him now.

Dad turned and screamed, "Just go!" as the man slammed into his back and they hit the ground, grappling in the mud. The man with the scar was coming at Dad from behind so I scooped up the rifle and swung it by the barrel like a club. The heavy stock struck him on the back of the head and sent him down again.

Dad reared back and threw a solid punch to the black man's face, .dropping him into the mud with his partner.

"Run!" Dad yelled again.

We took off, blind from the pounding rain that turned the world around us a featureless gray. Paolo brayed as we passed him. There was no other choice. We'd have to come back for him. We'd never escape with him in tow.

I couldn't tell if the men were chasing us or the woman, so I just ran, cradling the mud-covered rifle in my arms, desperately trying to keep up with Dad, who was little more than a flickering shadow darting ahead of me. The thunder pounded constantly, atomic blasts of it, following blue-white flares of lightning. Every time, I ducked instinctively, like I was expecting a shower of shrapnel to follow.

Who knows how long we ran, or how far. At some point I crashed into what felt like an oak tree. I tried to dodge around it, but then I looked up and saw it was Dad.

"Do you see them?" He had to lean right down by my ear and shout for me to hear him at all.

"I can't see anything!"

Dad turned all around, sheets of water coursing off his head and shoulders. I wanted to scream that it was pointless, that we needed to keep running, but then there was another flash of lightning and a *crack*, and for a second it seemed like there might be a ridge of some kind out ahead of us. Dad grabbed my elbow and pulled us toward it.

"Come on! Maybe there's shelter!"

By then, the ground had turned to a slurry of mud and rocks and wrecked grass. Every few steps my feet would sink into it and I'd have to pull myself out one foot at a time, terrified that I'd lose sight of Dad and be lost out in that gray nothing, forever.

As we ran, the ridge ahead of us became more and more solid, a looming black wall. I prayed for a cave, but even a good notch in the rock wall would have been enough to get us out of the rain and hide until morning. We were only about fifty feet from it when Dad came to an abrupt halt.

"Why are we stopping?!"

Dad didn't say anything, he simply pointed.

Between us and the ridge there was an immense gash in the earth, a gorge some thirty feet across and another thirty deep, with steep, muddy walls on our side and the ridge on the opposite. A boiling mess of muddy water, tree stumps, and trash raged at the bottom.

Dad searched left and right for a crossing, but there wasn't any. His shoulders slumped. Even through the curtain of rain I could see the sunken hollow of his eyes, deep red-lined pits that sat in skin as gray as the air around us.

"I'm sorry, Stephen. I swear to God, I'm so sorry."

I reached out for his arm, to tell him it was going to be okay, that we'd be fine, but before my fingers could even graze his soaked coat, the ground beneath his feet disappeared. What was solid ground turned to mud in an instant and he went flailing, flying backward. There was a flash of lightning as he fell, arms pinwheeling, his mouth open in a shocked O. There was nothing at his back but thirty feet of open air and, beyond that, the bared fangs of a raging river.

When the lightning subsided, he was gone.

FIVE

I didn't think, I just jumped, sliding down the muddy wall, then tumbling end over end when it collapsed beneath me. I hit a small piece of ground at the bottom, a tiny shore, and pulled myself up out of the mud.

"Dad!" I screamed, searching the river and the opposite shore for some sign of him, but it was useless. "Dad!"

Another lightning flash and I caught a glimpse of something large in the water, moving fast downstream. I tugged off my pack, stripped down to my shorts and T-shirt, and dove in.

The icy water ripped the breath out of me as soon as I hit it. I had to struggle to move and get my blood flowing again. It took all my strength to stay focused on the big shadow in the water downstream and avoid the outcroppings of rock and the logs that shot by. I knew it could have been anything — a tree, or a clot of mud and rock — but I dug my arms hard into the cold water, praying, pulling for it.

I was only a few feet away when a flash of something dark and a thrashing arm shot up out of the churn. *Yes!* I stabbed my arms into the water and managed to get ahold of the collar of his coat. I pulled him to me but only had him for a second before we slammed sideways into a rock jutting out of the water. Dad shot away again headfirst down the river. He wasn't moving. His body was limp, tossed about and swept away by the current.

The cold sank deeper into my body, seizing on my muscles, paralyzing them. I let out a scream and pushed off the rock I was stuck on, thrashing through the water. A surge in the current rocketed me forward. I was almost on him. I reached, missed, then reached again, feeling the barest whisper of his coat against my fingertips. The third time I caught him.

I scrambled forward, catching hold of his shoulder, hooking my arm under his armpit, and dragging him to me. Soaked with water, he was incredibly heavy. The current tried to suck him away and under, but I managed to draw him to my chest and kick off toward a shallow area at the edge of the river. I kicked and kicked, dragging us toward the shore, pushing Dad ahead of me and then climbing out after him.

I turned him over onto his stomach and leaned over him, putting all of my weight into his back, hoping to push out whatever water was in his lungs. He was bleeding from the back of his head. Thick clots of blood pooled at the base of his neck and then washed away, misty red in the rain. I was pretty sure his right arm was broken in more than one place, maybe a leg too. I turned him over onto his back. His skin was a ghastly blue-gray in the low light. His mouth was hanging open. A voice in my head, Grandpa's sandpaper rasp, told me he was dead.

I laid my ear up against his mouth and listened as hard as I could, clapping my hand over my other ear to block out the rain. At first there was nothing, just empty silence, but then there was a flutter, and the slightest rise in his chest. He was alive!

I pulled him farther from the edge of the water, his waterlogged clothes adding twenty pounds or more. The muscles in my arms and back and legs howled, but I made it to the ridge and found a deep depression in the rock. It wasn't as good as a cave, but it would have to do.

I dragged Dad in and laid him on his side in case he started throwing up water. I thought about trying to go back for our stuff. There were some medical supplies on the wagon — bandages, antiseptic — but God knew how far away it was, and the storm, if anything, was getting worse. Instead, I pushed myself into the hollow beside him.

Blood was pouring out of the gash on his head. I tore off my T-shirt and ripped it into strips with my teeth and used them to pack off and bind the wound, trying my best to ignore the soft broken feel at the back of his skull. My breath froze in my chest as the blood advanced through the cloth, eating through several layers before finally stopping and holding still. I breathed again.

I wanted to do something about his arm and leg, but what they needed was some sort of splint. That clearly wasn't possible, so I had to let it go. They looked bad, but not life threatening.

My biggest problem was the cold. The depression we were in only gave us a bit of shelter from the wind and the rain. There was no brush to pack around us and no possibility of a fire. I wasn't sure if it was cold enough to kill us, though I suspected if it fell another five to ten degrees during the night, it might be. I strained, trying to think of some other option, but finally had to admit that there was none.

I sat up with Dad all that night, clutching him to my chest and fighting the waves of exhaustion that threatened to drag me under. I couldn't sleep. I couldn't leave him alone. As the lightning slashed the dark and the rain poured around us, all I could think about was the bear.

I was seven. We were camped in dense forest way up north at the Canadian border, a day or two from the Northern Gathering. The trees in Canada were the biggest I had ever seen, standing close together in impenetrable ranks with thick, nut-brown hides and a tangle of branches and leaves that nearly blotted out the sun.

I didn't plan to wander off, but when we got to our campsite and Mom, Dad, and Grandpa began setting up, I saw a robin at the edge of the clearing. It flew off as I approached it but I kept on going, drawn toward a pile of smooth rocks or a splash of sunlight on the pine needle–covered ground. It was a beautiful morning, cool and misty, with only the first stirrings of animals to keep me company. Before I knew it the forest had closed behind me and I was alone. I wasn't scared. It was thrilling being off the path. I dodged through the trees, down a hill, and deeper into the woods. It grew dim and hushed all around, the air full with the smell of decaying things.

It wasn't long before I found the video game. It was one of the big stand-up ones that Dad said they used to have in arcades when he was a kid. It was sitting at an odd canted angle, half on, half off a thick tree root that had sprung out of the ground. It said MORTAL KOMBAT on its side and was covered with colorful pictures of gigantic men and women in masks grappling with one another. The paint was peeling off in places, revealing a rusty metal surface underneath. Who knew how it got there? We ran into things like it, strange misplaced relics, from time to time.

I crunched through fallen leaves and up onto a little metal step at the bottom that raised me higher so I was face-to-face with the machine. Mom said she had played these constantly when she was a kid, before her parents finally broke down and bought her a home system. Down by my knees were two slots for coins. I reached into my pocket and mimed dropping two in, then started jerking the hand controls around, imagining the characters fighting it out at my command, making the sounds of punches and kicks with my mouth.

Bam. Bam. Baf. Crash. Ugh!

Leaves crunched behind me.

A twig snapped.

My hands froze on the controls.

I saw his outline first, a great looming thing reflected in the glass of the game. When I turned, the bear was maybe fifteen feet away, staring at me through the low tree branches, his mouth hanging open, teeth glistening. I guessed he had to weigh five hundred pounds or more. The bear's head was lowered, his brown muzzle thrust out at me, sniffing. His blank black eyes were fixed at the center of my chest.

I thought my heart would crack a rib the way it was pounding. The thing lumbered forward, slow and awkward as a nightmare, until he halved the distance between us.

He was close enough now that his breath, smelling like the humid rot of a swamp, struck my chest like an open palm. His black-spotted tongue lolled around in his mouth and over the peaks of his fangs. The bear reared back, then opened his maw and roared. It went on and on and the sound of it, so close, dropped me to my knees in the grass. Everything inside me, everything I had ever felt, or thought, or hoped for, was pushed aside like a river tearing away soil and grass and trees, leaving only bedrock.

The bear raised one paw to close the remaining distance between us when an explosion rocked the air. The bear flinched, whipped its head backward, and roared, but then there was another explosion and the bear crumpled into a heap at my feet. His lungs filled once and then collapsed with a slow whine.

Someone was racing through the woods toward me, but I couldn't look away from the bear. I had never been so close to something so wild, yet so still. I reached out, brushed my hand along the rough grain of his fur, and started to cry.

Dad dropped to his knees beside me. The barrel of Grandpa's rifle was still smoking as he wrapped his arms around me, pulling me tight to his chest. I could feel his own heart pounding.

"You're safe," he said over and over, rocking me back and forth and crying too. "I'm here, Stephen, and you're safe. You're safe."

Safe.

The war of rain and lightning and thunder hammered on through-out the night. I looked up at the gorge's edge high above us, but I knew that no rescuer would appear. There was no one left.

There was only me.

I wrapped my arms around Dad as tight as I could, shivering, hoping our little bit of body heat would be enough to keep us alive until the rain stopped and the sun rose.

It had only been twenty-four hours since Grandpa died.

SIX

When morning came, the storm had passed. In its place was a bright day with a blue sky. Dad's eyes were closed and his mouth was hanging slightly open. I put my ear down to his mouth and waited. At first there was nothing, but then I made out his slow, ragged breathing. I sat back, relieved.

His lips were horribly dry and cracked, so I went down to the river and brought back as much water as I could in my cupped hands. It was dark and silty and I knew it could be polluted, but what choice did I have? I knelt down next to him, awkwardly trying to keep the water from spilling, then leaned forward to trickle some of the water down into his mouth. I stopped before the first drop fell.

Can he swallow? Or will the water just make him choke?

My hands and back cramped as I leaned over him, indecisive. It was too much of a chance. I splashed the water onto the rocks, then sat down with my back to him, facing the river, stewing with frustration.

Grandpa always said that a good plan will get you out of anything. But what plan could I make? I was at the bottom of a gorge with thirty-foot walls. Even if I could get out, where would I go? Back to the plane?

Certainly the slavers would have taken anything worthwhile that we left.

If Grandpa had been alive, or if Dad had been awake, then maybe we would have had a chance. They were the ones who came up with the plans. They were the ones who knew what to do. I just did what I was told. I ached for things to be the way they were.

I lifted my head out of my hands and watched the river course by, carrying with it leaves, trash, and shattered logs. A current of broken bones and tattered skin. I thought again of that day with the bear and the crack of Grandpa's rifle.

No one is coming. If I do nothing, we die.

I managed to push Dad to the back of the little cave, out of the glare of the sun. Then I knelt down beside him.

"I have to go," I told him, clinging to his arm. "But I'll be back, okay?"

I found my clothes, backpack, and the rifle at the base of the gorge and waded across the river to get them. After I washed the mud off my clothes, I put them back on. The rifle was caked with grit, useless. If I could find the cleaning kit back in our wagon, then maybe I could get it working again. I dug inside my soaked pack and lifted out my three books. Each was swollen to nearly double its size. Just touching the waterlogged paper caused it to slough off like dead skin.

My eyes burned, but I wouldn't cry. Not over that.

I threw the books aside, located my fire starter at the bottom of the pack, and stuck it in my back pocket. The wall was higher than I remembered, its face made of mud and half-dried dirt. Outcroppings of rock and tree roots sprouted here and there. It was so steep I got dizzy just looking at it.

I jammed my hands and feet into the mud and started, pain-stakingly, to pull myself up. For every two feet of progress I made, I'd slide at least a foot, but I didn't give up. I kept one of Grandpa's commandments running in my head the whole time. Food. Water. Shelter. Fire. That was all that was important. Find these things and live. Don't, and die.

Panting, I clawed my way to the top, then pulled myself over.

The land we had crossed the day before, with its carpet of sparkling grass and flowers, was now a plain of mud strewn with branches, rocks, and dead leaves. It was like the end of the world had returned, eager to finish its work.

I didn't know how far we had come or in what direction. The plane could have been anywhere. I started by walking directly away from the gorge and then, pretty sure that the ridge we saw the night before had always been on our right, turned so it was on my left and kept going. The sun dried my clothes until they became stiff and scratchy. I walked until I wanted more than anything to sit down and never move again, but there was something in me that kept going, no matter how much I wanted to stop.

Finally a dark shape appeared far up ahead. Through the rifle's scope I could see what I was sure was a wing emerging from the mud. It was still a mile or so off. I dropped my head and pushed on, trudging toward whatever small salvation might be there.

When I reached the plane, the first thing I did was check for Paolo. He was gone, of course. Only a few scrap pieces of leather and brass from his tack remained.

I squatted and held his reins in my hand, rubbing my finger over the rough surface. Mom had found him on an abandoned horse farm and we'd nursed him back to health. I wondered if the slavers had taken him or if he'd freed himself in the storm somehow and had gone looking for us. That idea of Paolo lost, wandering about in the storm hoping to find me and Dad, made me feel like I was drowning.

Our wagon was smashed to pieces. All that remained of our things were a few useless pieces of metal and a big water jug I knew would be too heavy to take back to camp. I took a long drink, then stepped carefully inside the plane, where, after digging around for a few moments, I found Dad's knife and slipped it underneath my belt.

Dad's pack was half buried in the mud outside. Luckily the waterproof bag where we kept our first-aid kit, water purifying tablets, and extra rounds for the rifle was intact. I pulled all of them out along with some beef jerky and the gun-cleaning kit. I tore off a hunk of jerky and muscled it down my throat. Even though it hit my empty stomach like a ball of lead, it made me feel solid and awake for the first time that day.

Before I closed up Dad's pack, I reached down to the bottom and hunted around until my fingers closed around the only photograph we owned. I pulled it out into the sun.

It was of me and Mom and Dad. There was a stand of trees behind us and, towering above it, the bright red tracks of a roller coaster, twisting like the unearthed skeleton of a dinosaur, and a sign that said WELCOME TO SIX FLAGS GREAT ADVENTURE! We were all grinning. I was maybe seven or eight, leaning against Mom's legs, her small hands resting lightly on my shoulders. She was caught mid-laugh, pretty and young-looking in her blue coat, her tree-bark curls poking out from the big straw hat she sometimes wore. Her cheeks were bright and rosy from the cold. Dad was next to Mom giving a goofy double thumbs-up to the camera.

The way the shot was framed, you could barely tell that the roller coaster was half covered in rust, only a few years away from collapsing, or that the rest of the amusement park was a no-man's-land filled with wild, rabid dogs.

It was taken as we'd traveled toward the Northern Gathering. This seedy little guy had been wandering around with an old camera, one of those automatic ones, the kind that develop the pictures themselves. He was making a small living trading pictures for food and supplies, trying to make as much as he could before the batteries or the film ran out and he'd be unable to replace them.

I traced my finger around Mom's face and then around the outline of us standing together, a cloudless blue sky behind us. I liked to imagine that the picture had been taken before the Collapse, that we were just a family taking a trip out to the amusement park where we would ride rides and eat popcorn, our laughter rising into the sky like balloons. At the end of the day we'd drive home in the gathering dark and I'd fall asleep, my head cradled in Mom's lap, her fingers lightly brushing the hair back from my forehead.

But then, as always, I looked down, just to Mom's left under the Six Flags sign. A couple years later, Dad and Grandpa would dig two graves there, one large and one small, while I watched.

There was a sudden, sharp pain in my left hand. When I opened it, a line of blood trickled down my wrist and dripped onto the ground. In the center of my palm there were four half-moon-shaped cuts from where my nails had dug into the flesh. I wiped the blood on my jeans and put the picture safely back in the pack. As I walked away from the plane, I stuffed my left hand deep down into my pocket, as though I was scared someone might see.

It was late afternoon by the time I got back to the gorge, loaded down with supplies and whatever little bits of wood I could find for a fire. Dad hadn't changed much. His breathing was shallow but regular. The first thing I did was unwind the T-shirt bandage around his head and check on his wound. The gash along the back of his skull still seeped blood, but slower than it had last night. I pulled some antiseptic out of the first-aid kit and smeared it over the wound, then packed it off and bound it with some clean bandages. Again I felt the shifting, broken feel at the back of his head, the bone plates sliding against each other, but there was nothing I could do about that.

I arranged the bits of wood and kindling I'd found but paused before lighting them up. We were on fairly open land. The smoke would go up like a beacon, visible to anyone for miles around, but I didn't see a choice. The wet and chill could kill us.

The fire I got going was smoky at first, but finally a decent flame started. I stripped off my clothes, then Dad's, and hung them from a crack in the rock wall by the fire to dry. I huddled up as close as I could to the flames. It was amazing how much difference being warm made. I cleaned and loaded the rifle until the stars emerged and spread across the sky.

It was quiet then, just the crackle of the fire and the soft ripple of the dwindling river below. The world felt enormous and as empty as a dry well. In my mind I ran through a picture show of campsites we had stayed in over the years: the mall in Virginia, the gas station in South Carolina. I finally settled on the cracked parking lot of a Kroger supermarket in Georgia. The last time we'd been there, years ago, daisies had begun to burst through the concrete. I imagined there were fields of them now. I saw myself unpacking our camp, laying out our bedrolls, and gathering wood for a fire while Dad fed Paolo and then got our dinner together, humming as he did it.

I sat for a while in that fantasy until darkness began to seep into the picture around the edges and I felt low and cold. My clothes were mostly dry by then so I dressed and turned to Dad, his clothes in hand. When I saw him there, still and broken on that rock, it was like a wave hit me out of nowhere.

Why did we have to help those people? You said nothing would change. You promised!

I snapped my left hand closed, urging my fingers deep into the half-moons. A sharp thrill of pain shot up my arm and chased the thoughts away, clearing my head. Blood ran down my hand, but I didn't care. The pain was a relief. It was easier.

My head fell back against the rock and my eyes closed. I was exhausted but I wouldn't let sleep come. *What now?* I thought. I had supplies. Dad seemed stable, but I couldn't feed him or give him water. I looked up at the gorge wall, black against the gray night sky, and my heart thrummed against my chest.

I have to get us out of here. But how?

After I got Dad dressed again I reached behind me and drew his arm over my head and down across my chest, holding on to it tightly, nestling my head into the crook of his elbow. I sat that way for a long time, shivering, until my eyes closed and I slipped off into sleep before I could stop it.

I don't know how long I slept, but it seemed like only minutes before I snapped awake to a soft shuffling sound from above us. I closed my eyes, trying to listen past the crackling of the fire.

Footsteps on the ridge above us.

Men. Four, maybe five, creeping along the shore of the river down-stream with one on the ridge. They were moving slowly and not talking.

My hand fell to the stock of the rifle.

Slavers.

SEVEN

Of course. Grandpa had told me a hundred times. Fuel was incredibly scarce so people who had vehicles never went far from the central place where they stored it. Dad and I had wandered right into the slavers' territory, stirred up a hornet's nest, and didn't even know it.

Seeing no other choice, I left Dad for an outcropping of rock a few feet upstream. I was too exposed with him. From where I was, I had a good view down the gorge and, since the fire was still going, anyone coming from downstream would be distracted by it and not see me. I pulled my boots on and checked the rifle. One round in the chamber and six more in the magazine. Despite the years of attempted training by Grandpa, I knew I wasn't a very good shot. I aimed the rifle downstream and waited, hoping that I could at least scare them off.

The men in the gorge materialized out of the darkness. Three of them. Creeping shadows, sweeping their guns back and forth. My hands grew slick on the rifle's stock. The cuts on my palm stung.

The man in the middle stepped into the outer circle of our firelight. He knelt down next to my backpack and started to go through it, balancing his shotgun on his knee, finger on the trigger. He wasn't one of the two from the plane. He was older, Dad's age maybe. The two others stayed hidden in the shadows behind him. After the man went through my bag, he looked to his left and that's when he saw Dad. He signaled to his friends, then brought his shotgun to his shoulder and crept toward the cave. The other two followed.

I brought my rifle over the lip of the outcropping. Icy sweat was pouring down my face and arms. The leader of the slavers set his gun down and reached out toward Dad. I had his back squarely in my sights, but I was paralyzed, too afraid, too uncertain, to act. I was seven years old again, on my knees before the great brown bulk of that bear, waiting for someone to appear and make it all go away.

But then there was a voice in the back of my head. Dad's.

You're not seven years old anymore, it said, *and you're not helpless.*

The pounding in my chest slowed. Suddenly everything seemed clear. I clicked the rifle's safety with my thumb, then stood up behind the rock and squeezed the trigger twice. My ears rang as the shots echoed off the canyon walls. The bullets slammed into the dirt inches from the leader's feet.

The three men jerked away from Dad, the man in the middle yelling at them all to run. He and one of the others scrambled into the shadows along the wall of the valley, but the third one, a tall skinny one with a flash of yellow hair, stepped forward and raised his rifle. I fired. I was sure I'd missed until I saw his leg buckle and he went down. Winged him. Just enough. He staggered back to the shadows but collapsed before he made it there, hitting the ground right behind the fire.

Shots came from my left, over by where the other two had ducked into the shadows. One bullet struck the wall behind me, sending a rain of gravel down over my head, and the other slammed into the dirt in front of me. I dropped down behind the rock.

"Jackson, no!"

I raised the rifle just as someone came out of the darkness downstream, running to the man on the ground, a rifle in his hand. I leveled the scope. His face was round, unlined, beardless, and framed in a tangle of reddish curls. The ground beneath me pulled away and I went icy inside.

My God. He's younger than me.

Sand crunched behind me.

I spun around. The last thing I saw was the wooden stock of a rifle flying toward the side of my head.

EIGHT

"I don't *care* what Caleb Henry would say."

"Marcus —"

"He's just a kid, Sam. He's not a damn spy."

I woke up the next morning to voices I didn't recognize. My head was pounding. My hands and feet were tied with lengths of rope. Three men were standing by the side of the stream with their heads down, talking low and passing around a bottle of water. My rifle was on the other side of the camp near Dad, who was in his place at the mouth of the cave, unmoved. I shifted my weight quietly and sat up, my head swimming as I did it.

"How do you know that?"

"We're half a day from home, Sam. If they're spies, they're the worst damn spies I've ever heard of. Besides, he could have killed Jackson and he didn't. He had him in his sights."

"That doesn't mean —"

"Look at them, Sam. What would Violet say? What would Maureen say, if she was still with us?"

They weren't slavers, I was fairly sure. Farmers maybe, traders, or — who knew? — maybe even salvagers like me and Dad. The man who'd gone through my backpack the night before stood in the center of the group. He was compact, bald with a band of messy black and gray hair around the sides. Next to him was the man he called Sam, a black man in his fifties who wore a sweat-stained New York Yankees ball cap and had a heavy belly and a thick mustache.

The kid I'd almost shot was next to him. He was heavyset with a pinched, worried-looking face. He kept his head down and his arms crossed over his chest, not meeting anyone's eye.

Whoever they were, I didn't know what they intended to do with me and, like Grandpa always said, if they weren't family, they were trouble. I scanned the ground around my feet and found a rock about the size of a small apple that came to a brutal point at one end. I leaned forward, slipped it into my palm, then pushed myself backward until I was up against the wall of the gorge.

The kid nudged the leader. "He's awake."

The bald man was about to step forward, but the one I had shot, a teenager with a shock of golden hair that fell over his eye, appeared out of nowhere.

"Who are you?" he spat. "What are you doing here?" I gripped the rock in my fist, ready to defend myself, but the bald man pushed him out of the way.

"He's just a kid, Will," he said. "Not much younger than you. Now step back and let me handle this."

"We oughta string him up, right here and now, Marcus."

The bald man, Marcus, looked around the bare walls of the crevasse. "String him up from *what?*"

"Marcus —"

"No one is getting strung up," Marcus said sternly, which only enraged Will more.

"He shot me!"

"He *grazed* you, Will," Sam said. "You were barely bleeding. You're not even limping."

Will ignored him and kept after Marcus. "He's a spy for Fort Leonard! They both are! When I get home, I'll tell my father. I'll tell everyone!"

Marcus took a step closer to Will until their chests were almost touching. Marcus was actually an inch or so shorter, but he had shoulders like a buffalo and something deep and forceful in him.

"Tell them anything you want, Will, but for right now, shut the hell up. You're giving me a headache."

The black man laughed at that, a booming "Ha!" that caused Will to shoot him a deadly look before he sneered and, with a chuckle, shook his head in a snotty attempt at saving face. In the end he skulked away downstream, kicking a charred log from the fire with his bad leg. Marcus turned his back on Will and squatted down in front of me. I jerked away instinctively.

Marcus held up his hands, palms out. "It's okay," he said. "Don't mean any harm. Will there's daddy owns a lot of cattle and things. Sometimes he thinks that means he's next in line to a throne we all keep trying to tell him doesn't exist."

Marcus smiled, obviously trying to put me at ease, but I just stared at him, turning the rock around in my palm.

"Looks like Sam gave you a hell of a knock there."

"Sorry," Sam said in a deep Northern accent. He dropped his paw of a hand on the kid's shoulder. "Couldn't let you shoot Jackson here. We've just gotten to like him."

Jackson shrugged out from under the man's hand, embarrassed. "Sam . . ."

"What do you people want?" I asked.

Marcus dropped his grin. "I'm Marcus Green," he said, then pointed to the kid who stood shyly in the background. "That's my son, Jackson. His highness there is Will Henry. Sam Turner's the man who gave you that tap on the head."

"Howdy," Sam said.

Marcus looked back at Sam. Something passed between them that ended with Sam looking off after Will, then nodding. Marcus slipped a hunting knife from a sheath on his belt.

I flinched backward, ready to swing the rock as best I could, but Marcus held his hands up again to steady me, then began sawing at the ropes around my wrists. I watched him carefully, even as the ropes popped open and he started on the ones at my feet.

"That your dad?"

Marcus waited, but I said nothing. Grandpa always said you should never tell anyone anything they didn't need to know.

"Well, whoever he is, he looks like he's hurt pretty bad."

Marcus looked up at me as he worked, like he was taking my measure. He was trying to talk himself into something, and the fight was going back and forth. When the ropes snapped under his knife, he glanced back at Sam again. Sam hesitated, then gave a reluctant nod.

"We can help you," Marcus said under his breath. "We have a town. It's not too far. My wife, Violet, is a doctor. Not one of those drunks running around claiming to be a doctor either — she's the real thing. Army doctor before the Collapse. We could bring you both back to town with us and she could take a look at your dad."

He was lying, of course. If they had medicine, why would they waste it on some guy they didn't even know? Still . . .

"I don't have anything to trade," I said.

"We're not asking for anything," Sam said. "Just offering our help."

I scanned their faces, searching for some sign of the deception I knew had to be there. But I wasn't Grandpa; I didn't have his eye. Whatever they wanted, whatever they were planning, I couldn't see what it was.

Not that it mattered. Small towns had begun to pop up in the last few years, but Grandpa had always kept us away from them. They were nothing but muddy collections of tumbledown shacks, he said, that stank of people living too close together and bred smallpox and dysentery. Besides that, they were targets for every slave trader, scavenger, or bandit around, like nails begging to be hammered down.

"We just want to be left alone," I said squarely to Marcus. "We can take care of ourselves."

"You sure?" Marcus asked.

I nodded. Marcus signaled to Jackson and he stepped forward, his eyes on the ground in front of me. He handed Marcus a small cardboard box, then retreated to the stream's edge.

"Looked like you were about out," Marcus said, handing me the box. "You take care of yourself now. Sorry for the trouble. We're heading west if you change your mind."

They gathered up their things and turned to head downstream. Jackson lagged behind them, and for the first time that morning, he raised his eyes to meet mine. His were light blue and big and, like a doe's, smart and skittish at the same time. He looked like he had something to say.

"What?"

Jackson shook his head. "Nothing. Sorry." Then he turned and followed the others out of our camp.

Only when they were out of sight did I reach for the cardboard box and open it up. Inside were four rows of five gleaming silver-jacketed bullets, set tip-down in a piece of white foam. I pulled one out and rolled the cold metal between my fingers. They were much newer than the ones we had, probably made right before the Collapse.

Footsteps clicked against the rock, echoing down the walls of the gorge, growing softer each second. It wouldn't be long until Dad and I were alone again.

With Dad the way he was, I'd never be able to get us out of there. I closed the box of bullets and struggled to my feet, my head pounding.

I knew that what I was doing was wrong. If Grandpa had been around, he'd have had a better answer, but he wasn't. It was just me.

"Marcus!" I called out as I ran down the shore. "Sam! Wait up!"

PART TWO

NINE

We headed west for the rest of that day, tumbling through the yellow grass just below a heavily cratered highway. A thin sheet of clouds, like dirty cotton, was smeared across the sky.

They had me wear a bandanna over my eyes all morning so I wouldn't know the path they were taking, but they let me take it off by the time the sun was halfway into the sky. Not that it mattered much. I had never been so far west in my life and had no clue where I was.

Marcus led the way with Jackson bringing up the rear. I was with Dad in their wood-slat wagon, sitting behind Sam and Will. Lying across from us was a buck Marcus said he'd shot earlier that morning. I tried not to look at it. Its stillness and empty, glasslike eyes caused something inside me to quake.

I scanned the area around us for salvage, eager for something familiar, but there was nothing useful on the path, just blowing trash and a few distant billboards and road signs.

I huddled down behind the front bench of the wagon and tended to Dad. He was lashed to a driftwood stretcher that Sam had improvised to get him out of the gorge. I raised his head into my lap and poured some water over his lips to wet them, careful that none of it went down his throat. I made sure Sam and Will were focused on the road, then took his arm in my hand and squeezed, praying that if some part of him was still awake he'd feel it and know I was there.

Jackson had abandoned his position as rear guard and was trailing along behind the wagon, his rifle too big for him and cradled awkwardly in his hands.

"You know, my mom's real good," he said. "Last year she fixed my friend Derrick's broken arm."

He waited for a response, but I ignored him, turning my attention back to Dad. I was relieved when Jackson finally let the wagon pull away. I couldn't seem to look at him without seeing his face framed in my scope the night before. The memory of my finger tensing on the trigger felt cold and dark inside me, like a stone at the bottom of a well.

"Hey, look at that!" Will called out, his golden hair fluttering in the wind. We were rolling past an island of gas stations and fast-food restaurants off the highway north of us. An Applebee's sat in the center of it all like a faded king, its red, white, and green striped awning in tatters. A pack of dogs, razor thin and rabid, was in the parking lot, snarling as they fought over bits of trash. "Looks like some friends of yours!"

"Will," Sam warned.

"No, seriously. Bet they even smell the same, like a mix of dead horse and an outhouse."

Will had raised holy hell when Marcus and Sam had told him I was coming, yelling about outsiders and spies and how I'd tell everyone where their town was.

"Guess they don't have bathtubs in Fort Leonard, huh, spy?"

I gritted my teeth. I didn't know what Fort Leonard was, or why he thought I was some sort of spy for them. I knew I should ignore him like

I'd ignored Jackson, but I found my fingers curling around the handle of Dad's knife instead.

Will was about to start up again when the wagon slammed to a halt, tossing him back into his place at the front. "Ow! Sam!"

"Oh gee, sorry, Will."

Sam turned and gave me a mischievous little grin as Will righted himself, cussing and spitting.

Marcus came striding back from his place at the head of the group, wiping sweat off his bald head with his sleeve. I hid the knife under my coat before he could see.

"It's time," Marcus said, and dropped a red bandanna on the wood rail at my shoulder — we must have been getting close. The whole thing seemed pretty ridiculous, but Marcus was nice enough about it, so I went along.

As I was about to tie on the bandanna again, I caught Jackson staring at me. He held his rifle tight to his chest, his arms straining, his finger along the trigger guard. His face had gone stony. Confused, I followed his eyes down to my lap and saw that my coat had brushed open, exposing the weapon in my hand. Our eyes met before his darted away, but in that second I saw that he was afraid. I eased the knife back into its sheath before tying the blindfold around my eyes, feeling strangely satisfied to be the one causing fear instead of the one feeling it.

The air grew steadily cooler and twilight settled around us. After a while, we came to a halt, and Sam and Will piled out of the wagon. There were shuffling footsteps and low voices up ahead, then the sound of something large brushing against the ground. I slipped the bandanna up over my eyes while their backs were turned and caught the four of them moving aside a group of small trees and brush to expose a rough path cutting into the woods ahead of us. Clever. I raced to pull the bandanna back down before they returned.

It was colder and darker in the woods. We were surrounded on all sides by creaking branches and animal calls. It was another hour or more of bouncing travel before we moved out onto open ground, where we flew downhill before coming to a stop.

There was a pause, then Sam loosened the knot of my blindfold so it fell to my shoulders.

We were at the bottom of a grass-covered valley, surrounded on all sides by deep forest. Ahead of us was a white stone wall that cut across the entire valley like a bright line of snow, with a heavy double iron gate at its center. Two words were engraved in deep letters on the white wall: SETTLER'S LANDING.

After Marcus opened the gates, Sam shook the reins and we rolled through. The gates made a rusty clank and then a deep final boom as they closed, hemming us in. A nervous flare bit through me. For a panicked moment, I wanted to leap out of the wagon and run. I took Dad's arm tight in my fist.

What have I gotten us into?

On the other side of the gates, the grass turned into black asphalt, not at all the cracked, bomb-ravaged stuff most highways had become, but smooth and neat, snaking away down the hill. The horses' hooves clicked as we followed it. The trees on either side of the road filtered the dying rays of sunlight so that they fell on us in shifting patterns of small shadows. It was achingly quiet. As we got farther in, I caught flashes of black and white and bright, unnatural colors peeking out through the trees.

I was about to ask what they were but before the breath could leave my lungs the first house emerged from the trees. It was set back about a hundred feet from the road, two stories, with bright yellow on top and brick on the bottom, the whole thing circled by a wide porch the color of beach sand. Glass glittered in the window frames and there were brass fixtures on the doors and casements. In front of the house, a man in a sweater and jeans was raking up leaves from the lawn. He waved as we passed.

"Better close your mouth before a bug flies in," Sam said to me as he waved back.

Will snickered. "It's like the spy's never seen a house before."

It was true. I hadn't. Not like this anyway. Grandpa said that in the days of P11, people tried to escape the disease by barricading themselves in their homes, praying it would pass them by like an ill wind but it rarely worked. Somehow the plague always slipped in, under the doorways or through the windows like a mist, and killed them as they lay in their beds or sat at their dinner tables. Grandpa said that people used to think their home was their castle, but the Eleventh Plague made them all tombs. Every house I had ever known stank of rot, desperation, and fear. I didn't go anywhere near them.

But these . . . They were like a nest full of bird's eggs, painted pale pink or blue or a green that was like the color of sun-bleached moss. Some even flew crisp-looking flags from their porches that fluttered and snapped in the breeze. I tried to find some flaw, some sign that this place had been through the same history that the rest of the country had, but I found, unbelievably, nothing. Part of me wondered if I was actually still lying with Dad at the bottom of that gorge, starved and delirious, imagining all of it.

"You all right back there, son?" Sam asked.

I nodded dumbly as he turned the wagon onto a side road where a green and white street sign said SETTLER'S LANDING TERRACE. The road led downhill to a two-pronged fork. Where the roads diverged was an open area like a park. It was grassy, with a few trees and low bushes scattered here and there. In the center were two large swing sets, a slide, and a big jungle gym made of multicolored lengths of steel tubing.

Sam pulled on the reins and brought the wagon to a halt in front of a white house north of the park. He looked around at the other houses and cleared his throat — nervously, I thought. Sam had agreed to bring me here, but he was worried about it, not as sure as Marcus that it was a good idea. It made me wonder again what I had gotten myself into.

"Okay," he said. "Here we are."

As soon as we stopped, Will jumped off the bench and leaned over the side of the wagon. "Don't get too comfortable, spy," he hissed. "They may be fooled, but I'm not. This is *our* town. I'll make sure you're not here long." He laughed, a self-satisfied little chuckle, then took off down the road.

"Will, you should let Violet look at that leg," Sam called, but Will didn't even turn back. His grievously wounded leg seemed to be causing him no trouble at all. Sam shook his head. "You ready?"

Sam offered me his hand but I ignored it and dropped onto the asphalt. Marcus had gone ahead into the house, so Sam and I lifted Dad out of the wagon before Jackson led the horses away. Dread settled over me as I followed Sam up the white house's stairs. The door seemed like a great set of jaws, ready to swallow me whole.

"You okay?" Sam asked.

"Fine," I said, sucking back the fear so he wouldn't see. "Let's go."

I held my breath as we stepped inside. I had never seen anything like the room we were in. It had clean white walls, a brick fireplace with an only slightly cracked marble mantel, and scuffed wood floors. All of it was lit with candles and small oil lamps that cast a dim amber glow. It smelled of sweet wood smoke and somewhere, faintly, what I thought was baking bread.

"Set him here."

Sam pointed to a cot just under a window beside the front door. We got Dad off the pallet and onto it just as Marcus hurried into the room from another part of the house, a small woman with curly black hair following him.

"This is Violet," Marcus said.

The woman pushed through us, snapping on a pair of latex gloves as she came. "What happened?" Her voice was sharp and flat as a shot.

"He fell," I said.

Violet dropped down by Dad's side. "How far?" When I didn't answer, she turned back. "How far?"

"I don't know. Ten, twenty feet? He was in the water and hit his head."

Violet gently slid her fingers behind Dad's head and closed her eyes, concentrating. "More like thirty feet, I think. He lost consciousness immediately?"

"I don't know. I think so."

Violet went to a wooden cabinet along the wall and pulled open one of about ten narrow drawers. Inside I saw rows of small glass bottles with white labels. Gleaming silver instruments lay beside them. I tried to get a better look, but Violet selected a few instruments, then snapped the drawer closed and came back to Dad's side.

She worked quietly, listening to Dad's heart, checking his temperature, pulling back his eyelids to stare into his eyes. Her movements were quick and precise but never rushed, as though she was moving methodically through some checklist in her head. Even when she unwrapped his head and the blood began to flow again, she didn't panic. Instead, she grabbed some clean bandages and went to work.

I couldn't watch. The way she poked and prodded at him made me feel sick and hot. I turned away; outside the window, I could see a group gathering in the park, a small assembly of women and children in old jeans and flannels. Some were tending the beginnings of a bonfire, while others set a collection of torches into the ground and opened up a large plastic folding table.

"It's Thanksgiving."

I turned to Marcus and Sam, standing behind me. "What?"

"Today," Marcus said. "At least we think it is. Anyway, that's what we got the deer for. Couldn't find a turkey. We're putting together a barbecue tonight out in the park. Why don't we all go? Violet will come get us when she's done."

I shook my head and turned back to Dad. If they thought I'd leave him alone so easily, they were crazy.

"Look, there's really nothing you can do here. Why don't we —"

"Marc, maybe it's better if he stays inside for the time being. Right?" Sam said it gently, but there was a trace of warning there.

"Why don't you go on ahead, Marcus?" Violet said. "You too, Sam. We'll be okay here."

"Vi —" Marcus started, then pulled back. "You sure?"

Violet examined me over her shoulder. Her lips lifted into a thin smile beneath her blue eyes and pink freckles.

"You're not going to be any trouble, are you?" she asked.

The way she was leaning over my father — was it a threat? His life was in her hands. I shook my head slowly but didn't speak.

"Okay," Marcus said, backing away from me. "Come on out if you get hungry."

Violet waved Marcus off over her shoulder, then the front door opened and shut again.

"Sit down if you like," she said.

I didn't move.

In the stillness of the room, I was aware every time Violet's instruments clanked together. I looked over to the mantel, where there were two rows of framed pictures. The frames were whole, but the pictures inside them were discolored, torn in places, and repaired. One showed a family, tanned and smiling and trim, posing on some tropical beach in front of a huge white boat, while another was of a mother and father sitting in lawn chairs out in front of a dilapidated trailer, a baby in an old stroller beside them.

"Those are our folks," Violet said as she worked. "The poor rednecks are mine. Marcus's are the ones with the yacht. I think they actually owned that island."

Looking at the faded pictures of their long-dead families, a chill moved through me.

"What's your name?" Violet asked, but I glared at the floor. "There's no harm in telling me your name. Unless you're Rumpelstiltskin, I guess. Are you Rumpelstiltskin?"

"Is he going to be okay?"

"Why don't you sit down? We can —"

"Just tell me when we can leave." My voice echoed in the small room, but Violet acted like she barely even heard me. Her flat expression never changed.

"Your dad's right arm and leg are broken in multiple places; so are a few ribs. He's dehydrated. He has what I think are infected cuts in various places. The worst of it is he took a pretty good blow to the head, enough to crack his skull. That put him in what people call a coma. That's when —"

"I know what a coma is. When will he wake up?"

Violet's eyes never wavered from mine.

"It could be five minutes from now," she said. "Or it could be five years. Or it could be never. I won't lie to you. In the old days there'd be more we could do. More tests so I could be sure. But now . . . it's serious. The head injury is bad, but those breaks could cause trouble too."

It was like she wasn't even speaking English, just voicing a twisted jumble of sounds. A dark weight settled on my chest, pressing down on my lungs. I felt sick. My head swam.

Violet took a breath, about to say more, but was interrupted by a pounding at the front door. She set her hand on my back as she passed by me and went to answer it. When the door opened, I caught a glimpse of an older man standing outside, tall and craggy looking with shining white hair.

"What were you two thinking?" he demanded as he tried to push his way in.

"Caleb, I don't have time to —"

"Where's Marcus?"

"He's getting the barbecue ready. I'm with a patient."

"That's exactly what I want to talk about. Will —"

The man started to force himself inside, but Violet planted her hand in the center of his chest and pushed him out onto the porch.

"If you want to talk, we talk outside."

Violet slammed the door behind her. The two of them were just outside the window, but I couldn't understand what they were saying. The man towered over her, beginning to shout, trying to intimidate her, but Violet didn't give an inch. She argued him down the stairs and out into their front yard.

I looked from the window down to Dad, and that's when what Violet said hit me. It was like I was in the middle of the ocean and my hands had slipped off the side of a lifeboat. I sucked in a deep breath. I had to be calm, like Grandpa. Strong, like Grandpa. This was reality, and I had to deal with it. How I felt wasn't important. My fingernails dug into my raw palm.

I stuffed my hand into my pocket as the door opened again. Violet swept in and went directly to the wooden cabinet. She drew something out that I couldn't see, then returned to Dad's side.

"That was Caleb," I said. "Will's father."

"That's right," she said.

"He doesn't want us here."

"I think that's putting it mildly."

"He's why Sam wasn't sure I should come here."

Violet looked at me steadily but said nothing.

"What did you tell him?"

"I told him that if my family wanted to share our home and food with you, it was our business." I watched as Violet lifted a needle into the candlelight and filled it with liquid from a small bottle. "But that I definitely, without a doubt, wouldn't use any of our medicines."

Once the needle was full, Violet flicked it with her finger, then slid it into Dad's arm and pushed the plunger. When she was done she turned back to me.

"What he doesn't know won't hurt him," she said with a wink. "These are antibiotics, in case there are infections and to protect against pneumonia." Her brow furrowed. "He needs blood thinners because of the breaks but . . . we ran out months ago."

"Why are you helping us?"

"When I was in med school," she explained, "one of my teachers told me that my only job was to treat the patient in front of me. He said I couldn't change the world, I could just treat what's in front of me."

Over the next hour or so, Violet fed Dad with a plastic tube threaded down his throat and then made some plaster and set his arm and leg in a cast, struggling to make the shattered bits of bone line up and lock into place.

I fell into a chair behind her, sinking into its deep cushions, while outside it slowly grew dark. A bright orange glow rose from the park. Maybe fifty men, women, and children converged around the bonfire. It had a large roasting spit built over it that Marcus and Sam were tending, turning the big deer around and around over the flame.

A string of about twenty small torches was set in the ground around the perimeter of the group, making flickering islands of light. The people milled around, laughing and talking, swimming in the glow.

"Who are you people?" My voice sounded strange and distant, like pieces of wreckage bobbing along on dark water. "What is this place?"

Violet smoothed a length of plaster-covered cloth across Dad's knee, then gave me a kind and soft smile over her shoulder.

"There'll be time for explanations later," she said. "I'll be done soon. When I am, we'll get you cleaned up, and then I should get you something to eat."

I shook my head. Violet persisted, but I didn't move. I wasn't being taken away from Dad.

Outside the window, people moved dreamily around the playground. Groups came together and apart, only to re-form again like beads of oil on water. All of them talking, hugging, throwing their heads back to laugh. All of it an eerie dumb show, silent to me in the house.

Violet continued working and I closed my eyes, surprised to find sleep overtaking me. I fought it for a moment, but it was too strong, too long in coming. I just prayed my dreams would find me back out on the trail with Dad, crashing through the grass with Paolo behind us, Dad talking a mile a minute, me bringing up the rear.

When I finally did sleep, though, I dreamed I was walking through the woods alone, late at night, my every step mirrored by an immense shadow with claws that lumbered by my side.

TEN

When I woke up, Violet was gone and there was a gnawing emptiness in my stomach. I couldn't even remember the last time I had eaten. As I sat up, I saw a note sitting on a table near Dad.

We're all at the barbecue. Come out and have something to eat when you get up. — Violet

Outside, the party had gotten smaller, but a group of twenty or so still milled around the fire.

There was some jerky in my pack, and maybe a few crumbs of hardtack had made it through. That would do. I looked around the room, but then remembered with a jolt that in my hurry to get Dad inside, I had left the pack outside. I could see it peeking over the lip of the wagon. Grandpa's rifle leaned against it. The realization that I had left them both sitting out there in the open made me forget my hunger for a moment. I could feel the sting of the beating Grandpa would have given me if he had seen. *Stupid.* I wished I could just make my bed on the floor next to Dad and go to sleep, but I couldn't leave my gear out there for anyone to take.

I struggled out of the chair, kneeling at Dad's bed on my way to the door. The dirt and splashes of blood that had lingered on his face were gone and his skin wasn't quite the waxy mask it had been. I tried to tell myself that he didn't look any different than he ordinarily did when he was asleep, but there was a stillness there, an absence that seemed vast. I squeezed his arm and leaned down next to his ear.

"I'll be right back," I whispered before stepping outside.

The hairs on my arm lifted in the cool air, and the spicy smell of wood smoke and roasted meat made my stomach roar, pushing the last remnants of sleep out of my head. I crept down the stairs and across the yard, easing up to the wagon, hoping not to be seen. When I got close enough, I drew my bag toward me. Unfortunately I forgot that Grandpa's rifle was leaning against it, so as soon as I pulled the pack away, the rifle fell with a clatter. My insides jumped.

"Hey."

I looked down. Jackson and two others were sitting near the wagon's tires, a litter of plates and half-eaten dinner all around them. There was a skinny kid with big glasses and another larger kid with thick curly hair. All of them were staring at me, three pairs of eyes burning in the dark.

"You get something to eat?" Jackson asked.

I clutched my pack to my chest. "I have food."

"We've got venison," Jackson said. "And some potatoes Derrick's mom made."

"They suck," the big kid, Derrick, said.

The kid with the glasses was sitting on the other side of Jackson. "My mom brought her blueberry pie," he said, which for some reason caused the big kid with curls to shoot him a leering grin.

"Oh, I *bet* she did, Martin," he said.

"Shut up, Derrick! That doesn't even make sense!"

"Oh yeah? You want to know what makes sense?"

"Oh, I don't know," Martin said. "My mom?"

Jackson pushed Derrick away and stood up by the wagon. "Ignore Derrick. He's obnoxious. You should stay and have some food."

"I'm fine."

I shouldered my pack and reached for the rifle, but before I could get away, Derrick leapt in front of me and started doing a spastic shuffle, jumping up and down and throwing his arms around at his sides like he was having a fit. I took a step backward.

"Uh . . . Derrick?" Jackson said, stepping up to my side. "What are you doing?"

"Well," Derrick said, panting, "I figured, uh, maybe the problem was that he didn't feel entirely at home yet, so I thought I'd perform the Settler's Landing Dance of Welcoming."

"You look like you're having a seizure," Martin said drily.

Derrick cackled and threw himself into the air, which I guessed was his big finish, since when he landed he swept his arms out in front of him and took a deep bow. Martin clapped sarcastically and Jackson laughed. When Derrick stood up again, he somehow had a plate of venison and potatoes in his hand. Where it came from, I had no idea, but when he held it out to me, the smell of it almost made me faint.

"Eat," he said. "Eat, my new and tiny little friend."

"What do you care if I eat or not?"

Derrick's grin froze.

"Just being friendly, man, that's all. You want it or not?"

I was about to turn and run back up the stairs into the Greens' house, but my hands moved before the rest of me could. Before I knew it, I had snatched the plate from him and dug my fingers into the pile of meat. It was rich and gamey and seeped into every part of my body.

I gulped it down, and when it was gone, I scooped up the potatoes and devoured those too, sucking the remains from my fingers. When I was done, I had to gasp for air. Jackson and the others stood there, jaws wide.

"Uh . . . you want us to go kill you something else?" Martin asked. "I think we have a horse that's lame."

Embarrassed, I pushed the plate at Derrick and grabbed the rifle out of the wagon. "Thanks," I mumbled.

"Hey, it's no problem, man. I'd do anything for the guy who shot Will Henry."

I turned, glaring at Jackson. "They know about that?"

Jackson flinched. "I—"

"Relax," Derrick said. "We just wish your aim had been a little better."

"Hey, you coming to school with us tomorrow?" Martin asked.

I looked at him, blank faced, sure I hadn't heard him correctly.

"School. You know. Teachers. Books." Derrick whacked Martin in the stomach. "Girls in tight sweaters."

"You all go to school?"

"Sure! How else are we going to get into a good college?"

The three of them laughed, but I didn't get it. The way they talked, like they were tossing a ball around in a game of keep-away, was confusing.

"So you wanna come?" Jackson asked.

I looked over my shoulder at Dad's window and shivered at the thought of him lying in that tomblike quiet. What if he woke up and I wasn't there? I shouldered the rifle and backed away from the three of them without a word.

Derrick called after me. "Okay! Take it easy. Come back anytime!"

Jackson pushed Derrick hard on the shoulder, knocking him off balance.

"What? I was being nice!"

"You were being a spaz."

I left them bickering, getting halfway across the road, when Marcus spoke up from behind me.

"Everyone? Everyone, can I have your attention please?"

Marcus was standing by the fire with Violet at his side, waving everyone closer together. Caleb Henry loomed in the background.

"Just for a second. Thanks, everybody. Um. I just wanted to say it's great that we could all be here like this tonight. It's Thanksgiving today, uh, we think, and I'm sure most of us remember that from back when we were kids. Every year we'd gather the whole family and spend the day together, eating and watching football and arguing."

"Was this back on the yacht, Green?" someone called, and a laugh rose up from the group.

Marcus chuckled. "Well, wherever it was, I don't remember ever feeling closer to my family than I did right then. And I don't think I've ever felt closer to all of you. We've done great work in the past year, haven't we?"

There was a general murmur of agreement from the assembled, a scattering of applause.

"New wells were dug, the crops came in a bit better than expected, and everybody's house is ready for the winter. But most of all, another summer has gone by and we're all still here, together and safe. We're lucky. Damn lucky, I think."

Just then Caleb edged Marcus out of the way and came forward. His face looked even rougher in the firelight, creased like an old map.

As soon as he stepped up, everyone went quiet. Caleb looked from person to person grimly, then began a prayer. Everyone lowered their heads as he spoke. His voice was dark and sharp.

"Lord, after the flood, many of us believed it would be the fire next time. All of us here saw that fire, and thanks to your grace we were among the few who found their way through it. As we struggle to please you, we are beset on all sides by those that would tear down all that we have built."

As Caleb spoke, his blue eyes searched the crowd. I wondered if he was looking for me.

"Today we give thanks and reaffirm that the price of your gift is vigilance and obedience to your will. Amen."

The crowd murmured "Amen" and then someone at the back of the group began singing a song that I didn't recognize at first. "Oh, say, can you see, by the dawn's early light . . ."

Even Jackson and his friends joined in. Some of the adults laid their hands over their hearts. I remembered it then from the few times Grandpa had sung it when he was drunk. The American national anthem. What were they singing that for?

"What so proudly we hail —"

"Leave me alone!" someone shouted.

The singing stopped and the group turned as one body to a mass of shadows that was swirling at the edge of the park.

"Oh no," Jackson said from behind me.

Derrick barked with laughter. "Here comes the show, ladies and gentlemen!"

As the group turned more into the light, I could make out a kid standing in the center of a circulating mob of five or six others, all of whom were jutting in and out at him like crows after a scattering of seed. The kid in the center was thrashing hard and had already put two kids on the ground, one clutching his knee to his chest, the other cradling his jaw. A third boy got up his courage and went in, only to get a kick between his legs that put him down howling.

"Nice one!" Derrick shouted.

"Stop it!" Marcus hollered as he rushed toward the scene. "Stop this right now! Jennifer!"

Jennifer?

Marcus grabbed the arm of the kid in the middle to pull him out of the melee. To my surprise, it wasn't a boy at all, but a black-haired girl of about sixteen, dressed in dirty jeans and a loose blue-and-red flannel shirt. As she stumbled closer to the firelight, her tan skin glowed like bronze. Marcus pulled her back just as she was going after one of the boys who was stupid enough to have gotten up off the ground.

"What have I told you?" Marcus yelled as he pulled her away. "What have I told you about fighting?"

The girl didn't argue with him, and instead took the time to kick one of the remaining boys firmly in the calf.

The group of adults broke up as Marcus came charging through with her in tow. Some of them went to pull their wounded sons off the ground and others gathered in a tight knot around Caleb Henry, sternly watching the proceedings and whispering among themselves.

As Marcus and the girl came closer, I got a better look at her. She had broad shoulders for a girl, inky black hair, and dark, almond-shaped eyes.

Chinese, I thought, gripping the stock of Grandpa's rifle. They were all supposed to be west of the Rockies. *What is she doing here? With them?*

"You could have walked away," Marcus said.

"And let them call me a murderer and a spy? Let them call me a Chink?"

"They're just words."

"They're just words to you!" she screamed, yanking her arm out of Marcus's grasp and stalking away. "I didn't start any damn war!"

I tensed up as she came toward me.

"Jenny!" Marcus called. "We'll say something. I'll talk to their parents!"

"Forget it. Just forget it!" Jenny stomped toward the wagon, her face screwed up in rage.

"Hey, Jenny, how's it goin'?"

"Shut up, Derrick!" she said, then whipped her head my way. "And what the hell are *you* looking at?!" she snapped as she shot past me.

Jenny tore across the park and into the Greens' house and returned several moments later with a big bag slung over her shoulder.

"Jenny!" Marcus barked. "Don't you just walk away! Jennifer Marie Green!"

She whirled around to face him. "It's Tan! My name is Jenny Tan!"

Jenny ran up the road, disappearing into the darkness. It was quiet then, like the aftermath of a storm. Most of the other parents had drifted off, injured sons in tow, leaving Caleb Henry and his grim circle.

"Beset on all sides," Caleb intoned, looking from the Greens to me. His blue eyes reflected the twisting fire. "Even from within."

Marcus was about to say something back, but Violet appeared at his shoulder and he swallowed whatever it was. Caleb grinned wolfishly, satisfied, and drifted out of the group, his followers trailing behind him like smoke.

Marcus stood in the middle of the road, his shoulders slumped, his hand clasped on the back of his neck. Violet rested her hand on his arm. He looked up wearily and nodded.

Jackson was sitting against the wagon. His knees were drawn up to his chest, head back, staring blankly up at the stars. I would have thought he was praying, except for how his hands were curled into bone-white fists. He saw me and forced a smile.

"Welcome to Settler's Landing."

Soon the park emptied and I followed the Greens inside.

"Jackets on the rack, everyone," Violet announced as we entered. Jackson and Marcus dutifully obeyed, stripping off their coats and hanging them just inside the door.

"If I don't keep at them, they're pigs," she said. Once Violet got me settled in the room with Dad, she disappeared into the kitchen with Marcus.

I stood by Dad's bed, pulling my thin blanket out of my backpack.

"Sorry for all that tonight," Jackson said from the doorway behind me. "You can pretty much bet that if Jenny sees calm water, she'll throw in the biggest rock she can."

"She's your . . . sister?" I asked, still amazed that a Chinese girl lived with them.

"Adopted, yeah. I was little, so I don't really remember, but Mom said we went through this town the day after some big fight and there she was, wrapped in this old Chinese army jacket she always wears. She was all cut up and bloody. Mom figured whoever her parents were must have left her, thinking she was a goner, or maybe they got killed themselves. Anyway, Mom fixed her up and took her along with us."

"So how does she know her real name is Tan?"

Jackson laughed. "She doesn't," he said. "That's the thing — she just made it up. Guess that's how much she didn't want to be one of us. Anyway, she'll go sleep it off in this old barn she goes to, out north of town. She'll be well rested and ready to embarrass us again soon enough."

I rolled my sweatshirt up into a pillow and laid it out on the blanket. Jackson stood behind me a little while longer, then stepped back into the hallway.

"Well . . . anyway, good night," he said.

Soon I heard the creaking of stairs and the soft shutting of a door. I blew out the candles scattered around the room and the house settled into darkness.

Even in the dark, Dad's skin was powdery and pale against his beard. His cheeks were sunken and there were hollows around his eyes. He looked like a stranger. An aching homesickness shot through me. There was so much that was new: these people, this place. I wished we could be back on the trail, just the two of us.

I closed my eyes, praying I'd drift off immediately, but of course I didn't. In fifteen years I had spent the night in tents and caves and abandoned buildings but never once in a house. I couldn't breathe. I wrestled the window over Dad's bed open, letting in the rhythmic chirp of crickets and the blow of the wind rustling through the trees.

Across the park, the other houses loomed in the moonlight, their unlit windows like blank, staring eyes. Looking at it all made me feel the whole Earth tilting underneath me. Every other time in my life when I felt like this, I would go to Dad and it seemed, with just a wave of his hand, he could make things right again.

Before I went to sleep, I leaned over his chest, straining to hear the soft pat of a heartbeat, but what was there was too soft and too far away to grasp.

I was on my own.

ELEVEN

I woke with a start before dawn, disoriented. But soon the memories of the day before fell into place and everything began to clear.

The house was quiet. Dad hadn't moved.

I pulled my blanket aside and rubbed the sleep out of my eyes, wondering what I was supposed to do next. No salvage to secure, no trail to start down. I felt like some great wheel was spinning inside me, but it had nowhere to go.

I slipped into my jeans and moved through the downstairs rooms, exploring. I found a sharpened stub of a pencil and an old nickel lying in a dusty corner and pocketed them. Other than that, there wasn't much I hadn't seen the night before. A few pieces of furniture. The pictures. The big wooden cabinet.

I froze, remembering the glass and shining metal, and how Violet had shut the drawer so quickly, like she didn't want me to see inside. I closed my eyes and listened to the house. Nothing. I slipped over to the cabinet and opened the top drawer. Inside there were gleaming rows of silver instruments: razors and scissors, picks and tweezers. I lifted out a large saw with brutal teeth. I set it down and moved to the next drawer.

There, lying on strips of green felt, were the rows of frosted glass bottles. They all had white labels, with words like MORPHINE and PENICILLIN written on them in precise black letters. Marcus said Violet had been an army doctor. I guessed maybe she had done a bit of salvaging too before the military broke up. Whatever the case, it was a gold mine. For a fraction of what was in that cabinet, we could get a new wagon and mule, maybe even a horse, and enough supplies to get us trading again.

A spring squeaked upstairs, followed by the sound of feet hitting the floor. I scrambled to make sure everything was in its place and then shut the drawers. When the Greens came downstairs, I was sitting innocently at Dad's side.

"How we doing this morning, Aloysius?" Marcus asked. He was standing in the doorway that led back to the kitchen, munching on a hard-boiled egg. He had a bowl of them in his hands.

"Who's Aloysius?"

"You are," Marcus said. "Well, at least until you tell us your real name." Marcus held the bowl out to me. "Egg?"

I hesitated for a second, but then the hunger took over.

"It's Stephen," I said as I plucked an egg from the bowl.

"You think about what you'd like to do today, Stephen?"

I glanced out the window. It was a bright fall morning, crisp. A full moon still hung in the sky, fading as the sun rose. Every part of me yearned to be out of the stifling closeness of the house.

"I should just stay here," I said. "With my dad."

"You sure?" Marcus asked. He gave me a moment, then turned back toward the kitchen. "Okay. Suit yourself." His boots echoed down the short hallway.

"Wait," I called before he could disappear. "Maybe . . ." My mind spun in place. Wouldn't Grandpa have given me a pounding if he knew

I was in a place like this and didn't take the time to do a little recon? I mean, who knew what else I'd find? "For all you've done for us . . . I can't pay you, but maybe I could work."

"I told you, there's no reason to —"

I turned my eyes from the window and set them on Marcus, unmoving. It was a look that, when Grandpa used it, said there would be no compromise, no discussion. To my surprise, it actually worked.

"Well, there's a little of the fall harvest left," Marcus conceded. "It's not much but —"

"It's fine," I said. A buzz of excitement lit through me. Just the idea of being out in the open air was a weight lifted off my shoulders.

"Vi!" Marcus called into the kitchen. "Gonna take Stephen out with me to the harvest."

"Who's Stephen?"

"Aloysius."

"Oh! He should rest!" she yelled back.

"Can't! Says he has to be our indentured servant."

"Okay, well, have him clean the gutters while you're out."

Marcus laughed. "Come on. I promise you, though, you'll regret this."

I pulled on my boots and coat and tucked a piece of jerky into my pocket for later. I started to follow Marcus but stopped at the foot of Dad's bed. Violet had removed the feeding tube from the night before, so he almost looked like he was just sleeping, his hands resting atop the clean white sheet. Could I really leave him here with these strangers? Then I remembered how Violet had cared for him, even defying Caleb to do it. I leaned down by Dad's ear quickly, so Marcus wouldn't see. "I'll be back," I whispered.

Marcus grabbed his coat off the rack by the door and then I followed him outside.

The second I stepped out the door I felt like I could breathe again. As we made our way deeper into the neighborhood, kids of all ages blew past us carrying salvaged backpacks and carpetbags. Groups of girls would meet up on the road and separate into age groups, the younger ones squealing and hugging, the older ones trying their best to seem unimpressed. The boys pushed one another, braying laughter loud as donkeys. I flinched as they thundered by and disappeared down a hill that dipped into the trees a few houses from Marcus's.

"Heading to school," Marcus said. "Welcome to join them, you know."

I shook my head at the thought of being shut up inside some room with the screeching horde. I could only imagine what Grandpa would say about running off to school when there was work to be done.

I cracked the egg Marcus had given me and ate it as I scanned the roadside and the yards along the way, looking for treasures like the ones in the Greens' house, but found little. The place was amazingly neat; only a few scattered toys lay about here and there, abandoned as kids raced to school. The houses, though . . . what was in all of these houses?

"Listen," Marcus said, stuffing his hands into the pockets of his jeans. "Sorry about Will and all. What are ya gonna do? Last month he accused Winona Lee of being a Fort Leonard spy. She's eighty-three."

"What is Fort Leonard anyway?" I asked. "Another town?"

"Barely. It's a little settlement that popped up to the north. The map says it's near a place called Fort Leonard. People have a bee in their bonnet since somebody saw a scout poking around east of here the other day. That's who we were out looking for when we spotted you and your dad."

I nodded, but didn't really get it. They brought me and Dad in, two complete strangers, when they were supposed to be out looking for a spy?

The houses thinned out and then the land opened up into five large fields that stretched out about as far as I could see. Most were barren at this point, but the closest one was still full of rows of thick green sprouts. A dozen or so adults circulated around them.

"Well, here we are," Marcus announced. "The land of plenty! Whole thing used to be the town golf course. Took us almost the whole first year to clear the ground. 'Bout killed us all, but it was worth it. We bring in a decent amount of wheat and corn and beans now. People mostly raise vegetables in their backyard gardens. Hey, Sam!"

Sam waved from where he was kneeling down in the rows of plants.

"We owe it all to Sam, actually. His people were farmers way back. He told us what was what."

Sam tipped his hat at the compliment. Marcus held out a handful of thin plastic bags to me. They said SAFEWAY in big red letters.

"Okay," he said. "You asked for it."

I took the bags and we picked two rows alongside Sam's. We were harvesting carrots and onions. I stripped off my coat and sweatshirt and got down on my knees. At first I worked just enough to cover my inspection of the area around me. There wasn't much to see though. A few farming implements, hoes and shovels mostly, sat nearby. I made a mental note of them.

I ranged out toward a fence that ran along the length of the fields. The branches of the brown-leaved trees squeezed through its narrow openings or surged over top like an advancing army. The fence was warped in places, bent inward from years of trying to hold the forest back. Farther east, the fence disappeared — torn down, I guessed, when they'd cleared the land.

"It used to be a gated community."

Sam was kneeling in the rows behind me, pushing his hands through the carrot leaves, picking and choosing. Marcus joined us from a few rows down.

"What's that?"

"Before the Collapse," Sam continued, "rich people like Marcus here's family liked to build these self-contained neighborhoods, surround them with fences and security and whatnot. You know, keep out the riffraff. Anyway, this whole place was built right before everything went bad. After that, the people living here closed themselves up. Cut access to the roads, let some of the forest grow back in. With so much going on, they were just forgotten."

I stopped my digging and sat back on my heels. "What happened to them?" I asked.

"P Eleven," Marcus said. "Sickness took all but the Henrys. You know? Your buddy Will? His family. They have this big house on the north side. They were here when all of us arrived. Had a hand in building the place, I think."

"Yeah," Sam said with a chuckle. "And they *still* think it's theirs."

The sun was out now in full. A flock of birds cut across the sky and landed on the field, pecking briefly at the earth before swarming away again. I looked around at the ten or fifteen people moving through the rows, pulling in a harvest like it was the most natural thing in the world.

It was sad in a way, standing there in the fields, watching them. They'd been lucky, incredibly lucky, but sooner or later I knew their luck would run out, just like it had for Dad and me. Just like it had for everybody. All it would take was one little mistake and they would be found and wiped out.

How could they not know how useless it all was?

"Lunch," Marcus announced a couple hours later, stretching his back. "You ready, Stephen? I bet Vi has something good for us."

"Maybe I'll keep going," I said, thinking of the house's awful stillness. "Is that okay?"

"You should come and eat."

"I'm fine, really. It's just . . . it's good to be *doing* something. You know?"

Marcus looked over at Sam, who just shrugged. "Kid wants to work."

"All right," Marcus said. "But not too much longer."

I handed Marcus my bags of carrots and he and Sam followed the others back toward the house. Once they were gone, I clapped the dirt off my hands, cut through the fields, and wound through the neighborhood's unfamiliar streets.

I ended up at the spur of a road leading down a hill, the same one the kids had streamed down earlier on their way to school. I looked over my shoulder: No one was around. I pulled the scrap of jerky from my pocket and chewed on it as I followed the road. Down at the bottom of the hill, there was a black parking lot, cut up into little slips with fading yellow paint. A low building, surrounded by a neatly trimmed yard that stretched behind it, was backed by a hill dotted with one large sycamore. Just behind a sidewalk that ringed the building there was an old sign that said in large black letters: SETTLER'S LANDING HIGH SCHOOL.

I kept close to the school's beige walls as I passed. Like all the buildings in the neighborhood, it was neat and well maintained, the brick foundation without a crack. The grass around it was short and free of weeds, and I found discarded kids' things here and there on the ground. A jump rope. A broken colored pencil. I took what I could and kept going.

I walked around the school, looking in the windows as I went. Inside there were empty classrooms filled with abandoned desks and chairs. I made it around to the back of the school, found a lone window, and peeked inside.

Desks and chairs sat in six neat rows far below. There was a kid at each desk, pencil in hand, leaning over a stack of papers and writing intently. The rows were broken up by age, the youngest in the front, oldest in the back. Jackson and his friends sat together toward the rear. Will Henry sat on the opposite side of the room behind them, dozing, surrounded by twins, two pale, greasy boys who reminded me of slugs, and a giant redheaded boy with a grove of acne covering his face.

All the rows faced a black chalkboard and a long wooden desk to my right. Sitting at the desk was a tall, thin man with steel-rimmed glasses, wearing a black suit that was a bit too tight and made him look like a scarecrow. He scanned the room, watching the quietly writing students.

"Freaky, huh?"

I whirled around, dropping my hand to the hilt of Dad's knife.

Jenny Tan lounged against the big sycamore behind me, wearing a green army jacket with a red star on the sleeve. She had a large pad of paper spread on her lap and a line of colored pencils in the grass next to her.

"You gonna stab me with that thing, or what?"

Suddenly feeling foolish, I jerked my hand away from the knife.

"So," she said. "You're the spy."

"I'm no spy," I said. "We're salvagers."

"Salvagers," she said, tilting her head against the tree trunk and studying me. "Never actually met one of you before. You travel around, right?" She nodded her head out toward the trees and the edge of town. "Out in the great beyond?"

I nodded. Jenny watched me a moment longer, then took a pencil off the ground and started drawing. She looked past me into the window of the school and then down again. I watched as she erased a line and redrew it, then smudged it with her thumb. Her eyebrows knitted together in concentration. Her hair, loose and tangled, framed her face like a deep shadow. I kept thinking of the hurricane she had been the night before, amazed at how she seemed like someone completely different now.

"How come you don't go to school with the rest of them?" I asked.

"And listen to Tuttle go blah-blah-blah-blah about history and math and the poetry of English guys who have been dead for a thousand years? No thanks. Only reason anybody goes is because it's what their parents remember doing when they were kids, so they're doomed to repeat it." Jenny looked up at me. Her eyes were deep brown and seemingly flecked with gold, like a hawk's. "Sounds kind of dumb, huh?"

I shrugged. "Guess so."

Jenny glanced down at my hand. "No dumber than reaching for a weapon every time you see a Chinese girl."

She sprang it like a bear trap. I scrambled for something to say, but when I opened my mouth, no words came.

"What? Your folks tell you to expect horns and a tail or something?"

"No. I —"

Jenny's grin grew wider, about to burst into a laugh. "Relax," she said. "I'm just messing with you. Hey, I'd probably reach for a knife if I saw me too."

A rumble came from inside the school. I turned to the window and saw the students were pushing back from their desks and stampeding toward the double doors at the back of the classroom.

"Uh-oh. Here comes the flood." Jenny tore the drawing out of her pad, crumpled it up, and tossed it to the ground. As she stood up and stretched, her Red Army jacket lifted, revealing a scar that was thick as a trench and curled across her middle and around her back.

"I don't know. Maybe I *will* go back to school on Monday," she said, letting the statement hang in the air for a moment before turning and giving me a quick look. "It's been a while since I annoyed Tuttle. Maybe I'll see ya around, tough guy."

Jenny gathered her things, then strode away on bare feet down the hill, just missing the torrent of bodies that roared into the playground outside the school. I turned to escape before they could reach me, stopping only to snatch Jenny's crumpled drawing off the ground, then dashing into the forest.

I tromped through the brush, not looking where I was going, simply trying to escape the strangeness of the day. She was right — I had never actually seen a Chinese person up close before, let alone talked to one. These were the people the United States had been at war with? The people who'd released P11 and killed millions? After the plague had passed and the Chinese troops had invaded, there'd been years of vicious fights between them and the survivors. My family had fled San Diego a year before I was born, though, so we mostly kept out of it. Still, we couldn't help but see the spreading aftermath.

Grandpa said the Chinese were subhuman. Savage, ugly, and vicious. *But if that's true,* I wondered, *how come when I look at Jenny, that's not what I see?*

I skimmed the edges of backyards as I went deeper into the woods. The neat lines of the houses were just visible through the trees, which were hanging over thick grass and vegetable patches. I thought again of the treasures Violet had laid out in that cabinet of hers. Drugs. Priceless medical instruments.

I wondered: *How is it possible that while we had nothing, these people are here with all of this?*

A twist of anger made me stop to catch my breath. The forest shifted around me in the wind. Something small skittered through dry leaves. Grandpa had told me a hundred times that life wasn't fair and that expecting it to be was for fools.

These people got lucky. That's all. It can't last. All that matters is that I have to be ready when Dad gets better so we can get on track again. We need supplies and things to trade.

But what?

I searched and searched for an answer, only to return to the same place each time.

There was only one thing to do.

I didn't like it, but the truth was we had never been in anywhere near this much trouble before and I was the only one who could save us.

A blackbird cawed loudly, startling me. The sun had dropped a couple degrees in the sky. I thought of Dad lying there all alone and started to go, but then I remembered Jenny's drawing still clenched in my hand. I turned the crumpled ball over, and before I knew it, my fingers were pulling it open. The paper crackled as I spread it open on the ground in front of me.

It wasn't what I expected at all. Inside was a nearly perfect sketch of the back of the school with the sky and drifting clouds in the background. The scrub and grass leading up to the brick wall were textured and deep. It all looked unbelievably real, like a photograph, except that on the other side of the window, instead of a class full of students, desks, and a teacher, there stood a lone, riderless horse.

Its head was bowed almost to the floor. It had no saddle or bridle, and its dark mane was long and tangled. The strangeness of it was overwhelming, but not in the same way that the town was. Looking at it made my pulse slow and my breathing run shallow and quiet for the first time since I'd arrived, like it was speaking to me in a language I could almost, but not quite, understand.

I traced the lines of the drawing with the tip of my finger, looping and slashing across the paper like Jenny had, trying to imagine what was in her head as she did it.

The blackbird cawed again, pulling me back into the world. *Waste of time*, I thought, and folded the paper up and shoved it in my pocket. I had no time to be looking at pictures.

I had work to do.

TWELVE

Late that night, once everyone had gone to sleep, I sat up in the darkness. I dressed as silently as I could, then gathered everything I needed — moving achingly slow to avoid making any sound — and crept out of town.

I followed the road up toward the white stone wall that seemed to glow in the moonlight. Luckily the gates had been left slightly open so I was able to slip past, avoiding the rusty creak that I was sure would have carried across the entire town. Once through, I headed for the woods on the other side of the grass plain.

It took me more than an hour to cross through the forest. When I stepped down onto the cracked remnant of the highway on the other side, my boots were caked in mud and my arms were raked with scratches from the thornbushes woven through the trees.

The land across the road was dark as slate. It seemed to stretch westward nearly forever, dotted with scattered families of trees, until it ran up against low mountains that loomed far off in the distance. Off to the north there were the remains of a casino called the Golden Acorn and a Starbucks. Their billboards stretched into the sky.

I made my way up the hill until I found an old lightning-struck tree. It was split down the middle with the very first showings of sprouts growing out of its charred interior. I stepped back into the cover of the woods behind it before I pulled the gauze-wrapped package from my coat pocket and opened it.

Two glass medicine bottles and a few stainless steel instruments, priceless at any trade gathering, glittered in my hand. A sharp stitch of guilt knotted in my chest. *I'm no thief,* I thought again. But the fact was that we were broke. No wagon. No supplies. Nothing to trade. I couldn't let that happen. With no one else around, it was my responsibility and mine alone.

I found a sharp, flat rock, pushed aside the leaves, and started digging into the soft ground until I had a wide hole cut about two feet deep into the earth. I set the gauze-wrapped medicines, along with the pencil and old nickel, carefully into the bottom. The way the gauze lay over the medicine bottles made them look like two bodies wrapped in a shroud.

I pushed the dirt over them quickly and sat back on the hill, leaning on my elbows, pulling in the cool air that tasted of wood smoke and decaying leaves. That pang of guilt hit me again. My hand moved around to my pocket and I laid Mom's picture out in a patch of moonlight.

Hours after we'd taken the picture and made it back to camp, I'd slipped into Mom and Dad's tent, squirming in between them. Mom lit a candle, opened one of our few books, and laid her arm across my back while Dad turned the pages. Mom would read a passage out loud and then I would read the next one, both of us quiet as could be, so as not to wake Grandpa.

I'd liked how, when I stumbled on words I didn't know or couldn't pronounce, Mom would reach for our battered dictionary and we'd go over the definition and sound it out, over and over until I had it down. It always felt to me like trudging up a tough and rocky hill, sweating and pushing until finally I made it up over the top to land that was flat and bright.

We made it through *Sounder*, *Charlie and the Chocolate Factory*, and *Great Expectations* that way, the words rolling from Mom's mouth in her high, clear voice that was like a bird's or a bell's. We'd read until my eyes drooped and the steady in and out of Mom's and Dad's breathing on either side would rock me to sleep.

Grandpa thought the idea of my learning to read was a waste of time, and in a way I'd agreed with him. I was going to be a trader like him and my dad — what use would reading really be?

Mom had said that maybe the world wouldn't always be like it was now. But even if it was, she said, sometimes it was important to do things there was no real use for. Like reading books and taking pictures.

She'd said we had to be more than what the world would make us.

A branch snapped and leaves rustled down to my left. I scanned the woods with my hand on the hilt of the knife, but everything was blurry, swirling like the forest was underwater. I reached my hand up to my eyes and it came back wet. I had been crying and didn't even realize it.

Stupid baby. I wiped the tears away with my dirty coat sleeve but still didn't see anything. *Probably nothing anyway. A deer. Maybe a stray dog.*

I swept leaves over the disturbed ground so it blended into the hillside, then marked the place by half burying the rock at the head of the hole. It didn't matter what Mom would have thought. Like Grandpa, she was gone, and I was here.

I surveyed the highway and the land beyond, all flat plains of black and gray. The stars, straining through the thick canopy above my head, shone like bits of broken glass.

As soon as Dad was better, all we'd have to do is stop here on the way out of town. Then we could trade for whatever supplies we needed. Everything would be back the way it was.

The only question was, what would I do until then?

THIRTEEN

"So what do they do down there?"

I was lingering by the window over Dad's bed a few days later, full from a breakfast of eggs and bacon and bread that Marcus had cooked and insisted I join them for. The sun was spread across the asphalt where it dipped into the woods a few houses down. Soon that road would be stocked with kids jostling and laughing on their way down to the school.

"Usual stuff. Math. English. Why? You want to —"

"No," I said quickly. "I was curious. I'll help you and Sam in the fields again."

"I bet we could do without you for a day or two."

Violet had changed Dad into a pair of Marcus's old pajamas that had white and blue stripes and a neat little collar. His face and beard were clean. There were shadows all along the white sheet that covered him. Dips and peaks. It was like he was buried under a drift of snow.

"What are you two talking about?" Violet appeared in the doorway behind us, drying her hands after doing the dishes in a wash bucket out on the porch.

"Stephen going to school this morning."

Violet glanced down at Dad and then fixed me with a no-nonsense gaze, her hands on her hips. "There's nothing you can do for your dad that I can't. I'm sorry, but that's the way it is. I'm sure he would want you to go to school if you could. Don't you think?"

"I —"

"Jackson," she called back into the kitchen. "You have some notebooks and things to give Stephen if he wanted to come to school with you?"

"On my desk!"

"Upstairs to the left," Violet said to me, turning back toward the kitchen. "Better get moving. Don't want you two to be late."

I was about to argue, to insist that I would stay behind with Dad, but there was something about the swift sureness of Violet's command that had me falling into place behind her and following her through the kitchen. Besides, I had to admit I was curious.

The kitchen was wide and open with tall windows all along the back looking out onto a porch. Jackson was sitting at the end of the long table with a big book that said AMERICAN HISTORY on the spine. He peeked over it as I came in, then away again as soon as I caught him.

"Next to the bed," he said. "Take a couple pencils too."

I nodded and looked up the length of the dark staircase that sat behind him. I took the rail and climbed slowly, feeling a strange leg-shaking vertigo. Once I reached the landing at the top of the stairs I saw his open door, went through, and was instantly struck dumb. To my left there was a bed, an actual bed, neatly situated under a curtained window with a little nightstand next to it. The bed was crisply made with a bright red blanket and two pillows.

Standing there, I felt the same eerie sense as when I saw the pictures of their long-gone families. Everything they had was left over from the last inhabitants of the town. After they had died, the Greens and the others swept in, tidied up, and took their places. Slept in their beds. Cooked in their kitchens. Started their lives all over again.

I stepped farther in. Next to the bed was a shelf that, incredibly, held at least thirty paperback and hardcover books. I stepped closer and ran my finger along each book's cracked spine. The same hunger I felt when Marcus laid down that first plate of eggs and bacon that morning twisted inside of me. I felt a stab of jealousy again — How could they have so much? — so I made myself look away. That's when I noticed that there was a second room across the hall. From where I stood, I could just see the corner of a bed and a bureau with its drawers hanging open. Clothes, bits of paper, and nubs of pencils littered the floor.

Jenny's room?

I scooped up a notebook and a couple pencils from Jackson's desk and crossed the hall, lingering at Jenny's door and listening. Glass clinked together as Violet put the dishes away. Jackson talked low to Marcus downstairs. I slipped inside.

Light flooded in from the one bare window, harsh and glaring on the bone-white walls. Where Jackson's was clean and orderly and spare, hers was a junkyard. There was a bed stripped of its blanket with a couple coverless pillows and a balled-up sheet. Old clothes lay among dishes that were covered in congealed candle wax. A big hardback book was spread-eagled on the floor. It said CHEMISTRY in black letters.

Her mattress was small with thin blue pinstripes. I could imagine Jenny lying there, her hair spread out like a thick black cloud, staring up at the ceiling and waiting (like me?) for sleep that wouldn't come.

I remembered Jenny's body stretching in the sun, her heavy scar glowing white like a vein in marble, a sketch of a smile on her lips.

Violet's voice drifted up the stairs. "Stephen?"

As I pulled myself out of the room, I caught sight of a spot to one side of the door where the wall had been crushed inward. I stepped up for a closer look. The hole was in the shape of a small fist. Smeared traces of blood lay where knuckles would have bit into the plaster. I opened my own hand and looked at it.

In the center of my palm were the four half-moon slashes I had made the morning after Dad's accident. I reached my hand out, laid it over the hole in the wall, and closed my eyes.

"Stephen? You okay?"

It sounded like Violet was at the foot of the stairs now. Any second she'd come up to check on me.

"Coming!" I called, feeling strangely drained as I ran down the stairs to where Violet was waiting with two metal pails. I scrambled for an explanation for what I had been doing, but she handed one pail to Jackson and one to me. Puzzled, I peered inside and found a few big lumps wrapped in cloth.

"Your lunch," she said helpfully.

"Oh," I said and stood there awkwardly for a moment. Just over her shoulder I could almost see the edge of her big medicine cabinet. "Well . . . thanks."

Violet pulled at my collar, fussing with my clothes to get them straight. "If I had known you were going, I would have heated up enough water for a bath. Marcus, I don't know. . . ."

"He'll be fine."

Jackson was hovering by the door, impatient.

"I'll be fine," I said. As I started to go, Violet turned me around and pulled me into a warm hug. Close up, she smelled like baked bread and dried flowers.

She said nothing, just held on, her breath rising and falling, matching the swell of my own. The feeling was familiar, nice at first, but as it lingered it was like being embraced by a ghost and I had to push myself away.

"We better . . . we should go. Right, Jackson?" I blew past him, not waiting for a response, and threw myself into the front door, relieved to feel the blast of fresh air that hit me as soon as I was outside.

"God!" Jackson said when he caught up to me. "She's always doing stuff like that!"

I had my head down, watching my old boots slap against the asphalt, trying to swallow the thick lump in my throat and shake the warm feeling of Violet's arms around me.

"It's okay," I said. "Moms are like that, I guess."

Jackson and I fell in with a torrent of kids that pushed us faster toward the turn in the road that led to school. Jackson tried to explain the school day to me as we went, but I only caught bits of it. Six class periods broken up by lunch. Something about math. A buzzing nervousness had come over me. I craned my head toward the safety of the Greens' house, wondering if I could turn back before it was too late.

"Hey, look, there's Derrick and Martin!"

Martin looked half asleep. He stared blankly at the road in front of him, glasses slightly askew and shirt untucked, his chopped-up crew cut glistening wet. Derrick, on the other hand, reminded me of corn popping in a skillet. He bounced from toe to toe as though he could barely contain himself.

"Guys!" Derrick shouted. *"Compadres! Mis amigos! Como estás?"*

"Hey, Derrick," Jackson said.

"Well, if it isn't my little friend with the big appetite," Derrick said to me. "What's up, my man?"

Head cottony with nerves, I didn't know what to say. I hitched my shoulders noncommittally.

"Awesome. We all ready for a big day of learning?"

The double doors to the school loomed ahead of us, and the crowd swept us right toward them. Derrick knocked a few little ones out of the way. I took a deep breath, and in we went.

We were herded into a narrow hallway lined with metal lockers and doors to other rooms. I had never seen so many people my own age in one place before. I marveled at their clean clothes and the way they coursed through the hall, full of purpose. As with the houses the day I came to town, I searched for any sign that these people had grown up in the same world I did, but found nothing.

As I studied them, I was being watched too. When I caught them looking, they'd wrinkle their noses before turning away to whisper to their friends. A girl in a gray skirt pointed out my ratty old coat and giggled. I faked like I was cold and pulled it tight around me, hoping to hide the rest of my clothes.

Once we were inside the classroom, Jackson, Martin, and Derrick took desks about halfway back. Jackson pointed to an empty chair in front of him.

"Sit here," he said.

All around me, kids were writing in their notebooks, desperately trying to finish their homework, I guessed, like Jackson had done that morning. The ones who weren't working were talking. The roar of it came in waves, building and building until the entire room was shouting at once. It sounded to me like glass grinding against glass. *Why does everyone talk so much here?* I wondered. *What is there to say?* I almost put my head down on the desk and covered my ears, but the last thing I needed was to stand out even more. I looked up to my right. Above a set of tall bookshelves I could see the blue sky and the waving branches of the sycamore tree out of the window.

"What are *you* doing here?"

At first I didn't realize anyone was talking to me, but then someone's knee bumped roughly into my side.

"Hey! Spy! I'm talking to you."

I looked up. Will Henry. He was wearing a black T-shirt and a pair of jeans that bulged a bit around the thigh where I guessed a bandage was. He was with his three friends, the two sluggy twins and zit-covered mountain of a redhead.

"I said, what are you doing here?" Somehow Will's eyes glittered but were utterly blank at the same time. My hand fell beneath my coat and closed around the handle of my knife. When I didn't say anything, Will snatched the notebook out of my hands and held it up to Jackson.

"You give him this, Greeny? You and your folks? How many of these you think we have left? And you give one to some spy?"

Will planted his fists on my desk and leaned over me.

"These things are for us," he said. "Not you."

"Leave him alone, Will!"

I turned and was surprised to see that Jackson was up out of his seat. Derrick and Martin rose tentatively to join him.

"What are you going to do?" Will continued, leaning toward him. Even though he was a whole row of desks away, Jackson took one nervous step back, which clearly delighted Will. "You and your folks gonna save this stray too? What? Was the first one not pathetic enough for you?"

Every part of me tensed, desperate to shoot up out of my chair and knock Will into the wall behind him. I struggled to stay calm even as he leaned over me, his face inches from mine.

"How about you, spy? You gonna do something?"

My cheeks burned and the wounds on my hand throbbed as I gripped the rough leather of the knife's hilt.

The doors at the back of the classroom flew open and slammed against the wall.

"Class, settle down! Settle down, everyone!" the teacher called as he rushed in past us to the front of the room. "Mr. Henry, take your friends and sit."

"Mr. Tuttle —" Will began, pointing at me.

"No time, Mr. Henry," Tuttle said, distracted with papers at his desk. "Sit or find yourself in detention."

Will glanced at Tuttle. "You're lucky, spy," he said as he tossed the notebook over his shoulder to one of his friends. "Come on, guys. Kid's stinking up this side of the room anyway."

The redhead gave me a vacant, moist-eyed glare while one of the slug twins nudged my desk so my pencils fell to the ground with a clatter. I waited until they were back at their seats before bending to pick them up, but when I did, Jackson was already holding them out to me.

"Here you go."

"Thanks." I turned away from him and rearranged my things. It was odd how Jackson and the others had stood up for me the way they had. Getting backed up like that by people who weren't family didn't make sense. It felt good, but I couldn't afford to be careless. Nobody did anything for free.

"Class, I will need your attention . . . now."

Tuttle smacked his ruler across the desk and there was a rustle of bodies as everyone dropped into their seats and shot to attention. He surveyed the room, moving from face to face and making little marks on a sheet of paper until his eyes fell on me.

"And who is this?"

"Stephen," Jackson piped up from behind me. "Stephen, uh . . ." Jackson tapped my shoulder.

"Quinn," I said.

"Stephen Quinn. He's new."

Tuttle glanced at Jackson. "Yes, I can see that he's new, Mr. Green. If he wasn't, I would not have expressed surprise upon seeing him, would I?"

"Um —"

"Rhetorical question, Mr. Green. Now. Quinn. Stephen. I am Mr. Tuttle. Have you been in school before?"

I cleared my throat and tried to sit up straighter. "No sir."

"Can you read? Do you know your numbers?"

"Yes sir."

"The Pledge of Allegiance?"

"The pledge of allegiance to what?"

The class laughed all around me. I felt my cheeks go red and hot.

"Well, you'll have a lot of catching up to do, but I can't afford to slow down." Tuttle went back to marking his paper, then nodded toward Jackson and Martin. "Mr. Green and Mr. Stantz will help you."

"Hey, what about me?"

Tuttle glared at Derrick. "I think Mr. Quinn would do well to pay as little attention to you as possible on educational matters. Don't you agree, Mr. Waverly?"

"Yes! Absolutely!" Derrick said. "Good call, sir."

Tuttle gave him a withering look, then stepped back to the blackboard behind him. It was covered by some kind of pull-down screen. The class groaned as he reached for it.

"Yes, class," Tuttle said. "That's right. If you were able to better control yourselves, these little tests wouldn't be necessary. So take out your —"

Before Tuttle could finish, the doors behind us burst open again, smacking against the walls. The class turned as one body toward the sound as Jenny Tan strode barefoot into the classroom. She carried a tattered notebook. A nub of pencil was stuck behind one ear.

"Well, well, well, this is quite an honor," Tuttle deadpanned. "We haven't been graced with your presence in weeks. So nice of you to join us today, Miss Green."

"It's Tan," Jenny said as she plopped down into an open seat toward the back of the class and put her bare feet up on the chair in front of her. "And you're welcome."

A ripple of laughter went through the classroom. Jackson had his eyes closed tight and his head in his hands. Irritation pulsed off him in waves. Tuttle slapped his ruler down on the corner of his desk.

"I won't have any more disruptions."

Jenny raised her hands, palms up, as if to say he wouldn't get any from her. Tuttle considered her a moment, made a notation on his sheet, then stepped back to pull on the screen in front of the blackboard. It shot up toward the ceiling, revealing a long list of questions written in chalk. Jenny bent over her desk, laying her chin in the palm of one hand while she dug into the wood of her desk with her fingernail.

Jackson handed me a sheet of paper from his notebook as the rest of the class picked up their pencils and began writing. Jenny flicked her hair out of her face, turning just enough to catch me staring at her. It was like being stuck out in the open as lightning flashed all around me. I knew I should look away, and quickly, but I froze.

Jenny raised one eyebrow, and when I still didn't look away, she jutted her face out at me, bugging her big brown eyes and making a show of staring back. I looked away immediately, up at the test questions, trying to calm the thrill of nerves in my stomach.

I was surprised to find that the test was on *Great Expectations*, a book I had actually read and more or less remembered. I made a stab at the questions, but it was hard to concentrate. I could feel Jenny across the room. It was like her body had this gravity all its own and it was pulling at me, trying to make me turn. I thought of her drawing spread across that rumpled paper. The riderless horse, motionless but somehow pulsing with movement and life.

Jackson nudged the back of my shoulder. "Ten minutes, Steve," he whispered. "Come on."

I shook thoughts of Jenny out of my head and forced myself to focus. The test was a fill-in-the-blank thing and time was ticking down, but I rushed to fill in the last answer just as Tuttle pulled the screen back down in front of the questions.

"Now, class," Tuttle said as he collected papers. "We will continue our discussion of algebra. Turn to page two twenty-three. . . ."

Jackson nudged me again. When I turned, he was holding a folded piece of paper. He jerked his thumb over toward Jenny, who was bent over her notebook, drawing in the margins. I took the paper and unfolded it.

It was a short note, just two lines long, but when I was done reading, it felt like something had sucked every last wisp of breath out of my lungs.

Across the room, Jenny was smiling in a way that reminded me of a wolf.

The note said, in a jagged scrawl:

I saw what you buried in the woods Friday night.
You are a naughty naughty boy.

FOURTEEN

As soon as Tuttle dismissed us for the day, I jumped out of my seat and ran for the door.

"Hey!" Jackson cried. "Where are you going? We've got a game!"

I ignored him. Jenny had started to leave before "Class dismissed" had even left Tuttle's mouth. I raced down the hallway behind her, but by the time I made it through the school's front doors and outside she was gone.

The doors behind me opened again and someone rammed into my shoulder, pitching me forward. I turned around just in time to see a golden flash of blond and Will's grinning face.

"You oughta watch where you stand. I think some people are trying to walk this way."

Will and his friends laughed.

That's it.

I grabbed two handfuls of Will's shirt and spun him around, slamming him into the wall. An icy thrill went through me as his eyes bulged with surprise and fear. I was about to cock my fist when someone grabbed my elbow.

"Stephen, don't," a voice said. "Tuttle."

As soon as he said it, Tuttle appeared behind us like a pillar of black smoke. "Mr. Green, Mr. Quinn, Mr. Henry. What's going on here?"

"Nothing, sir," Jackson said quickly. "Right, Stephen?"

Jackson gave me a nudge and I managed to back away from Will and agree through gritted teeth that everything was fine.

"Good," Tuttle said. "Mr. Henry?"

Will jumped forward with barely disguised glee. "He's got a knife, sir," he said, pointing at my waist. "He keeps threatening us with it and it's making all of us feel really unsafe."

"That's not true! I didn't —"

Before I could say anything else, Tuttle pulled aside my coat and yanked the knife straight out of its sheath.

"I see," Tuttle said, turning the dark blade over in his hands. "Mr. Henry, you and your friends are dismissed."

"But —"

"You're dismissed."

Will's glare bloomed into a wide smile. He held up one finger and mouthed the words *strike one* behind Tuttle's back before he and his friends glided lazily up the hill and away from the school.

"You three may go as well," Tuttle said to Jackson, Martin, and Derrick. As they left, I caught Jackson's eye. He had a strange, worried look on his face but motioned that I should follow them toward the field east of the school when I was done.

"It's old," Tuttle said as he turned the leather-wrapped handle of the knife over in his hands. "Older than you. Your father's?"

I nodded.

"I thought as much," he said quietly. "He's hurt, I understand."

I nodded, struggling to swallow something bitter that had risen in my throat.

"I see," Tuttle said. He ran his finger gently along the knife's blade. "I will not have chaos in this place, Mr. Quinn. There's enough of that on the outside. To discourage it, there are a range of punishments I have for my students. Would you like to know what they are?"

I stood my ground, saying nothing.

"There is detention. There is extra homework and cleaning of the schoolhouse. If that doesn't work, there is brief but vigorous corporal punishment. Now, for someone such as yourself, someone who has no ties to this town, I believe there is another option, the one I hear that Caleb Henry and a few others are already eager to exercise. Expulsion. From school and, if needed, from the town. I believe that would be something you or your father could ill afford, would it not?"

Tuttle waited for an answer. An ember burned down in the pit of my stomach. My fingernails stabbed into my palms. For this man who I didn't know, had never met, to have that kind of power over me and my dad . . . it took every ounce of my strength to shake my head.

"I thought not. Luckily for you, there is another option."

Tuttle turned the knife's hilt back toward me.

"The stern warning. Take it home and do not bring it to my class again. Do you understand?"

I paused, expecting some sort of trick, then took the knife from him. Tuttle clasped his hands behind his back and stepped down to the concrete sidewalk.

"I'll be watching you, Mr. Quinn," he said over his shoulder. Then he was gone.

I fell against the brick wall behind me and clamped my eyes shut, grimacing from the spiky seed of a headache that was sprouting in the back of my skull. *What was I thinking? First Jenny sees me burying that stuff in the woods and now this?* Will said he'd make sure Dad and I weren't here long, and now it was pretty clear how he intended to make that happen. In coming to school, I couldn't have helped him any more if I had tried. I should have seen it. I let my head fall hard onto the brick behind me, relishing the dull shock of the pain.

"Well, *that* was kind of awesome."

I opened my eyes. Derrick was grinning madly and bouncing on the balls of his feet. Martin and Jackson were behind him.

"Just what we all needed before a little baseball game, right? Excitement!"

His voice was like broken glass in my head. I pushed off the brick wall and blew past the three of them without a word.

"Hey! Where you going?" Derrick cried as he jogged alongside me, trailed by the others. "We need you! You can even play second base!"

"Leave me alone, Derrick."

"But —"

"I don't want to play some stupid game, okay?"

"*Stupid* — are you kidding me? Have you ever played baseball before? I mean, what the hell have you been doing all these years?"

"Gee, Derrick, maybe he's been spending all his time looking for food and shelter and stuff."

"Valid point, Green!" Derrick said, and darted in closer to me, sticking his face right in mine. "But you don't have to look for food and shelter right now, do you?"

I glared at him, but he kept going.

"Okay, I get it. Crappy day for you. No question," Derrick went on. "And I know that most people would back off at this point and let you go and gather your thoughts or whatever, but I can't. My mom says it's 'cause I've got, like, this thing in my head that makes it so once I get on something I can't let it go, and I get kinda hyper about it. She said when she was a kid they'd have doped me to the gills on this stuff called Ritalin, but now — ha! — everyone has to just put up with me!"

"It's true," Jackson said. "He won't stop bothering you until you play or one of you dies."

"Ha! Nice one, Green. Steve, look, seriously —"

"I said leave me ALONE!" I planted my palms on Derrick's chest and pushed him so hard he stumbled and fell back into the grass.

Everything went quiet except the sound of blood pounding in my ears.

Derrick looked up at me with huge eyes. Jackson and Martin were motionless, just behind me, waiting.

"Steve," Jackson said, his voice tremulous. "Hey, come on, we were just trying to —"

I turned and shot him a hard glare. He staggered backward as I tore past Derrick and up the road.

The Greens were both gone when I got back to the house. I slammed the door behind me and threw my coat in a heap by Dad's bed, fuming.

How could I have been so stupid? School. What was I thinking?

My fingernails found the scabs on my palm and sank in. I gritted my teeth. I wanted to break something. The chair by the fireplace. The frames on the mantel filled with pictures of idiotic smiling boaters, tanned and lying about in the sun, with no idea that their world was about to come crashing down around them.

I wondered how it would feel if I put my hand through the window above Dad. The glass would tear through my skin and scrape along the bones, maybe shattering them. I flinched at the idea of it, but still my hand collapsed into a fist and drew back. Just then, there was a rattle next to me as Dad's chest rose slightly and then fell again.

My fist fell open. Will wanted me kicked out of here, and hadn't I helped him enough already?

I break something, maybe Marcus gets mad, maybe that's strike two. . . .

I sucked in an angry breath, and slowly the redness that clouded my vision flowed out of me, replaced by something cold and dark, something empty.

"You okay?"

Startled, I turned to see Violet standing in the doorway, a big medical book tucked under her arm. I found a nearby chair and pulled it up to Dad's bedside. I sat with my back to her as a tidal surge of guilt rocked through me. *This is where I should have been the whole time.* I took Dad's hand in mine. It was light as a handful of grass.

"I imagine they're getting a game started over there. I'm surprised you didn't join them."

I glanced over my shoulder. Violet was sitting in a chair just behind me. She had grabbed an old ball cap off a nearby table and had pulled it down over her hair. The book lay open in her lap.

"It *is* the national sport, you know."

"It *was* the national sport," I said. "I don't understand why you people talk about America like it still exists. My grandfather would say it was" — I searched for the phrase. I had heard it a thousand times growing up, generally whenever one of us suggested a slightly shorter hike or a little more sleep — "like square dancing on the *Titanic.*"

Violet's book closed softly behind me. I didn't move. My eyelids felt heavy watching Dad's shallow breathing rise and fall.

Outside, the remaining leaves of fall swayed in the fading sun. Two kids, a boy and a girl with wide, bright faces, were playing out in the park. I looked away and my eye fell on Violet's cabinet, the cabinet that only I knew was lighter a few bottles.

"Why are you people helping us?"

"Why wouldn't we?"

"You don't know us," I said, surprised at the wave of disgust rising in me. "You're giving us medicine, food, your home, and you're just getting in trouble for it. It's stupid."

"You're what was put in front of us," she said.

"That's not an answer."

Violet crossed her arms and looked out the window over my shoulder. "Because there was a time when people helped each other," she said. "And that made the world a little bit better. Not perfect, but better. We'd like to think we can have that time back."

"But what if you're wrong?" I asked.

Violet shrugged. "Maybe we *are* on the deck of the *Titanic*," she said. "Maybe the Collapse isn't over and this will all be gone tomorrow. I don't know. What I *do* know is what it's like out there, we all do, and even if I can only have a little break from it, if I can be the kind of person I was before all this happened, then I'm going to take it. Even if it's just for a day."

Violet tossed the baseball cap into my lap.

"You know what I mean?"

She left without another word, entering the kitchen and leaving me alone.

I shifted in my chair. Outside, leaves swayed across the blue sky. Dad lay before me, as still as ever. I turned Violet's threadbare cap over and over in my hands.

There was a squeal of laughter and the two kids flew by the window. They were maybe six or seven years old, the girl with a long stream of golden hair. The boy was taller and thin as a sapling. They were both holding sticks that had colored streamers attached to the ends so as they went by they were a streak of red and purple and blond, like a flight of brightly colored birds. I pulled the cap down over my head and watched as they banked into the sunshine and disappeared into the park.

FIFTEEN

I skipped school the next day and spent it searching for Jenny but had no luck finding her. I ended up standing in the field east of the school, watching Jackson and the rest gather for their daily baseball game, choosing sides, lining up, swinging their bats through the crisp air.

I had never played baseball, but with how much Dad talked about it I almost felt like I had. He pitched throughout high school and was a passionate Padres fan. Sometimes to keep us entertained on the road, he'd recount major games he had seen in painstaking detail. I stuffed my hands in my pockets and let myself drift closer to the game, finally finding a spot to sit in the grass.

No harm in watching, I thought. *Just for a few minutes.*

Derrick and Jackson's team was lining up for the first at bat. Martin threw a battered plastic helmet to a broad-shouldered girl, and she took a few practice swings before making her way to the plate. She hunkered down, eyeing the tall pitcher sharply, and let the bat hover over her shoulder. She was ice-cold and didn't move an inch on his first two pitches but unloaded completely on his third and sent the ball rocketing into the blue sky. She made it to second, then stopped, cheating out toward third.

"Carrie V."

Jackson had strayed from the game and was standing just a few feet in front of me. I half expected him to tell me to beat it, given how I'd acted after school the previous day. But he just stood there and watched the game, his hands in the pockets of a worn pair of khaki pants. Soon he eased down next to me. I set my palms in the grass, ready to get up and walk away, but for some reason I didn't. I just sat there, watching.

"She's one of our best. The pitcher is her boyfriend, John Carter. She knows him inside and out. Almost always gets a hit off him."

Jackson turned to face me over his shoulder.

"You can play, you know. If you want."

"I gotta get back to my dad."

A shrimpy kid with long hair made his way nervously to home plate with the encouragement of his teammates. "Stan," Jackson said. "Not our best player. Hey, where were you today?"

"I was out," I said, quickly. "Just . . . looking around."

"So what did it say?" Jackson asked.

"What?"

"The note. The one Jenny made me give you that got you tearing out of school."

"Oh. Nothing. She was" — I scrambled for a lie that might sound even slightly convincing — "messing with me."

It sounded weak. Jackson gave me a little sideways look, then returned to watching the game. "Yeah," he said. "That's Jenny, all right. She can't leave well enough alone."

It was silent for a moment as Stan took a couple practice swings. I felt another twinge of guilt. Jackson didn't have to come over and talk to me, not after how much of a jerk I had been.

"I was looking at your books," I said. "The other day. It's a really good collection."

Jackson turned back. "Thanks. I do chores for people and they give me books in return. You like to read? You can borrow them anytime if you want."

"Thanks," I said. "That'd be great."

Jackson nodded and turned back as Stan took a couple practice swings, then lifted the bat over his shoulder. The ball came streaking toward him. For some reason Stan stepped closer to the base as he swung, bringing his right leg into the path of the oncoming ball. Jackson saw it just as I did.

"Oh, this is *not* going to be good."

The ball slammed into Stan's thigh and he went down cursing.

"Every other time," Jackson said. "I swear, the kid gets hit by the ball more than he hits it. Aw, man, now we're one man down. I better go. See ya, Steve."

Jackson hopped up and ran to his team, stopping to check in on Stan, who was sitting on the sidelines. I stripped off my coat and lay in the grass, watching as Jackson and Derrick conferred. They seemed to be having some kind of argument. Derrick was waving his arms and refusing some request of Jackson's, but Jackson kept at him until Derrick finally relented. He turned away and began waving to someone behind me to join the game. I looked back, but no one was there.

Oh no.

"Hey! Steve! Hey! Over here! Yoo-hoo!"

I tried to ignore him, but Derrick made it nearly impossible. Soon he was jumping up and down on his toes and calling in a high-pitched squeal. The whole team was watching now, and a rush of embarrassment hit me. I started to retreat back to the Greens', but something made me stop and look around.

The grass, holding on despite the coming of fall, was thick and green. There was the slightest chill and the smell of wood smoke in the air. Where was I going? Back inside the tomb? To my dad, who, no matter how much I wanted to, I couldn't help? It was true that soon all of this would be gone and we would rejoin the trail, but I was here now. This was my world. Would it really hurt to live in it, just for a day?

Before I knew it, the grass seemed to be moving under my feet. I trotted, head down, toward the game.

"It's okay, everybody!" Derrick shouted as I reached the edge of the field, hanging back from the team. "Our savior is here! Steve will fill in for Stan."

"Can he even play?" someone shouted from back in the lineup.

"Can he play?" Derrick repeated, dumbstruck. "He's a heckuva lot better than any of us. His dad was an actual New York Yankee before the Collapse. Taught him everything he knew."

The flash of embarrassment hit again as the team erupted into a chorus of *oohs* and *aahs*.

Derrick leaned in. "You, uh, do know how to play, right?" he whispered.

"In theory."

"Well, you're still one up on Stan," Derrick said. "Anyway, you're at bat!"

"Oh wait, maybe someone else should —"

But Derrick was already pushing the bat into my hand. He and the others were cheering me from behind the fence to home plate. I felt like I was being pushed onstage to star in a play I didn't know any of the words to.

"Hit and run!" Derrick shouted. "Just hit and run!"

"Tear the cover off it, Steve!" Jackson yelled.

"Don't suck," Stan called from the bench.

My stomach quivered, but I found myself raising the bat to my shoulder, readying myself for a fresh disaster. I took a deep breath and got into a slight crouch, eyes on the pitcher. He nodded at the catcher behind me, then started his windup. Before I could move an inch, the ball slapped into the catcher's glove.

"Well done," he said, smirking as he tossed the ball to the pitcher. "I think you're a natural."

"It's okay, Steve!" Jackson shouted. "That one wasn't yours!"

The pitcher turned back, a big grin on his face. I raised the bat and crouched, scowling. He wound up and threw, but this time it was like everything slowed down. I could see the white ball tumbling toward me. The voices behind me elongated. I brought the bat around in a quick arc, and as it connected with the ball there was a sweet, sharp *crack*. The ball sailed out into the field, over the head of the pitcher, into the outfield.

Dopey and amazed, I watched as the ball lifted into the sky and over the trees whose top branches moved in the wind like hands waving good-bye. I turned back to my team, bat dangling from my hand, eager to share this incredible triumph, but they were all standing on the tips of their toes, looks of terrified anticipation on their faces.

"Don't just stand there, you moron!" Carrie screamed from second, shattering the moment. "Run!"

Oh! Right! Now I run!

The bat clattered at my feet as I took off. I passed first base easily, then skidded in to second. The baseman there was pivoting toward the outfield and raising his glove, his eyes squinting to track the ball headed his way. In a second he'd have me, so as I got closer I threw my shoulder out and it connected with his right arm. It knocked him off balance enough to make him miss the throw. The ball bounced off his glove and bobbled into the outfield. While he was scrambling for it, I was leaving him behind and making for third base in a cloud of dust.

Carrie waved her hands wildly to get me to stop, but it was like there was this engine in me that was running nearly out of control and there was no way I could stop it even if I wanted to. It felt too good: my feet ripping into the soft dirt, my lungs and legs pumping madly, the distant sound of cheering. Finally Carrie was forced to abandon her base and run for home. Following her, I rounded third, digging in and pushing myself faster. I was halfway there when I caught some movement out of the corner of my eye — an arm reeling back to throw a ball.

"Dive!" Jackson shouted.

I threw my arms out in front of me without thinking, as though I was diving into a huge, clear lake, and I sailed across the next few feet, weightless, stretching for home. When the ground leapt up to meet me, it was like jumping headfirst into concrete. The impact rang through me and I got a face full of dirt, grass, and bits of rock. When I could move again, I rolled painfully to my side and saw the catcher standing there with the ball in his hand.

He dropped his arm to tag me, but stopped when he saw my outstretched fingers, straining, but definitely, without a doubt, touching the flat gray rock that was home.

We played until the sun sank behind the trees and cast gold-streaked shadows across the field, then we gathered up our equipment and started the walk back to town. I trailed behind the main pack with Jackson, Derrick, and the other side's pitcher, John Carter.

"You did good, Steve," Derrick said. "I mean, you kind of tanked after that first run, but —"

I surprised myself by giving Derrick a playful shove, knocking him into Jackson. He was right — after that first run, I had struck out three times in a row. When it was time for us to play defense, I was stuck safely way out in right field.

"So you really never played before?" John asked.

"No. Never."

"Not anything?"

I scooped up a pebble from the road and skipped it down the asphalt. "Dad found this old football once, out behind a Walmart. We'd play catch with that sometimes."

Up ahead, Carrie drifted toward the four of us, falling in next to John and taking his hand. "You guys up for going to the quarry?"

John said sure, but Derrick hedged. "I don't know. I really have to do my homework and then get right to bed."

"Shut up, Derrick," Carrie said. "What about you, Steve? It's just this place out to the east, like a manmade pond. We go there after games sometimes."

I looked over my shoulder, back to where Dad lay in a deep coma at the Greens' house, but the tug I felt toward him seemed fainter than it had before. I knew he was safe since Violet was with him. And hadn't she said he would have wanted me to go to school if I could? Well, maybe he would want this too. Me playing baseball. Me with people my own age. Having a life a little bit like he must have had back before the Collapse.

"Yo!" Carrie called out. "Everybody! Quarry!"

We continued up the hill and then moved out to the east of town, past the fields and into the trees as night began to settle around us. After a while the path opened up into a circular clearing, the ground at the center of it falling away in rocky steps, leading down to a pool of water that was dotted with the reflections of stars that were just beginning to appear.

Everyone scattered when we got there, breaking up into smaller groups of two or three or four and finding places around the pool. One kid, the third baseman from the other team, dipped his hand into the water and pulled out a net that was filled with mason jars. He unscrewed the top off one, took a long drink of whatever was inside, then passed it around the circle.

When it came to me I dipped my nose in and caught the smell of rotten fruit and a nose-singeing tang of alcohol. Home brew. Grandpa used to trade for it sometimes when we had some salvage to spare, and he would get blisteringly drunk on it after dinner. Mom would generally lead me into the tent for a reading lesson whenever he got going.

I took a small sip, then winced. "So, how did all of you end up here?" I asked.

"We were coming north from Georgia," Martin said from his place behind me. "And we ran into, like, this entire ex-US army regiment. Dad decided we'd go through these caves he found to get around them. Took us five days. Five days with no food. My brother" — Martin's voice hitched, then he continued — "he was really freaking out. Cried the whole time until we found our way out. We had no idea where we were, but a few weeks later, we found Derrick and his folks. And then Jackson and his. Now here we are."

As soon as he stopped talking, Martin stared down into the dark water, his face cloudy and distant. I knew why, of course, could tell from the millisecond stumble after he said "my brother." It was the same one I always made after saying "my mother." Somehow between that story and now, his brother was lost. I nudged Martin with the edge of the jar and held it out to him.

"Thanks," he said.

Others told their stories and as they did I looked around the group, noticing things I hadn't seen before. A long jagged scar along the forearm of the blond kid who played right field. A deep smudgelike burn mark peeking out from under the sweater of the redheaded girl sitting on the other side of me. The more I looked, the more I saw them, those telltale marks of lives lived after the Collapse. How had I not noticed them before? Was it possible that they all had lives like mine at some point until they came here?

What would have happened, I wondered, if Dad had stood up to Grandpa when I was little and insisted we leave the trail? Could we have ended up here? Would we be living in houses and going to school and cookouts and baseball games?

Would Mom still be alive?

The redheaded girl tapped my arm with a second jar of home brew that had made its way around the circle. I shook my head and she passed it along down the line.

"I'm Wendy, by the way," she said quietly, her small fingers grazing my arm. "You okay?"

"Yeah, I'm —"

"Cann-on-ball!"

There was a gigantic splash that soaked all of us. When I looked up, Derrick was shooting to the surface of the churning water, in his underwear, a dopey smile on his face. Two of the mason jars sat empty where he had been sitting. Jeers came from every corner of the quarry, but they were all mixed with laughter.

"Derrick!"

"Derrick, you jerk!"

"You got us all wet!"

Derrick laughed a deep stuttering laugh and floated lazily on his back.

Wendy shook her great head full of curls and chuckled. "Love, hate. Love, hate. That's all it ever is with him."

"Okay!" Carrie said, rising unsteadily from John's lap. "I think that's our cue, babe."

John offered me his hand. "Hey, man, good job today."

"Thanks. You too." Carrie dragged John up and the two of them said their good-byes and headed down the path to town with their arms around each other's waists. Soon, other couples emerged from the woods and drifted home.

"Well," Jackson said, "I guess we should go pull him out."

Martin and Jackson and I stripped off our shoes, rolled our pant legs up high, and went in after Derrick. Luckily by that time he was pretty tired, so it wasn't too hard to catch him. The trick was getting his bulk out of there and to shore while he mumbled over and over how much he loved us.

"Really, honestly, totally, you dudes are awesome. Just awesome," he said, struggling with his pants.

After we finally got Derrick up and dressed, but before we could get him moving down the path, he lurched forward and grabbed me up into a soggy bear hug, pushing us away from the others.

"This is what it's like, Steve," he whispered intently only inches from my ear. His breath was heavy with the sweet cherry smell of the home brew.

"What what's like, Derrick?"

He pulled back slightly and for a moment didn't seem drunk at all. His eyes were clear and focused.

"This is what it's like to have friends," he whispered.

I stood there in the silence as a grin grew across Derrick's face and then he fell into Wendy's and Martin's arms. "Home, friends! Take me to my home! And you! Wendy! Off with your pants! You too, Marty!"

He giggled as Wendy and Martin led him down the path back to town. I stood there motionless, surrounded in the rhythmic chatter of the grasshoppers and cicadas and the gentle lapping of the quarry's water. Everything seemed to hang in perfect balance, all of it strange and welcome at the same time.

This is what it's like to have friends.

"You okay?"

Jackson was standing in the shadows, waiting.

"Yeah," I said. "Sure."

We left the quarry and made our way through the woods to Jackson's house. Before we got there, though, we slowed without a word and stopped in the park across the street. Jackson sat on one of the swings and I climbed up onto the jungle gym next to him.

To our left, the road wound out of town and away like a ribbon. The pinpricks of candlelight in the windows around us gave the neighborhood the look of a constellation come to Earth.

"So how'd you guys end up here?" I asked. "You never said."

Jackson twisted the toe of his sneaker into the dirt. For a second I thought he hadn't heard me. "We were in, I don't know, Kentucky, I think, with some other families in a little tent city. Mom and Dad were out doing some hunting, and Jenny and I were by this stream downhill from the camp playing Go Fish with some cards she had made. The sun had just gone down and it was all orange and gold." Jackson's fingers curled tight around the swing's chain. "That's when we heard them coming. There were maybe fifteen of them. Twenty. They looked just like us. Maybe a little better off. They came into camp, all smiles, asking if they could have some water from the stream. Nice as could be.

"The man who I guess was their leader was walking with Mr. Simms. Mr. Simms was a friend of my dad's and was in charge of us when Mom and Dad were away. He was older than my folks and lost his whole family to P Eleven and kind of adopted all of us.

"Anyway, the new group's leader, this big hulk of a guy, put his arm around Mr. Simms's shoulder as they walked. After a few steps he pulled Mr. Simms close and said, 'Knock, knock,' which is the start to this old joke. When Mr. Simms said, 'Who's there?' the man reached into his jacket, pulled out a gun, and pressed the barrel right into Mr. Simms's temple."

Jackson's voice caught in his throat. His eyes were far away, remembering. "I saw him do it and I thought, 'Oh, this is a joke. It's a joke.' But then the man pulled the trigger and there was this explosion and Mr. Simms . . . dropped."

Jackson's Adam's apple rose and fell and his lips pressed into a tight line.

"Everyone froze. All of us. There wasn't a sound, just Mr. Simms hitting the ground. Jenny and I stood there watching this fan of blood spread out around his head. Then someone screamed and then everyone was screaming and rushing to their tents for their guns or to escape, but it was too late. The man and his people were everywhere, shooting anyone they could, laughing like it was all this big game, like the rest of us weren't even real.

"There were about twenty-five, maybe thirty, of us in all. Men and women. Some kids me and Jenny's age. The leader and his group killed all but us and a couple others. Then they put their guns away, took whatever supplies we had, and strolled back out of town."

A cold wind blew across the playground and made the trees around us moan. Jackson dug his hands into his jacket pockets.

"Whole thing didn't take but five minutes. When Mom and Dad came back, we took our things and ran as fast as we could, but no matter how far away we got, I thought they were right around the corner, ready to pop out again, just . . . smiling and shooting."

By now the dark of night was settling in. Everything around us — the trees, the houses, the curves of the land — was looming shapes, like animals prowling beneath dark water.

Jackson looked back at me, but I didn't know what to say to him. If we were friends, like Derrick had said, what did friends do? What did they say?

"Guess somebody like you has never felt like that," Jackson said quietly, turning away from me. "Afraid."

Shadows of leaves played over Jackson's drawn, pale face. I stared down at my lap. Something ached deep in my chest. The idea that I had never been afraid was ridiculous but I knew what Grandpa would have said. Never admit fear. Never admit weakness.

"I'm afraid all the time," I said. "After my mom died, I couldn't sleep. Not for months. I'd lie awake at night and think about Dad or Grandpa getting sick. One of them dying. Dad told me we'd be fine. He said nothing would ever change again, but then Grandpa died and he . . ."

I shut my mouth tight and closed my eyes. Saying all of that, thinking it, even, made the whole ugly mess real all over again. It was like this darkness that I could keep at bay most of the time, but if I got too close, if I touched it, it would seize up and have me.

"Hey."

I opened my eyes with a start. Jackson had left the swing and was standing right beside me.

"You're here now," he said. "We both are, right? No matter what happens. Me and my folks, all of us, we won't let anything happen to you."

I looked away from him, along the houses and up the street. How could I tell him that it would only be a matter of time before all of this was gone and we were scattered to the wind? Did a friend say that?

"Probably time for dinner, isn't it?" I said, slipping off the jungle gym.

Jackson lagged behind as I crossed the park and went up the stairs and into the house. The fireplace smelled smoky and warm. Timbers creaked above me. I stood by Dad's bed, looking down at him. His chest rose and fell weakly as he breathed.

"We've been here five years now," Jackson said from behind me in the hallway that led to the kitchen, half in and half out of the light. "I don't know if it'll be forever, but we've almost been wiped out by storms and droughts and bad crops and a hundred other things, and we've always made it. We just stuck together and never gave up."

Later that night, when I closed my eyes and headed to sleep, it was as though I could feel all of them: Marcus and Violet and Dad and Jackson and, somewhere outside in places of their own, Derrick and Martin and

Wendy and Carrie and Jenny too. I felt each of them like blooms of heat pulsing out in the night, separate but connected.

Instead of the tomblike stillness of the previous nights, the house felt warm around me, like all of us were settled underneath a thick blanket with the cold winds and the world safely outside.

Was Jackson right? Was it real? Could it last?

I didn't know. But right then, lying there in that quiet and warmth, I hoped. For the first time, I hoped.

SIXTEEN

The next morning before school I helped Violet carry tin buckets of hot water from the fire out back to a white tub in the bathroom upstairs. She said she figured *I* must be dying for a bath — meaning *she* was dying for me to take a bath but wanted to save my feelings. It was a good effort. And a few whiffs of myself confirmed that it was probably past due.

Once we were done and she was gone, I stripped and lowered myself into the tub. The homemade lye soap Violet gave me felt like it was taking a layer of skin off with the dirt. As I scrubbed, I thought how easy it must have been when she and my dad were my age, back before the Collapse. Turn a faucet and out came hot water. Flick a switch and there was light. It must have seemed like magic.

When I was done, Violet came back in with a razor and a pair of scissors. She cut my hair and shaved the light fall of whiskers on my cheeks, then sent me off to Jenny's room. There I found a pair of nearly new-looking jeans, a red button-up shirt, and a handmade black wool sweater. There was even a slightly scuffed pair of brown hiking boots. On the floor next to the bed were my old clothes: a dirty, heavily patched heap of greasy cloth I had been wearing almost daily for the last year or two. I knew every hole, every tear, every patch, wrinkle, and worn spot.

I lifted my old pants and turned them over. Sewn on the right knee was a rectangular scrap of red cloth with gold ducks on it. Dad had put the patch on when I'd worn through the knee a few months ago. The square of cloth had come from one of Mom's old dresses, her favorite one. After she died, Grandpa had insisted we trade her clothes away, but Dad had kept that one dress, hiding it like I hid my books.

Standing there, I didn't think I could do it — throw aside these old things for the new. I told myself I was being crazy. If I'd come across these new clothes on the trail, I'd have taken them. And if I'd come across my old clothes, I would've walked right on by.

"Stephen?" Violet called from downstairs. "You okay?"

I dressed quickly in the new clothes before heading out into the hall. When I turned to close the door, there were my old clothes, blue and black with a flash of red and gold. Dad's knife lying on top in its sheath.

They're just clothes, I told myself and shut the door.

When I came downstairs, Violet was sitting at Dad's side with a bowl of oatmeal in her lap.

"Hey, Violet, I . . ."

When Violet turned back, I saw the feeding tube down Dad's throat. He lay there, his mouth unnaturally wide, his teeth clamped down on the hard plastic. Something shuddered inside me, seeing him like that. Part of me wanted to run over and tear it out of him, to make her leave him alone, but I marshaled myself and crossed the floor slowly until I was just behind her.

"How's he doing?"

Violet spooned the last bit of food down the tube.

"About the same," she said. "I wish I could say more, but without tests . . ."

"I've been talking to him at night."

"That's good." Violet looked back over her shoulder and smiled. "You look really great, Stephen."

I pulled awkwardly at the new clothes. "Thanks."

"You ready?"

Jackson had just come down the stairs and was standing behind me.

I moved to the bed and squeezed Dad's hand tight. "Thanks," I said again to Violet before leaving with Jackson.

"Mr. Waverly!" Jackson announced cheerily as Martin and an extremely bleary-looking Derrick joined us. Jackson clapped him on the back. "How's it going, buddy?! Rough night last night?"

"Ugghhhh," Derrick groaned and halfheartedly pushed Jackson away. He trudged along behind us, grumbling as we made our way to school.

"You playing today?" Martin asked me.

"I don't know," I shrugged. "Stunk pretty badly at the end of the game yesterday."

"Yeah," Derrick said. "In fact, I think he was lying when he told me he was descended from a real New York Yankee. Don't let him play, Martin."

"We're not letting *you* play," Jackson said.

"Why not?"

"You're a mess."

"Quinn, buddy, I was just kidding about how much you suck. Defend me here. Am I a mess?"

I regarded Derrick carefully. His hair was a greasy tumbleweed. All his clothes were rumpled. "Definitely. A total mess."

"Ha!" Martin laughed and punched me in the arm.

"I liked you better when you didn't talk," Derrick grumbled.

Carrie and Wendy mixed in with us at the bottom of the hill as we all filed in behind the mass of little ones.

"Lookin' awful snazzy there, Steve," Carrie said with a grin.

"Oh," I said, looking down at my new clothes, strangely embarrassed. "Thanks. Marcus's old things."

Wendy reached across and drew her finger across the hair that fell just above my eyebrows. "Your hair's out of your face too," she said. "I can see your eyes."

I didn't know what to say. She was wearing a pink and white sweater and jeans, her hair loose and flowing coppery over her shoulders. I was surprised to find myself nervous as she fell into place next to me.

Once we got to school we all split up and the rest of that morning was pretty uneventful. Tuttle lectured and while everyone else was struggling to stay awake I leaned over my paper and took careful notes. He talked about math and poetry and the Holy Roman Empire. I had no idea there was so much world out there to learn about. At noon he let us out for lunch.

It had grown colder in the past few hours and some clouds had begun to pile up, signs of fall moving headlong toward winter. All of us spilled out onto the yard, pulling our lunches out of bags and buckets. The little ones immediately swarmed around the slide and swing sets, fighting over who got to do what first.

"Okay!" Martin announced as he pulled a wrinkled sheet of paper out of his back pocket. "Time to make the lineup! Waverly is benched!"

"What? No way!"

"Quinn is taking your place."

"You know," Derrick said. "You people don't appreciate me. I'm gonna start hanging out with Will Henry."

"Oh go take a bath, Derrick," Wendy said.

I laughed and the lineup talk went on. They all seemed so comfortable with each other, laughing and joking, trading mock punches. I looked around at everyone else in the school yard as they ate their lunches in their own small groups. The inside jokes and chatter of each one joined with the others into a low roar that somehow didn't seem as grating as it had just a few days earlier.

I turned back to the negotiations, and when I did, I saw Jenny. She was sitting under the big sycamore, facing away from the school, in her torn-up jeans and Red Army jacket with her knees pulled up in front of her, sketching furiously in her sketch pad.

My body tensed immediately. The note. I had almost forgotten. I tried to stay calm, nibbling at my sandwich and keeping my eye on her, waiting for an opportunity. All the noise and movement below her — the laughing and yelling and flirting, the squeak of the old swing sets — didn't seem to distract her in the least. She drew with great looping strokes and slashes, leaning down into the pad like she was wrestling with it and just barely winning.

When she was done, Jenny dropped the sketch pad on the grass and stretched out against the tree. She reached up and tucked a length of hair behind her ear, leaving the rest of it to blow over her face like smoke drifting over beach sand.

"I don't know why she even bothers coming."

Jackson had moved out of the lineup negotiations and was eyeing Jenny too.

"Does she always just sit up there drawing and stuff?"

"No, that one's new," he said. "She just started coming to school again the other day."

Up the hill Jenny leaned over her sketch pad, erasing, drawing again. I thought of that lone horse, locked in the classroom.

"Sometimes I wish . . ." Jackson's forehead wrinkled, his lips hardening into a tense slit as he watched her. Whatever he was going to say, he pulled it back before it could get loose.

"What?"

"Sometimes I wish she would go," Jackson said, his voice a harsh whisper. "Just leave. Before she does something that gets us all thrown out of here."

"Would they really do that?"

Jackson eyed me a moment like he was trying to make a decision.

"There was a family," he said, "a few years back. The Krycheks. Had a little girl, like nine, I think. Mr. Krychek used to be a soldier, but all he did was drink by the time he got here. He hid it pretty well for a while, but it got worse. One night he was drinking out in the woods and tried to build a fire. It went out of control and got within a few feet of spreading to the houses. Caleb called a meeting about it the next day. Mom and Dad tried to speak up for them, but Caleb had more than half the town ready to vote against them *and* anyone willing to stand up for them. In the end it was pretty much unanimous."

"Your parents . . . ?"

"Dad voted to send them away. He didn't want to but . . . I mean, the guy was dangerous, right? What choice did he have? Let the whole town get destroyed? Get us thrown out too?"

"What about your mom?"

Jackson's eyes went unfocused as he drew his fingertip aimlessly through the dirt. "She was . . . sick, I think. Didn't make the vote that day."

"What happened to them? The Krycheks?"

Jackson didn't look up. He shrugged. "Dad and some others insisted they at least give them some supplies but . . . it was the middle of January."

He didn't need to say any more. Middle of the winter and the dad a drunk and dragging along a nine-year-old. Only one thing could have happened. I looked down at the remains of my sandwich but wasn't hungry anymore. I could see that family clear as anything, huddled together and snow-blind, making their slow way out of town. A sick shudder went right through me.

I jumped as the bell rang and everyone started packing up their lunch things and heading inside.

"Let's go!" Derrick shouted, throwing up his arms. "It's time to learn, people!"

Jackson lingered by the door. "You coming?" he asked.

"Yeah," I said. "Sure. Just a second. I'll catch up."

The doors slammed behind them and the yard was quiet and empty.

Just me and Jenny.

Jackson's story hung with me. Now more than ever I had to be careful. If Jenny was going to be a threat to me, I needed to deal with it. I looked around, making sure I was alone before stalking up the hill. Jenny didn't notice me as I drew near, too busy sketching the landscape in front of her. The trees looked almost alive on her paper, caught in mid-sway against the gray clouds, the horizon ominous in the distance.

"You're different," she said without turning. "Your clothes and hair and stuff."

I froze. Jenny looked me up and down over her shoulder. Her dark eyes made me feel like I was a fish wriggling on the end of a spear.

"It was, uh . . . Violet. She gave me some clothes."

"Figures," Jenny smirked. "You look like one of *them* now. You come up here for a reason?"

I cleared my throat and tried to force myself back to business. "The note."

"Which note?" she asked innocently. "A? B? C major?"

"Your note."

"Oh, *my* note!"

"Jenny, whatever you think you saw —"

"Oh please," Jenny said with a flirtatious lilt. "Let's not play games that aren't any fun."

I felt my legs go weak. My mind was wiped clear like Tuttle's blackboard. Jenny chuckled.

"I need to know what you want," I said, trying to find the steel in my voice that was always in Grandpa's, but only managed what sounded like a strained squeak. For a second I thought Jenny would laugh, but she didn't. She dropped her pencil and shifted around, looking up at me like she was awaiting a lecture.

"Have you always been a scavenger?" she asked.

"I'm not —"

"Salvager. Whatever. You go north to south, right? To those trade gatherings?"

"Jenny, the note. I —"

"Do you take the same route every time or do you mix it up?"

One time Dad told me about how when they were building the railroads way back when, there would sometimes be a mountain in their way and they'd have to decide whether to load it up with dynamite and blow it up or just go around. I had the feeling that this was one of those times and I was pretty sure I didn't have anywhere near enough dynamite for the first option. If I wanted the information, it looked like I was going to have to play along.

"It changes."

"Why?"

"If you keep to one path, people can predict it. Set ambushes."

"Smart. How close do you get to the coast?"

"Not close."

"Why? Is it dangerous?"

"Some. Mostly it's just rubble."

"What about the West Coast? What have you heard about it?"

"Nobody goes there anymore," I said.

"Why?"

I gave her a look like it was obvious.

"What? Because that's where my scary Chinese brothers and sisters are?"

I crossed my arms over my chest. "Jenny —"

"You ever seen them?"

"No."

"So what are they *doing* out there?"

Jenny chewed on the end of her pencil, squinting a little in the sun.

"You like your life, Quinn?" she asked, throwing me off base with the sudden change in tack. "Wandering about this war-torn land of ours?"

No one had ever asked me anything like that before. Did I like my life? What kind of question was that?

"It's just . . . it's my life."

"Well, it's not a rock. You can have an opinion about it."

"You like yours?"

"I like parts of it."

"Which ones?"

"The parts where I get to break things."

"Why? Because that makes you feel like you're in control of something?"

For the very first time, I stopped her cold. It took everything in me not to throw my arms into the air in celebration. Jenny looked up at me blank-eyed, wriggling on a spear of her own. Slowly a smile grew at the corners of her lips.

"Oh Stephen," she said. "You *are* a pistol."

"What do you want, Jenny?"

Jenny's eyes glinted in the sunlight.

"I want a lot of things, Quinn. I'm just trying to decide which of them you can provide." She flicked her eyes to our left. "Uh-oh. Feel like a tussle?"

"Huh?" I turned and there was Will Henry, the redheaded giant, and one of the slug twins barreling our way.

"Come on," I said, backing away down the hill. "Let's get out of here."

"What? Are you kidding?"

"No, seriously, Jenny. They're trying to get me thrown —"

But Jenny wasn't listening. She jumped up and ran right at them. Will stormed on ahead.

"This isn't about you, Jenny," he said.

"Is it about the uses of symbolism in Melville's *Moby-Dick*?"

"What?"

As Will stopped to figure that one out, Jenny punched him in the face. A hard right, slamming into his jaw. It rocked him, but he came right back at her. Jenny laughed and danced away.

I edged back down the hill toward school. If Jenny wanted to fight, that was her business. I needed to play it safe, for me and Dad. For the Greens.

"This is my town," Will spat. "People like you and the spy aren't welcome, Chink."

Will planted both hands on Jenny's chest and shoved her to the ground. She landed with a dull thump.

I didn't even think. I just launched myself at him, slipping a fist past him and landing it in his stomach. He made a satisfying *oof* sound but recovered fast, throwing a punch that connected squarely with my jaw and spun me around. The next thing I knew, I was on the ground with a mouth full of grass. My head was ringing. I rolled over and all I could see was a wide expanse of cloudy sky cut in half by the dark shadow of Will Henry towering over me.

"You. Don't. Belong. Here," he growled.

Something behind me roared and Jenny flew past me, throwing herself at Will, her fingers stretched out like claws. He tried to shrink out of the way, but she got her arms around his neck and forced him to the ground. My vision was still a little hazy, but I could make out the two guys who were behind Will stepping forward and reaching for Jenny. I forced myself up, taking a fistful of dirt and grass with me. I threw the clump in Big Red's face and threw myself at the other one, using my body like a battering ram. I hit the slug twin full in the chest with my shoulder and he went down. Once we were on the ground, I brought my knee up between his legs. He howled, then curled up on his side, moaning.

I pulled myself on top of him, cocked my fist, and gave him a good one right on the nose. There was a sick crunch and blood spurted out between us. I reared back again, but someone's hands were on my shoulders, pulling me up and away from him.

It was the big redhead. He was strong but slow. I wriggled out of his grasp and got to my feet, backing away and getting my hands up in front of my face. I could hear another fight going on to my left. I wanted to look and see how Jenny was doing, to see if she needed help, but I had troubles of my own. Big Red was sizing me up, deciding on his next move. It was probably the dumbest thing he could have done. While he was thinking, I was moving.

I threw myself at him headfirst, right into his stomach. Even though I was pretty sure I knocked the wind out of him, he didn't go down. I kept pushing forward, hoping to get him off balance, but he grabbed my shoulders and used my momentum to toss me down instead. I hit with a thud, my head slamming into the dirt. I reeled again and a wave of nausea hit me. I reached for my knife, realizing too late that it was sitting on Jenny's floor guarding a pile of old clothes.

I tried to get up, but my arms felt like jelly, and before I could do anything else, Big Red was down on one knee beside me. He pulled his fist back, blocking out everything else in my vision. It was a pale comet hurtling toward me.

But then a look of surprise came over his face and his whole body shot back away from me, like he'd been grabbed up by an angel. There was shouting and a commotion, but my head was too swimmy to make it all out.

Someone grabbed my shoulder and tried to push me up, but it was no use. I was like a rag doll filled with lead.

There was a voice in my ear, close and rushed. "Come on, get up. We have to get out of here."

The world snapped into focus. Jenny was leaning over me. Her bottom lip was split and trailing blood down her chin and neck, soaking the top of her T-shirt. Her right eye was surrounded by a red and black bruise and nearly swollen shut.

"Did we win?"

"Ha! You are a pistol, Stephen," she said as she pulled me up. "Now let's get out of here."

"Jenny Tan!"

"Oh crap."

Tuttle stormed up the hill toward us, clutching his wooden ruler like a sword. He was being led by the second of the slug twins. I saw the plan immediately: Will starts a fight, then sends one of them to get Tuttle, no doubt blaming it on me and Jenny. *Idiot*, I cursed myself.

He was followed by a group of students, all excited to see what was going on. In the middle of the pack were Derrick, Martin, and, finally, Jackson. As soon as Jackson saw Jenny and me together, he stopped cold. The group broke around him, but he didn't move.

He was staring at my hands.

They were covered in dirt and bruises and blood. The new clothes Violet had given me just that morning were torn and stained. Jackson looked from me to Jenny and back again, his body rigid with anger, his hands knotted into fists. I knew what was going through his head. The last straw. A calm day was smashed to pieces and maybe this time it would lead to a vote that would turn his world upside down. I wanted to say something, tell Jackson it wasn't my fault, that it was Jenny, that it was Will, that everything would be okay, but before I could do anything, Tuttle barked, "Enough. Detention for both of you."

"But what about them?" Jenny asked.

Tuttle ignored her. He whirled around, sending the mass of kids behind him scurrying back toward the school. Jackson didn't move at first, but then Martin tapped him on the shoulder, whispered something, and pulled him away.

"You're done," Will said as he passed me, flashing that easy wolfish grin. He and his friends strolled down the hill in Tuttle's wake.

My hand curled into a fist so tight I nearly broke a bone.

"Easy, tiger," Jenny said. She laid her hand on my shoulder, but I jerked away.

"Get away from me."

"Oh come on. We'll get ours."

"Our what?"

Jenny's lips brushed my ear as she whispered, "Revenge, Stephen. We'll get our revenge."

"I don't want revenge," I said, pushing away from her down the hill. "I just want you to leave me alone."

SEVENTEEN

When the classroom was empty except for me and Jenny, Tuttle regarded us over the rim of his steel glasses. *"American History,"* he said. "Chapters one through three."

"Read them?" I asked.

"Copy them."

I opened the book and flipped through the pages. Chapters one through three were about twenty densely worded pages. My bruised knuckles ached at the thought of it. Tuttle leaned over a stack of papers, making quick little check and X marks down the length of them. I couldn't concentrate. Every time I tried, I saw Jackson's face growing more and more angry as he looked from me to Jenny after the fight. I had tried to explain, tried to pass him a note even, but he'd ignored me, that hard fury like a wall between us. *Stupid*, I thought, over and over. *Why didn't I just walk away?*

What made it worse was Jenny, twirling a pencil in her bruised fingers, totally unconcerned.

Tuttle cleared his throat and I leaned over my paper. I swallowed the anger as best I could and started to write. I only had two pages done before something bumped against the side of my boot. When I looked down there was a folded piece of paper lying on the floor. I checked on Tuttle, then leaned down and picked it up, unfolding it onto my notebook.

How are the war wounds, tough guy?

Jenny had her head down in her book, copying away, the slightest shadow of a smile on her bruised face. I refolded the paper and went back to work, ignoring her. Minutes later another piece of paper knocked against my foot.

Awww, what's wrong, pal? Mad at me?

Leave me alone, I scrawled across the paper in heavy black letters before kicking it back to her.

Oh come on, Stephen, she wrote back. *You've been dying to hit somebody since the night you got here.*

Well, thanks, I wrote. *Now I'm in detention. Everybody hates me, and your whole family, my dad, and I are all one step closer to getting thrown out of here.*

She answered: *The sky's not going to fall because of one little fight! No one's going to throw you out. Jackson and his band of doofuses will get over it.*

I made sure Tuttle was still busy grading before writing back, *And if they don't?*

I could feel Jenny shaking her head as she read it. When the paper returned it was nearly torn through.

*Food for thought. If someone can't handle seeing who you are —
are they really your friends?*

She was wrong, of course. Jackson and the others were my friends, and fighting those guys was not who I was. Jenny hadn't been there at the game or the quarry. She didn't know.

What would you know about who I really am? I wrote back.

Jenny wrote something immediately, then quickly erased it. Almost an hour passed before she kicked the paper back.

Sometimes I can't sleep, she wrote, her messy scrawl replaced by small deliberate letters. *Because it's like I can feel the whole world spinning so fast beneath me, and I'm thinking, what am I doing here? Is this where I belong? Do I belong anywhere? Some nights it gets so loud in my head that I want to break something, anything, everything, just to make it stop.*

I didn't move for several minutes. I just stared down at the words, the letters so tight, so precise and dark, they looked like they might rupture at any moment and tear the page to pieces. My pencil was near my fingers, and in one strange moment I thought, *Did I write that, or did she?*

I checked on Tuttle, then looked back at Jenny, but she was slipping out of her chair and heading toward the door.

"Miss Green," Tuttle called out, but she ignored him, didn't even correct him. "Miss Green, come back here!"

I wanted to stop her too, but the double doors behind me flew open and slammed shut. Tuttle settled into his chair, and I was surprised to see a strange look on his face, almost concerned. Maybe even a little bit sad.

"This does·not mean that you are excused, Mr. Quinn," he said when he caught me looking at him. "Get back to work."

I read Jenny's note twice more before I did, lingering over each word. Tuttle cleared his throat pointedly, and I folded the piece of paper and put it in my pocket so I could finish my work. About an hour later, I finished the assignment and, my hand cramped into a claw, I set it on Tuttle's desk before turning to leave.

"A moment, Mr. Quinn."

I returned to my desk and slumped down while Tuttle took his time making a neat stack of graded papers and sliding it into a leather folder. The waiting was driving me crazy.

"Mr. Tuttle, we were just defending our —"

Tuttle held up his hand to silence me. He slipped a paper out of his folder, then crossed the room and dropped it on my desk. It was my *Great Expectations* quiz. Down one side of the paper was a long column of check marks and a single X. A large *A* was written at the top of the page.

"The question you must ask yourself, Mr. Quinn," Tuttle intoned, towering above me, "is this: Are you a boy or a man? Human being or savage?"

Tuttle's cool blue eyes were on me, unwavering.

"Obviously you've never had to make that choice before. Running around the ruins of this world as your sort of people do, you acted on instinct and self-preservation — an animal — no doubt quivering before rainstorms and amazed by fire and shiny objects. But you're here now, Mr. Quinn, and this is civilization, so now you *do* have a choice. So, what do you want to be?"

Tuttle waited for an answer.

"The fact that you pause does not fill me with confidence."

"Look, as soon as my dad is better, we're leaving, so you don't have to bother."

Tuttle surprised me by folding his long body down into the cramped desk in front of me. He twisted around to face me, his knees nearly pressing into his chest. "Do you like to learn?" he asked.

"I like to read."

Tuttle's thin lips curled into a tight smile. "Yes. So do I. Sometimes it doesn't seem like the world has much use for people like us, does it?

No, most of the world only has time for people who can build or break things. It won't always be that way, I think. A time will come when society, as it always has, will turn for its salvation to the learned. Now, to my surprise, you appear to be intellectually capable, but the question remains: Do you *want* to be one of them?"

It was a ridiculous question. Did I want to be one of the learned? I tried to think of an answer that would satisfy him, but he might as well have been asking me if I wanted to be an astronaut.

"The times we live in, Mr. Quinn, are teetering between the chaos behind us — an infancy made up of smoke and terror and withering plague — and what adulthood lies ahead for us. Wisdom? Peace? Oblivion? Whatever it is, to get there we must let go of the past. It is dead and gone. It will never return and it cannot be changed. All we have now is one another and whatever new thing we make together."

Tuttle unfolded himself from the desk and strode to a shelf along the wall. He pulled down a small stack of books, then laid it on my desk. *Mechanical Engineering. Chinese History. World Political Systems.*

"If you have a desire to be more than what you are, if you want the world to be more than it is, study these in addition to your regular work. If not, please feel free to escape to a warm cocoon of petty violence and team sports."

With that, Tuttle turned his back on me and planted himself at his desk to begin grading a new stack of papers. The books sat in front of me; I ran my fingers across their glossy covers.

This is how we got here in the first place, Grandpa would have said, sneering at the books. But then there was Dad's voice, whispering to me that night in the plane as we watched a doomed woman and boy.

Grandpa is gone.

In my head, it sounded like a fallen leaf blowing across a grave.

Out of the corner of my eye, I saw a thin smile grow on Tuttle's lips as I scooped the books up into my arms, and dashed into the twilight.

EIGHTEEN

I crossed the park, balancing the stack of books in my aching hands, strangely excited to start reading them, when the Greens' front door flew open and out walked Caleb Henry.

It was like I hit a wall.

Caleb was masked by the shadows of the porch at first, so all I could see was his tall frame in jeans, a flannel shirt, and boots. As he descended the stairs and stepped out into the yard, though, it was clear that he was smiling. He didn't acknowledge me or make a sound as he glided up the street.

My arms went weak underneath the pile of books. My stomach churned. *Of course. Where else would Will have gone after the fight?*

The Greens' door hung open. No candles had been lit yet, even though it was edging past twilight and into early evening. Inside it was gray and hushed. I set the books down by my bedroll and the neat bundle Violet had made of my old clothes and Dad's knife while I was away. Then, once I'd checked on Dad, I crossed the room and entered the short hallway that led into the kitchen.

Marcus and Violet were sitting next to each other in the gloom at the kitchen table. Marcus was hunched over a mug, his hands clamped around it, while Violet sat back in her chair, one hand covering her mouth and chin. The shadows of the room deepened the lines on their ashen faces. I kept to the darkness of the hall and listened.

"What choice do we have, Vi?"

"They can vote if they want to vote," Violet said. "We're not giving him up. We're not like that, Marcus. You're not like that."

"But what if we fight them again and Caleb decides to come after us this time?"

Violet had no answer. Her silence hung heavy as stone.

I backed away from the door. Whatever the people of the town thought of Jenny, she was family to the Greens and maybe that protected her. It wouldn't be the same with me or Dad. We were outsiders. Little better than vagrants, no matter how Violet tried to dress me up.

I eased back to the front room, then dropped to my knees alongside Dad's bed. I ripped my bedroll up off the floor and began shoving it along with the rest of my supplies into my backpack. I had put that pack together a million times, but my hands were clumsy now, rushed. I reached for the rifle's cleaning kit, but my knuckles slammed into one of the bed's legs and a jolt of fresh pain rocketed up my arm. Finally I just stuffed everything inside and yanked the flap closed.

There on my knees, I was eye level with the stack of books Tuttle had given me. Politics. History. Science. Little pieces of a larger world.

Useless, Grandpa's voice said deep inside me, disgusted, stronger than ever. I yanked my bag off the floor and stood up over Dad. A wave of sadness reared up. I told myself that Violet would take care of him, that if I didn't protect them, they couldn't protect him, but it was no use. The wave was too big and coming too fast.

How many days had it been now since Grandpa was gone? Eight? Nine? How was it possible that everything could have fallen apart so quickly? That our lives could turn over, again and again, in such a tiny packet of time? I longed for my old life, following Dad and Grandpa without question. Pack the wagon. Scan for salvage. Then make our way from landmark to landmark, a slumping mall and its rusted attendees, a parking lot cracked with yellow flowers.

I wondered if this was what it was like when the end of the world came. A sudden overturning that made every day like stepping alone into an empty room — everything you longed for, every handhold you used to pull yourself along, vanished.

My pack was heavy as I lifted it up onto my back and cinched the straps tight around my arms and middle. I threaded Dad's knife onto my belt and checked that the rifle was loaded before hanging it over my shoulder and walking toward the door.

"Stephen."

I stopped where I was. Violet was standing in the hallway, with Marcus in the dimness behind her.

"You're not leaving. We won't let you. We'll —"

Violet leaned forward, but Marcus's hand shot out from the dark and clamped around her wrist.

My eyes locked on Marcus's hand, rough and tan. It seemed to glow in the low light as he held her back.

"I'll be fine," I said. "Just take care of my dad."

I took the doorknob, but something stopped me before I could turn it. Dad was lying there in his bed, pale and still as always. There was a twist deep in my chest, a hand wrenching at my heart. There was something I still had to do.

"The second night I was here," I said, "I stole two bottles of medicine and some instruments. There's a lightning-struck tree overlooking the highway a couple miles to the west. You'll find them buried just behind it." I looked back at Violet and Marcus. Neither of them had moved. "Thanks," I said. "For everything."

Before either of them could say anything, I forced myself out the door and closed it softly behind me.

When I reached the foot of the steps, I turned and looked up at the house. Jackson's window glowed with a candle's flame. I hoped he was there, reading quietly in the calm of his room with no idea how close he'd come to another overturning, this one far worse than the last. I wished I could have said good-bye. I wished I could have explained.

I went out past the houses and driveways and neglected mailboxes until I came to the town's iron gates and let myself through with a rusty squeak. I stood on the other side, facing the long plain and the wall of the forest.

Where to now?

I put my hands in my pockets to warm them and skimmed the edge of a piece of folded paper I had forgotten was there.

Jenny's note.

I pulled it out and opened it. The dark letters shone in the moonlight.

. . . it's like I can feel the whole world spinning so fast beneath me, and I'm thinking, what am I doing here? Is this where I belong?

I folded the piece of paper, returned it to my pocket, and got moving.

NINETEEN

The trees grew thicker as I went, choked with deadfall and thornbushes. I pulled myself over the fence that marked the northern edge of town. All around me were the night sounds of the woods: owls hooting and lizards skittering through the underbrush. Farther out were the heavier steps of larger things — deer or wolves or bears — making their own way through the dark.

I leapt over a fast-running stream and then stepped out into a clearing, caught in the silvery wash of the moon. On the far side were the remains of a barn. Its arid wood slats were pockmarked with nail holes and overgrown with moss and creeping vines. There was a large ragged hole in the roof.

The whole place was surrounded by rusting farm implements, hoes and shovels and pitchforks, and what I thought was an old tractor that was covered in vines and weeds.

This old barn, Jackson had said. *North of town.*

I crept up to the barn and slipped in through half-opened doors. The inside was lit with a few flickering candles that sat near an old mattress in one corner. I looked around but there was no one there, just piles of hay bound into moldering blocks against the walls, and rakes and a long rusty scythe hanging on pegs. Something rustled in the loft above me.

"Jenny?"

An owl exploded out through the hole in the ceiling, startling me enough that I almost cried out. I steadied myself and crossed the barn to the mattress. It was covered with a quilt and a couple thin pillows. Scattered around it were scraps of paper, clothes and stubs of old candles, another dog-eared chemistry book. Near the head of the bed was Jenny's sketch pad.

I peered into the dark corners of the barn to make sure I was alone, then set the rifle to the side and knelt down. I opened the sketch pad, tipping its face into the candlelight. The drawings at the beginning were mostly of people. Tuttle glowered from one page, surrounded by a dark halo, his ruler in hand. Sam sat in soft candlelight holding a pipe, a half smile on his face and a book draped over one knee. As I got toward the end, the people began to disappear and were replaced by trees, the barn, the school building, empty fields. If there were any people at all, they were seen from far away, their backs turned — dark, faceless walls.

"What are you doing here?"

I twisted around so fast I lost my balance and fell in a heap onto the bed, scrambling backward away from the voice. When I looked up, Jenny was standing over me in a bloodstained T-shirt, with a cat's grin and a black eye.

"Nice squeal, tough guy."

"I didn't —"

"Whatever." Jenny snatched the sketch pad off the floor next to me. "What are you doing here?"

I stood up warily, awkward in my backpack and coat. I searched the ground for an explanation.

"I was . . . walking."

Jenny turned and peered into the dark outside the doors.

"There's no one else here," I said. "It's just me."

"I thought you were pissed at me."

I shrugged. Jenny set the sketch pad on a pile behind the bed.

"How's your hand?"

I raised my right hand into the light and flexed my fingers. The bleeding had stopped, leaving my knuckles crusted with dirt and blood. The joints ground together when I moved them.

"We should clean it up," Jenny said. She retrieved a plastic box from her bedside and stood in front of me. I just looked at her. "What? You want gangrene? Sit down."

I slipped out of my coat and pack and did as she said, sitting down on the edge of her bed. Jenny grabbed my hand, examined it, then started scrubbing away with a rag. I hissed and tried to pull back but Jenny held my wrist tight.

"Take it easy, you big baby. If it's not clean, I'll have to amputate."

I held my breath as she worked the dirt out of my wounds. Once my hand was clean, she spread some ointment from a small tube on it.

"How come Violet's not doing this for you?"

"Caleb was there when I got back after detention."

Jenny looked up with one arched eyebrow.

"They were going to have a vote tomorrow," I said. "I left before they could."

Jenny stopped what she was doing. Her dark eyes smoldered and she cursed under her breath. "I'm sorry. I shouldn't have —"

"You didn't make me do anything."

"Your dad, is he — ?"

"He's with Violet."

"Good," Jenny said. "They won't mess with her about a patient. Wouldn't dare."

Jenny tossed the tube of ointment back in the kit and took out a roll of gauze. She began carefully winding the bandage around my hand.

"Well, at least we denied them the pleasure of tossing us out," she said. "That's something, right?"

"Yeah, that'll show 'em."

Jenny smiled and her breathing slowed as she looped the bandage around my fingers and across my palm. It was strange to see her hard surface swept away. Before, she seemed like a giant. A hurricane. Here she was just a girl. The air around her felt still.

"So you're not going back?" she asked.

"No. You?"

Jenny glanced up at the rafters. "And leave all of this? It's easier for everybody if I don't. No place for me in their American fantasy camp." She shook her head with a dark laugh. "I mean, it's hilarious, right? Baseball games. Thanksgiving. American flags. They're the ones responsible for blowing all that stuff up in the first place, and now they love it so much and want it all back? They even took Fort Leonard and built themselves a little nemesis."

"Marcus and Violet aren't like that."

Jenny looked up from under her black hair. "No?"

"They took me in," I said. "Took you in too. They didn't have to do that."

"I know," she said quietly. "They mean well, I know they do, it's just . . . they only go so far. You know? They get right up to the edge and then back off."

I thought of Marcus's hand on Violet's wrist, holding her back. Violet yielding.

"Like with the Krycheks."

"Jackson told you about that? I'm surprised. It doesn't exactly paint Mommy and Daddy in the best light. I don't know. Maybe it's as far as they *can* go. Maybe it's safer to just keep things as they are."

Jenny secured the bandage with a pin, then put the rest of the gauze away and snapped the med kit closed.

"Well, I think you're all set. Should heal up in a few days."

"So no amputation, then."

"I'll keep my eye on it."

I took my hand back, a little sorry to see it leave the cradle of her palm. We sat there, silently, on the edge of her bed. I needed to go find a camp for the night, needed to search for supplies, but I didn't move. An owl hooted outside. The candlelight flickered.

"How is he?" Jenny asked. "Your dad?"

Her question brought a wave that reared up over me again. My throat constricted and there was a burning in my eyes that I had to fight back. But then Jenny drew closer and laid the flat of her palm against my back. Every curve of it, warm and rough, spread across my ribs and spine. There was maybe an inch between my leg and the calloused plain of her bare foot. A pulse of heat came off her, carrying along with it the scent of pine and spicy earth.

Everything in me calmed. The heat and noise faded away.

"Ever since we got here, I've been saying, 'when he wakes up,' and 'when he's better.' It's like I've been trying to pretend that Violet didn't say he might never wake up."

"Violet can be wrong," Jenny said. "She's not perfect. I mean, there used to be, like, tests and instruments and things that told us what was going to happen to us, but not anymore. Right? Now we don't know much of anything. The future just goes in whatever direction it wants."

She was right. I thought of the churn of the river tearing through rock and dirt. Who knew where it would go? What it would wipe away? Who it would spare?

"Did you really mean that stuff you said in the note?" I asked. "The stuff about the world spinning?"

"Yeah," Jenny said. "I did."

"What do you do about it?"

Jenny stretched across the bed behind me, curling around my back, and dug into a bag on the other side.

"What are you doing?"

When Jenny sat up, her hand was closed into a fist. "What I like to do in times like these. When the world's got you down."

"What?"

Jenny opened her hand into the candlelight. A pile of fat paper cylinders sat in her palm. There was a twisted white fuse attached to each one.

"If you thought punching people was good," she said, "wait till you try blowing things up."

Sitting there in the palm of her hand, the little explosives seemed distant, almost imaginary, but a tingling started through my whole body anyway, like that moment when my bat connected with the ball and I ran the bases.

"What did you have in mind?" I asked.

Jenny's grin shone all the way to the corners of her lips.

TWENTY

Minutes later I was running through the woods behind Jenny. There was no path I could see, so I had to struggle to keep an eye on her as she ran, slick as a deer, in and out of the pools of moonlight that littered the forest floor.

She knew the woods better than I did and made a game out of staying ahead of me so that I could follow but never quite catch up. It wasn't until we both had to slow down to scale the Settler's Landing fence that I got anywhere near her. She dropped down into a crouch just behind a thick stand of trees. When I came up, Jenny put her finger to her lips and motioned for me to get down. Both of us were breathing heavily, pushing out thick plumes of white steam.

"Where are we?" I whispered.

Jenny motioned forward with her chin. "Take a look."

In the clearing ahead was a house totally unlike all the others in Settler's Landing. It was enormous, more of a mansion than a house, with towering white walls and columns flanking the front door like marble generals. Two windows in the upper stories glowed with yellow light and filled the yard with a flickering glow.

"Casa de Henry," Jenny said.

"What are we doing here?"

Just then the lights in the upper windows went out. "Come on. We have to go around back."

Jenny took off deeper into the woods, heading to the rear of the house. As we moved around it, its size became even more overwhelming. The walls stretched back another hundred feet or so.

Behind the house there was a collection of fenced enclosures that looked recently built, homemade from scrap pieces of wood, split logs, and scavenged chicken wire. One held chickens, another pigs, and a third sheep.

"The horses and about twenty cows, mean suckers, are in different enclosures on the other side of the trees, but this'll do," Jenny told me.

"Do for what?"

Jenny wasn't listening. She had started to dig around in her bag.

"Take these." She dropped a handful of the fused cylinders into my hand.

"You want me to blow up the sheep?"

Jenny slapped me on the side of the head. "No! We're not gonna hurt them."

"But —"

"Look, the word *explosive*, when applied to these things, is a little grand. They're more like firecrackers."

"Jenny, I don't know. If we get caught —"

"What? We already tossed *ourselves* out of town. Right? Look, I swear to you, they'll never know it's us. Besides, what we are about to do is incredibly obnoxious but more or less harmless."

"What *are* we about to do?"

She smiled a razory smile. "We are going to make sure Will Henry has a really, really crappy night. Now go around to the sheep pen, open the gates, and toss them in. Oh! Matches."

Jenny shoved a cardboard box of matches in my hand and darted out from behind the tree to a spot between the pig and chicken enclosures. I made my way to the sheep's pen, one eye always on the house in case a light came on. I ducked down by the gate. Most of the sheep were in a knot at the center of their pen and didn't even raise their heads as I approached. I slipped the rope loop that held the gate closed up over a post. There was a sharp squeak from the hinge as I opened it that made my heart freeze. One sheep raised its head with mild curiosity but then lowered it again.

I shuffled the bundle of firecrackers in my palm. It was crazy. Utterly crazy. I peeked over the fence. Jenny was poised at the pig pen, firecrackers in hand. I swallowed hard and turned back to the sheep standing placidly in the mud. I saw Will Henry pushing Jenny to the ground. I saw his gold hair and his vicious smile.

I lit the fuse as Jenny struck hers, then tossed my bundle about five feet behind the biggest knot of sheep. One turned back toward the sparking pile of firecrackers.

"Baaaaa."

The explosions were so much bigger than I thought they'd be — a fast procession of booms, sizzles, and cracks, followed by great showers of sparks, red and green and yellow, shooting up into the sky and exploding again, creating umbrellas of fire that lit up the yard like a new sun.

"Cool!" Jenny exclaimed as she slid into the dirt next to me. "I had no idea they were going to do *that*."

The animals completely lost their minds. I had never heard anything like it — the clucking, the oinking, the . . . whatever it is that sheep do was deafening. In seconds they were on the move, pouring out of the gates of their pens. Most of them headed right for the Henrys' huge and beautiful home. Candles flared throughout the house and I could imagine what was going on inside: a confused jumble of Henrys shouting over the squeals of the animals, trying to get dressed, reaching for guns.

"Um, Jenny, I think we better get out of here."

Just then the back door opened and Will came running out in his underwear, a shotgun in one hand and a flashlight in the other. He was joined by a mix of relations, a group of much older brothers and a small girl with blond hair I guessed was his sister.

The animals made right for them, a tidal wave of flesh that curled around their legs, knocked them off balance, then scattered out in all directions. The smaller ones leapt onto the fine white porch and covered everything with a layer of mud and panicked excrement. A few even made it through the back door and into the house, eliciting a chorus of screams and smashing pots and pans. But the bulk of the animals tore right into the woods, crushing through the brush and disappearing. Caleb emerged from the house and shouted at the others to get after them. Will tried to comply but right then a particularly terrified sheep knocked him into the mud.

"Yes!" Jenny said. "Mission accomplished!"

"Hey! Who's there?!"

The beam of a big flashlight was coming Jenny's way. It would hit her any second.

I leapt up out of the brush. "Bow down to your new masters!" I yelled. "Fort Leonard forever!"

The flashlight jerked away and we took off into the woods, laughing just as a shotgun exploded behind us. We ran flat out, leaping over streams and dodging walls of thornbushes, pausing only long enough to fling ourselves up over the fence before racing on again. Even when the sounds of the stampeding livestock and the panicked Henrys were lost in the thicket behind us we kept running. Jenny was ahead of me when the barn appeared in front of us.

As we crossed the clearing, I gave a burst of speed and was right at her heels. I grabbed hold of her arm and tried to pull her back, but our momentum sent us both careening into the wall, landing hard enough to make the whole barn shudder. Jenny hit first and I piled into her, trapping her with my arms. She twisted around so her back was pressed up against the wall.

"I still won," she panted.

Her cheeks were bright red from the cold and slashed with strands of black hair.

The next thing I knew, we were kissing. I don't know if she started it or I did. My elbows collapsed, making a cage around her, pressing our bodies together so that when we fought for air our chests crashed together.

Her hands clasped around my back, pulling me in tight. My hand found her hip, then rose up until it touched the smooth fault line of her scar.

Her skin felt like it was on fire beneath my fingertips.

TWENTY-ONE

When I woke it was barely light out and freezing. Winter had finally arrived. Even in my sweater, flannel shirt, and jeans, I shivered as I pushed myself up on my elbows. Jenny was sitting on the floor of the barn, dressed in jeans and a black sweater, scribbling away on her sketch pad.

"Aren't you cold?"

She shrugged, focused on the paper in her lap, sketching, frowning, erasing, and starting over again. In the sunlight her black eye from the day before looked even worse, an oil slick spread of blue, black, and gray. I turned on my side and watched her, pulling the blanket up over my shoulder.

"What are you doing?"

"Drawing," she said without looking up.

"What?"

"You."

"Think you could make me taller?"

Jenny smiled. I turned on my back and rubbed the sleep out of my eyes.

"What do you do them for? The drawings. Do you sell them or trade them or something?"

"Oh yeah, I supply the entire town with moody line drawings."

"Seriously."

"I don't know. Violet found this set of drawing pencils somewhere and gave them to me. Everything seems a little quieter when I draw. Nothing else manages it. If I didn't, I think a lot more people around here would be sporting black eyes."

I looked up and traced the dusty lines of the timbers stretching across the ceiling, wishing I had something like that, something that would still the nameless feeling that was growing inside of me like a storm cloud, like something just barely forgotten.

Dad.

It was the first night of my entire life that I had spent apart from him. *And for what?* I thought bitterly, memories of the night before swarming in. *So I could run around having fun while he lay there alone in that house? What if our little prank made things even worse?*

I closed my eyes and saw a glint of gold shining in the dark. My grandfather's fist falling from the sky. Alive or dead, he was still there. His voice still in my ear. Our survival was all on me — and what was I doing about it?

I drew myself up out of the bed.

"What are you doing?" Jenny asked as I slipped one boot on and hunted for the other. "Uh, hello? Question here."

"I should be out looking for supplies," I said. "Making camp somewhere."

"Funny, it seemed like you were making camp here."

My fingers froze on the strap of my backpack. I stood there stupidly, unable to move. It was like all the bones had tumbled out of my body. *How could I make her understand?*

"Talk to me, Stephen," Jenny said quietly. She was looking up at me over the edge of her pad. Her eyes, liquid and sharp at the same time. It was like she was always one step ahead of me. Grandpa had told me a hundred times to keep quiet. To keep things to myself. But I couldn't anymore.

"I just . . . I keep thinking I'm going to be . . ."

"What?"

A white star, crowned in gold, fell, and I shook from its impact.

". . . punished," I said.

"For what? Having fun? Being with me? Why would you think that?"

Jenny's pencil clattered to the floor as she charged across the room and knocked me back onto the bed. She threw her legs over my chest, holding me down.

"Jenny . . ."

She took both my wrists in her calloused hands, pinning me. Her hair fell down around us like a curtain, blocking out the rest of the world.

"No one is going to be punished for something as dumb as stampeding some pigs or wrestling with me. Not by God, not by anybody."

"Jenny, let me up."

"The world is not all on you," Jenny said, pushing me down, suddenly fierce. "I know it feels that way, but it's not. Not anymore." She dipped her head down and kissed me. "Not for either of us. Okay? Now say that the world isn't going to end if Little Stevie Quinn has some fun."

"Jenny —"

"Say it! I mean, you did have fun blowing things up and kissing me last night, right?"

Fun wasn't the word. Not even close. Suddenly Grandpa and that flash of gold seemed far away.

"Say it," Jenny repeated, a whisper, her face inches from mine. "The world isn't going to end."

I watched her lips move and matched them carefully, syllable for syllable. Something about it felt secret and shameful, but I said it anyway.

"The world isn't going to end."

Jenny's lips fell onto mine, and then we lay there gazing dreamily up at the high ceiling for I don't know how long. One of us would laugh and then the other, for no reason we could put a name to. Thoughts entered my mind and I said them and they all seemed to make sense to her.

The sun mounted steadily outside, filling the barn with an amber light.

"What time do you think it is?" I asked.

"Are you saying time doesn't cease to have meaning when we're together?"

"Seriously."

"I don't know," she said sleepily. "A little after dawn, I guess? Why?"

I turned so our faces were just inches apart on separate pillows. "I want to go back over to the Greens' for a second. Before everyone gets up."

"For what?"

"To see Dad. And get some books."

"Books?"

I paused. I had said it without thinking. I knew the mocking that I was in for, but what could I do?

"Some, uh, books Tuttle gave me."

Jenny chuckled. "He totally got to you with the save the world thing, didn't he?"

"He did not!"

"He did! You're going to help usher in a new golden age of mankind."

"I am not!" I said, and then, when her laughter had faded, "I don't know. I was mad when I left, so I didn't take them. But now I guess . . . I've just never had anything like that before. School and stuff, I mean. It's kind of cool knowing things other than how to avoid dying."

"No, I get that," she said, then added with a smirk, "you're coming back though, right? This isn't some clever little ploy?"

I laughed, struck for a second by the strange sound of it and how easy it felt when I was with her. Once I got myself together I stood there at the edge of the bed, hands stuffed in my pockets.

How does this work? Do I kiss her before I leave?

Over and over again I was falling into worlds I didn't know the rules for.

"So . . . I'll, uh, see ya later."

Jenny rolled her eyes at my awkwardness. I took a last look at her lying there in the half-light, then turned toward the door, knowing that if I didn't leave right away, I never would.

"I want to come with you when you go."

I stopped in my tracks inches from the door.

"When your dad is better," she said. "I want to come. I was going to be all subtle about it. At one point I was even going to blackmail you, since I spied on you burying all that stuff of Violet's that night, but now I thought I'd just come out with it."

Jenny rose up out of bed and moved toward me.

"Look, like you saw last night, I'm kind of a tactical genius, right? And I know where all the good stuff in this town is, so I could help you pick up some salvage before we go. What do you think?"

Jenny's face was inches from mine, but I was too stunned to say anything.

"You don't want me to," she said flatly.

"It's not that."

"What? You don't think I can handle it?" Jenny teased. "I could destroy you in a heartbeat."

"I know."

"Don't worry, Stephen — it's not like I'm asking you to marry me or anything."

"No, I didn't — I just mean . . ." I struggled, trying to come up with a reason her offer was so confusing. "Why would you *want* to?"

"Why? Because I can't live in this stupid twentieth-century museum anymore. I don't belong here, and neither do you! I want to be out there in the real world. With you."

"Jenny, it's not —"

"What? Easy? Safe? Uh, yeah, no kidding. We were out there for ten years before we came here and we saw all the same things you did. Worse, maybe."

I thought of that morning by the stream. She and Jackson playing cards and all the blood that followed. Who was I to tell her what the real world was?

"I know it will be dangerous," she said. "I just think sitting here in this barn playing dumb pranks isn't living. With or without you, I'm leaving. I'd rather it be with you. And I think that's what you want too."

She was right. I knew it as soon as she suggested it. I knew exactly what Grandpa would think, what he would say, but right then I didn't care. The idea of walking out of town without her seemed impossible.

"Yeah," I said. "Yeah. Okay."

"Ha!" she exclaimed. "Nice! It'll be great, you'll see. And your dad is totally gonna love me. Don't you think?"

"Yeah, I kind of have a feeling he might."

Jenny popped up on her toes and kissed me again, holding it longer this time, slipping her arms around my back so our bodies pressed tight together. "Still want to go get those books?"

I smiled. Our foreheads met, making a close little pyramid. "Yep."

"Jerk."

"I'll come back as soon as I get them."

By the time I got to the door, Jenny already had her sketch pad in her hands, drawing, lost in it. Her dark hair was a tangled mess, and in the growing light of the morning, her skin glowed. Her sweater slipped away from her shoulder, revealing a tiny island chain of freckles. I watched her for a second and then slipped out the door into the cold morning air.

I stood for a moment in the barnyard, then made for a path that cut like an arrow into the woods. Everything seemed golden and crisp around me and I felt I was close to touching something I had never seen, or even hoped for. The future.

TWENTY-TWO

I avoided the main road, following the decaying perimeter fence as it wound through the woods before jumping it and heading toward Settler's Landing. My steps felt lighter than usual as I walked through the bare trees. It was funny trying to imagine Jenny out with me and Dad on the trail. Somehow I couldn't see her trudging along, donkey in tow, picking up scrap.

Maybe we won't even go back on the trail.

I stopped dead in the middle of the woods, surprised by the thought. I rolled it around in my head like it was a jewel I had just discovered.

Was it possible? After all, Dad had been talking about it before the accident, and now with Jenny along, maybe we really could make a new start. Settle somewhere. Go west and see what there was to see. There was a whole world out there.

I laughed a little to myself. The idea would have terrified me just weeks ago. How had that changed? Was it Jenny? Was it Settler's Landing? Did it even matter? Hope was hope and I'd take it.

I clambered down a hill and leapt over a stream. The trees opened up above me. The sky was thick with looming gray clouds. The way the temperature was dropping, I wondered if I might actually see snow this year.

Usually we were down in Florida by this time of year, since real winter storms could sometimes last for weeks on end. The last time I'd seen snow was during a freak storm years before. We had just gotten to the Canadian camp in early April, when the day suddenly grew cold and snow began to fall. It had seemed like a miracle. The trading camp had buzzed around us, everyone rushing to celebrate before it was gone. There'd been a bonfire and food roasting on spits and a three-man band whose music had floated above the camp.

Mom and Dad and I had stayed behind while Grandpa went out looking for tobacco. We'd gathered around our campfire in a semicircle of folding chairs, cooking a skinny chicken on a spit, a plastic tarp angled over us to keep the snow off. We knew from experience that several hours from that moment we would have to take refuge to escape the drunkenness and the fights that inevitably broke out after a big party, but that was later. Right then the air was full of laughter and music and the clean-smelling snow that had painted the muddy camp around us a fresh, brilliant white. I had *The Lord of the Rings* on my lap but was listening to Dad talk about his days as a theater usher in San Diego while Mom talked of wild party after wild party and teased him for being a nerd.

"So how did you guys meet?" I'd asked that night.

Mom had glanced at Dad. I was maybe eight then and they'd only recently started talking to me about the Collapse and the war.

"P Eleven had just started up," Dad said. "There were rumors about a quarantine in San Diego, so your grandparents and I piled into the car, using Grandpa's military ID to get us through the roadblocks. We thought we'd head out east to this old army installation in the desert to wait things out. On our way out of town, we stopped for gas at the station your mom's parents owned."

"By then my whole family was gone," Mom said. "My sister, Sarah, went first, then Dad, then Mom."

Mom's face had darkened, remembering it.

"I heard the bell ding as your dad and his folks pulled up. I came out from behind the station to meet them. I was filthy. It's funny — I was such a prissy little thing when I was little, playing dolls and insisting everything I owned be as pink and frilly as possible. But by that point, I barely bothered to wipe the dirt off my face before going to fill up their gas."

Dad had held out his hand, stretching it across the space between them, and Mom had taken it.

"I pumped it for your grandpa, and when I was done, he dug down into his pocket to pay, but all he had was a hundred. When I told him I didn't have change for a hundred, he started yelling and screaming, claiming I was trying to cheat him! I laughed. I was like . . . the world is coming to an *end*, man! I mean, the sky is *falling*! I just buried my entire family out in the desert, and you're having an aneurysm over your eleven dollars and fifty cents in change? Finally I just said forget it. Go with God, Ebenezer!

"So he took his hundred and jumped in the car, but by that point your father here had gotten out of the car and said he wasn't getting in until his dad agreed to take me with them. Well, if you thought your grandfather had been impolite before, imagine the tidal wave of profanity that erupted when number one son decided to stage a little coup. Your grandpa screamed and hollered, he stamped his feet, even hit him! Can you believe that? Hitting something as adorable as your father? Didn't matter, though. Your dad was a brick wall. He wouldn't give an inch. Not one inch. I hadn't said two words to him yet! And here he was . . . my noble man."

"Why'd you do it, Dad?"

Dad had locked eyes with Mom over the orange flames. The snow swirled behind him.

"I don't know," he said. "Didn't really even think about doing it till then. It was just . . . the second I saw her, it was like a jigsaw puzzle. You know? You've got all these pieces and, on its own, each piece is a splotch of blue or a bit of green. But then a bunch of them click into place and you've got the sky or the grass and the whole thing just makes sense."

I'd recognized the look that came over his face then. He got it a lot when looking at Mom. It was like he was seeing her as she was right then, bright and rosy in the fire's glow, but at the same time seeing her as she was on the day they met, and when they'd first kissed, and when they'd snuck away from Grandpa to be married, and then as he imagined she might be ten years down the line, then twenty, then thirty, and finally as the old woman he had no idea she would never have the chance to become.

It was like he was looking at his whole life with her in that one moment.

I stepped out of the tree line and into the Greens' backyard. There were no candles lit in the windows and I couldn't hear any sign of movement from inside. Still, I skirted around the edge of their backyard garden toward the front door. I knew they wouldn't mind my coming, but I thought it would be better if they didn't see me. Hiding behind the corner of the house, I peeked out into the neighborhood.

It seemed strangely quiet, empty, almost as if everyone who lived there had picked up and moved on the night before. I told myself it was just my imagination.

I came out around the side of the house and went up the front steps, letting myself inside. Dad lay in his usual place, looking exactly as he had the night before. His face, more and more drawn as the days passed, was still framed with his great swirls of black hair, shot through with veins of white.

He had become a different person the day he met Mom, like a switch had been flipped inside him. He stood up to Grandpa in a way he never had before, and then they somehow managed to hold on to each other as the world tore itself to shreds around them. They even had me when the idea of bringing another person into that wreck of a world must have seemed crazy at best.

I thought maybe the man he was back in the plane, the one who rescued those two people, was the man Mom knew emerging again after being so long without her, the man who wouldn't admit that the world was really over.

She would have been so proud of him.

I realized, maybe for the first time, that I was too.

"Jenny wants to come with us when we go," I said quietly, my hand on his shoulder. "I think you'll like her. I was thinking maybe we won't even go back on the trail. You know? Like you said before we came here? Maybe we'll find someplace to have a house. Maybe we'll —"

I stopped myself short. It was fine when it was all in my head, but it felt foolish to imagine that life out loud.

Driving back the sadness I could feel swelling inside me, I knelt down by his bed and collected the books, piling them up in my arms.

"I'll be back soon," I said.

I reached for the doorknob, but as I did I noticed the coatrack that hung on the wall next to the door frame. Something about it struck me, but for a second I didn't understand what or why. And then I got it.

It was empty.

Each time I had seen the Greens come inside, they would take off their jackets and hang them on the coatrack's pegs. If Jackson or Marcus ever forgot, Violet would ride him until he took it from wherever he dropped it and hung it up.

The Greens should have been upstairs, maybe a half hour or so from getting up and starting their day. So why was the coatrack empty?

I set my books on the floor and stepped into the kitchen, listening intently for any sound coming from upstairs. Nothing. From the bottom of the stairs, I could see Jackson's door hanging open into the hall. The stairs creaked as I made my way up, but there was no answering sound from any of the rooms. There were clothes scattered on Jackson's floor and his bed was disheveled, like he had gotten up and dressed in a hurry. I made my way to the end of the hall, to Marcus and Violet's room, and found it the same way.

So what? Something came up and they all decided to get an early start. It's nothing.

It made sense, but I didn't believe it. Maybe it was that weird abandoned feeling I'd noticed as soon as I'd gotten to town this morning. I went downstairs and peeked out the front door. Just as I did, a door opened and slammed shut somewhere across the park. A man ran from his house and then down the road that led to the school.

I closed the Greens' door behind me and eased out onto the porch. I knew I should take my books and go back to Jenny. After all, what happened in this town was no longer my business but, curious, I went down the road toward the school.

I reached the edge of the parking lot just as the man threw open the school's front doors and disappeared inside. I circled around the side of the building, looking in each window as I had that first day, but saw nothing until I came around to the back of the school and looked in the window above the main classroom.

The room was packed with what I was sure was every single resident of Settler's Landing. A hundred people or more. The desks and chairs were pushed aside and everyone stood facing Tuttle's empty desk in tight groups. A murmur rose and fell in waves. I eased the window open.

Violet and Jackson were at the front of the mob. Violet stood behind Jackson with her hands on his shoulders. His face was cast down and his arms were crossed tightly over his chest. He leaned into his mom the way a scared child would. That was how everyone looked, afraid and waiting.

The doors at the back of the classroom flew open and Tuttle came in, followed by Caleb and Will and, behind them, Marcus. They all looked tired and pale. Their clothes were dirty and in some places torn. Each one of them was armed. The crowd hushed instantly as Caleb swept in front of Tuttle's desk. He bowed his head, his hands clasped tightly in front of him.

"Poison," Caleb said simply, letting it hang in the air without explanation. "The people of Israel were beset on all sides by the godless. Animals, starving and hungry for destruction. Unable to stand against the people of God in the field, they conspired to come into their land in parties of two or three as spies."

Caleb paused, searching the crowd. I pushed farther away from the window.

"The people of Israel took them to their heart. They dressed them in their clothes and gave them food and water and fellowship. After all, they thought, there were so few of them, what harm could there be? The people of God grew proud of their kindness and generosity, barely noticing the poison that had infected them, like a brackish stream pouring into a clear lake, until soon the water all around them was murky and foul. The people of God said to one another, 'But where is our home? Where is the land of God that was?' This is how the weak and the profane destroy the strong and the righteous."

The crowd held its breath as he scanned its faces.

"Last night, our home was attacked."

The crowd didn't move, except for some parents who pulled their children tighter.

"Two or more raiders from Fort Leonard, perhaps guided here by former members of our own community, came for our livestock, firing their weapons into the air to start a stampede. Whether their goal was to steal them or to simply run them off in order to weaken us before a larger assault, we don't know. My family gave chase but was unable to overcome them."

My first instinct was to laugh, it was so ridiculous, but the reaction from the crowd made it clear that this was deadly serious.

"Like you all, I know the danger of the world around us," Caleb continued, his voice softening, growing warm, "how it presses against us every day. For years now we have been safe in our anonymity, blessed by God in this place, but I fear, I fear deeply, that such a time may be coming to an end. These new times will demand not only vigilance but also action. It's my opinion that we cannot sit idly, waiting to be attacked again. If we are to be truly safe, we must act now before the danger grows. It gives me no pleasure to say this, but I propose the only course of action I feel is responsible. We must gather a force and, as quickly as possible, move to end the threat of Fort Leonard once and for all."

The people of Settler's Landing didn't hold back. Their agreement was absolute and automatic in a way that was frightening. Men yelled. Some stomped their feet and pounded on the walls. Down in the crowd, I saw Derrick and Martin and Wendy and the rest, all of them with their parents, and all of them shouting their approval.

Down at the front of the group, though, Jackson melted even farther into Violet's body, his skin waxy and pale as he imagined, I was sure, what was to come.

Caleb soaked in their approval as Sam entered the room, a rifle slung over his shoulder. He looked haggard, his clothes in disarray and a salt-and-pepper growth of stubble on his ashen face. Marcus leaned in, nodding, as Sam whispered to him. The two then slipped out the doors together and I moved away from the window to follow them. I thought that if I had the chance to stop the madness, this was it.

By the time I made it around to the parking lot, Sam and Marcus were talking to a small group of armed men. They spoke briefly, then Sam took the men east over the hill and out of sight. Marcus quickened his pace across the lot and toward town.

"Marcus!" I cried out. "Marcus, wait!"

Marcus turned back. "What are you doing here? You shouldn't be here, Stephen —"

"It was us," I said, catching my breath.

. "What?"

"Me and Jenny. At the Henrys' last night. We didn't mean anything by it. It was just a stupid prank to get back at Will and them."

Marcus checked behind us, then yanked me off the road toward the shelter of the trees. "Someone said they were from Fort Leonard."

"That was me. It was dumb. I know. I'm sorry. Look, just tell Caleb. Tell him it was us. We'll go, we'll really leave this time. There's no reason to do what he's saying. Build an army? Marcus, that's insane."

"It's too late, Stephen."

"No it's not. Go back in there and tell them."

"No," he barked, almost knocking me back. "Caleb came and got a group of us right after it happened last night and we went out to Fort Leonard."

Something sunk inside me.

"What did you do?"

Marcus drew a shaky breath, then dropped his eyes to the ground between us.

"Marcus, what happened?"

"We found their settlement early this morning. Figured out one of the buildings was a food storehouse. Caleb had the idea we should raid it like we thought they'd done to us. It seemed simple; the whole town looked to be asleep, but . . . there were two guards. They fired at us. Caleb shot one. I got the other."

I jumped as the school doors boomed open behind us and the crowd started pouring into the lot out front.

"Maybe we can talk to them," I said. "Talk to Caleb, explain. Maybe —"

"The people at Fort Leonard were getting together before we even left," he said. "It won't be long before they come looking for us. Our only chance now is to get them before they can get us."

The rumble of the crowd grew louder as it reached the road.

"You should go. Take Jenny and get out of here. Go to the old casino on the other side of the highway. We'll come get you when things have calmed down."

"But, Marcus —"

"Did you listen to that speech? He thinks you two were a part of it, Stephen. That you helped them. We tried to tell him you weren't any harm, but I don't know what he's going to do. Just go, Stephen. Get back to Jenny. Now!"

Marcus left to join the mob as it swarmed up the hill. I slipped into the woods and ran as fast as I could, throwing myself over the fence and dashing off again. Jenny had been alone for more than an hour. The trees rushed by me as I ran leaping over rocks and brush.

I was little more than a mile out when I first smelled smoke.

The air thickened the closer I got. My eyes stung. My heart pounded and I ran until my legs burned, ran until I blew through the trees and came out into the clearing where I was faced with a wall of flame and gray smoke.

Jenny's barn was on fire.

TWENTY-THREE

"Jenny!"

I threw myself into the doors of the barn, scorching my hands and choking on a lungful of smoke.

"Jenny!"

Flames were spreading up the walls and tearing into the roof of the barn. I dropped low where the air was clearer and covered my mouth and nose with my sleeve. My eyes stung but I searched the barn, yelling her name as loud as I could. There was a flash of movement by the bed. I raced toward it, finding Jenny on the ground, coughing, her legs pinned under a pile of charred wood from the partially collapsed ceiling. She was trying to get out from under it but was weak and barely able to move. I grabbed her under her arms and pulled but she cried out.

There was a *whoosh* as the wall next to us caught fire, exploding into a curtain of red and orange. The smoke swelled and thickened.

I dropped to my knees at Jenny's waist and thrust my hands into the smoldering pile of wood, ignoring the feel of my fingers searing as I threw the timbers off. I shook Jenny by the shoulders, but by then she was unconscious.

I looked all around me. The doors I'd come in had caught fire, as had the walls on every side. Fire flowed over the ceiling. I was trapped. The old wood of the barn, dry and weak from years of neglect, popped and hissed, burning as easily as paper.

I rolled Jenny onto her back, then muscled her up over my shoulder. The ceiling groaned louder. There was no time to waste.

I stood up, eyes watering and lungs aching, then dropped my head and shoulder and ran as fast as I could, straight at one of the burning walls. There was a panicked instant when it resisted, but then the wood cracked and flames gouged into my shoulder and cheek.

Our momentum carried us out of the barn and to the tree line, where I stumbled and Jenny went spilling out into the brush. I collapsed, coughing and heaving beside her. Jenny moaned. Her one good eye was open, but barely. She was breathing.

"You're going to be okay," I said. "We're going to be fine."

"I thought it was Will and them," she rasped. "But it wasn't. It was a group of men. They didn't even say anything, they just —"

"It's okay," I said.

There was a crash behind us as part of another wall fell in. The relief of safety washed away, though, when I realized that everything we owned — my pack and supplies, Jenny's clothes, Grandpa's rifle — was all in the barn. We couldn't go back to Settler's Landing and without shelter or supplies, and with winter coming on fast, we were dead.

I could still make out the hole in the wall I had broken through, a splintering oval wreathed in flame. Fire had spread nearly everywhere, but the roof still hadn't come down. I had seconds. If that.

"What are you doing?" Jenny said as I pushed away from her. "Stephen!"

I ran for the barn and took a deep breath before jumping through the gap, stumbling toward what was left of the bed. My lips were sealed tight and my fingers pinched my nose closed. If I tried to take a breath, I was dead. I tripped over a pile of timbers and landed hard. The smoke had dropped almost to the level of the floor. I felt around wildly, squinting into the gray clouds until my fingers hit the side of my pack. I pulled it to me and threw it over my shoulder. My knife was in its sheath next to it. I stuffed it into my back pocket.

There was a *crack* behind me and the sound of falling wood. I caught sight of the rifle lying next to Jenny's sketch pad, its barrel pointed toward me. I reached for it but the red-hot metal singed my fingers and I had to yank them back.

There was a growl above me. The roof was coming down. I reached out again and my fingers closed around Jenny's sketch pad. I scrambled to my feet and ran toward the opening in the wall. The growl above me turned into a long moan. There was a *whoosh* and the wall behind me collapsed. Then the ceiling started to come down, forcing the smoke and heat down on my shoulders like two giant hands. Burning wood fell at my heels, popping and hissing.

The way before me was closing off. All I could see was gray and livid yellow. I thought of Jenny, lying out there alone, and threw myself into the air.

TWENTY-FOUR

We stumbled through the woods, our arms clasped around each other, until we crossed the highway and came to the parking lot that surrounded the Golden Acorn casino.

When we got there, I eased Jenny down inside. The lobby was musty and cold. A jumble of gaming tables, chairs, and slot machines, most of which had been stripped of anything useful years ago, littered the main room. I followed a corridor that branched off to one side and was lined on either wall with rows of identical-looking doors. I pushed on each one until I found a door that gave. The room was empty except for a mattress that lay on the concrete floor, stripped of sheets and its metal frame, and the husk of what used to be a giant television set. It wasn't much. I pulled the curtains back and saw that the big glass window on one wall was still intact. It would do.

I brought Jenny inside the room and we collapsed on the bed, both of us covered in small burns and soot. Jenny's legs had gotten the worst of it. I pulled out my first-aid kit and carefully cleaned and dressed her wounds. We'd have to keep an eye on them, but for now they didn't look serious.

Jenny patched me up and then we drank the rest of the water in my canteen. After that we were exhausted and lay down, our arms draped over each other.

Soon Jenny was asleep, but I lay awake for hours as the land outside and the hotel room around us dropped into deeper and deeper darkness.

For some reason I kept seeing the quarry. Me and Jackson surrounded by all his friends. My friends. I skipped back to earlier that day and felt the jolt as I connected with that ball and ran the bases. I felt the wind against my skin and heard the sound of those voices cheering me on.

But all of that was gone now, wasn't it?

I looked over at Jenny, who was sleeping fitfully, burned and slashed, and my nails dug into my palm. I grimaced at the pain but welcomed it. Because it had been me, hadn't it? I was the one who sent those people to Jenny's with torches in hand. If they had killed Jenny, it would have been my fault. If there was a war, it would be my war. The people of Settler's Landing were a bomb, but I was the one who lit the fuse.

I rolled out of bed and drew the curtains aside. I thought of Dad lying all alone at the Greens' and felt low and sick. If the war came to Settler's Landing, it would come for him too.

"They won't come here."

I turned away from the window. Jenny was sitting up on the mattress, watching me.

"Who?"

"Will and his family. They won't follow us here."

"Why not?"

"The square pegs are out of the round holes. They can do what they want now."

I leaned against the windowsill. "Do you think they'll really do it? Start a war?"

Jenny winced as she drew her burned legs up to her chest and wrapped her arms around them. Her face filled with moonlight as she peered out the window.

"I think they want the world to be like it was when they were our age. Maybe a war is just the last piece of the puzzle."

I left the window and pulled out my old bedroll, spreading the small blanket as best I could over us both. We sat up, huddled close together. Jenny laid her head on my shoulder.

"I shouldn't have gotten you involved," she said. "In any of it. The fight with Will. The thing at the Henrys'. It was stupid of me."

"You didn't know what would happen."

"I didn't care," Jenny said, a knife-edge of bitterness in her voice. She turned and stared out the window, her back to me. "Maybe I just wanted to get back at them and didn't care who got hurt in the process."

I reached out until my hand found hers and clasped it tight. She turned. Her cheek was silver in the moonlight.

"Come on," she said. "Let's get out of here."

We left the casino and Jenny led me down to a billboard on the side of the road. It was the tallest one I had ever seen and dwarfed the trees around it. We climbed to the very top, up rusty and vine-covered handholds — past the smiling, tanned family that claimed AT&T cell phones would keep them connected forever — and sat looking out over the miles of empty land around us.

The night had turned cold with banks of heavy clouds rolling in. Jenny craned her long neck and looked up at a field of stars that glittered in the black. If you looked close, it was almost as though you could see the stars moving, a sparkling dome, turning and turning.

"Used to be you couldn't even see them," Jenny said. "With the cities and their lights and pollution and all. At least that's what Violet said."

Jenny picked a leaf off a nearby tree and let it drop, watching as it helicoptered down through the emptiness. Jenny leaned into me against the cold and we sat and watched the moon. Far off in the distance the barest wisp of smoke rose like a ribbon from someone's campfire.

"Do you ever wonder what they're doing out there?"

"Who?"

"All the other people," Jenny said. "I mean, there's a whole world out there, right? Whole other countries. Who knows, maybe there's some place out there where the Collapse never even happened. Where people are just going about their lives."

Was it possible? Since we shared a border, P11 hit Mexico and Canada as badly as it did us. But what about everyone else? Were there places that the Collapse never touched? I looked out into the night and wondered.

"If you could make it so it never happened," Jenny said, "would you?"

I tried to imagine it. The Collapse. The horror of P11. What would this place be like if none of it ever happened? I imagined vast crowds of people packed shoulder to shoulder, scurrying about like ants, our silent world wiped away by electric lights and movie theaters and televisions and cars.

What would our lives be like? Jenny and I never would have met, for one thing. She would be thousands of miles away with a different name and a different family. And since my mom and dad only met because of the war, would I even have existed at all? I knew it was wrong not to wish all that death away; but how could I long for a life, a world, that I never even knew?

"I don't know," I said.

Jenny raised her lips to my ear.

"I wouldn't," she breathed.

Later, we walked back to the casino and slipped into bed. As Jenny slept, I laid my head on her chest and listened to the thrum of her heart. It sounded like a bird's wings beating at the air.

I opened my eyes hours later, fully awake, and stared up into the darkness. Jenny was on her side, breathing low and steadily. I dressed quietly and felt my way out of the room and down the hall to the brighter gaming area, navigating toward the front door. The edges around it seemed curiously bright for the hour.

I stepped up to it. Outside, the whole world had changed.

As we slept, the first snow of the year had fallen with a vengeance. It covered everything with a coat of white that was already inches thick. The snow fell lightly now with a musical clink as one crystal stuck to another and settled. With the full moon just visible through some cracks in the clouds the whole place glowed almost as light as day. I buttoned up my coat and made my way across the parking lot, my steps crunching and my breath a white plume trailing behind me.

I had no destination in mind, but I felt this pull to keep going so I followed the highway south for a while, then veered off into the trees.

There, I found a circle of land isolated from the snow by the heavy canopy of tree limbs.

I cleared a plot of ground, then knelt down and assembled a pile of brittle leaves and twigs for a fire. The movements Grandpa had showed me years before effortlessly flowed back to me. Soon a spark caught off the fire starter I had in my pocket and the leaves smoldered. I leaned in close and blew on it gently until smoke puffed up and a bit of flame peeked out. This was the most delicate time. Get excited, add too much wood too fast, and the whole thing would be suffocated. Go too slow and the flame would starve and die. I added thin twigs at first, until the flames grew and could sustain themselves, then layered on thicker branches. I watched it burn, the warmth and familiarity of it flowing over me.

"We're better off now," Grandpa had said one night as we sat together across a fire. He was shaping a tree branch into the trigger of a small game trap with his knife while Dad slept fitfully behind us. I was hugging my knees, my head down, my throat sore, exhausted from crying and wishing I could disappear.

I was ten. Two newly dug graves, one large and one small, throbbed in the darkness behind us.

For months I had watched Mom's stomach grow, drunk with wonder. Dad had sat me down and patiently, if awkwardly, explained exactly what was going on, but it meant nothing to me. Clearly, this little person, this little world growing inside her, couldn't be anything but a miracle. I tried to picture having a brother or a sister. Someone to talk to, to play with, to foist chores off on, to torture in more ways than I could imagine. It was too good to be true.

"What are we going to call it?" I asked Mom one day. "How about Frodo?"

"We're not calling the baby Frodo."

"Why not?"

"How about Agnes?" Mom suggested.

"Boring."

Dad piped up."Hildegard?"

"Blech."

"Oh! Oh!" Dad hopped on his toes. "If it's a boy? Elvis. Aaron. Presley."

Grandpa, of course, was furious. It would be another mouth to feed. It would slow us down. He went on and on, but as tough as he was, Mom was tougher. She said if everybody thought like that, then the human race was going to disappear pretty fast.

We had planned on being at the Northern Gathering when the baby came — Dad said there were women there who knew about these things — but we were a month's hike away at best when Mom grasped her stomach and announced that it was time.

"But can't we stop it?" I'd asked. "Delay it or something?"

"Nope! When it comes, it comes!"

Dad was trying to seem unconcerned, dashing around to make Mom more comfortable, but I could tell he was worried. Mom too. Usually she joked through the worst of times — she always said that's what joking was for — but as she lay there on the grass that morning, her face was cut with lines of tension and sweat as she strained and cried out and fought. It was as though she was drowning and trying, more and more desperately, to claw her way to the surface of the churning water. Dad tried to help and so did I, but it was no use. There was so much blood.

Three hours into her labor, Mom's cries stopped.

Her face went slack.

"Bev?"

Dad knelt by her side.

"Bev?"

Her hand slipped from his, like a dove tumbling out of the sky.

Late that night, after the graves had been dug and Dad was finally asleep, I sat alone with Grandpa around that fire as he whittled at a piece of wood with his old hunting knife.

"Learn from this," he croaked.

"Learn what?" My voice sounded far away, like it was floating some-where far above my head.

Grandpa glanced over his shoulder where the skeleton frames of the roller coasters rose into the sky. He turned and spit thickly into the fire.

He wasn't at all the stick figure he would become in just a few years. He was a twisted piece of metal, scarred and pitted and hard. His knife-edge crew cut was thick and gray. Even in the light of the fire his eyes were like pale blue marbles, small and cold.

"She's better off now."

Grandpa's ring glinted as he carved a bloodless gash in the wood and looked at me across the flames.

"We made a mess of things before you were born," he said. "P Eleven was just what we deserved. It was no plague. It was a blessing. Surviving it, that's the real plague. But soon it'll just be . . . silence."

Now, as my own fire hissed and sputtered, I wondered: *Was he right? Is this how we were meant to live — like animals? Living and dying and hoping for nothing until one day we all disappear?*

If we were, then what? Should I just go? On my own? Right then? Violet probably hadn't retrieved her medicines yet. I could take them, get my pack while Jenny slept, and disappear. Dad would be safe in Violet's hands. Jenny would be fine on her own. Maybe if we all went our separate ways, if we stayed low to the ground, no towns, no family, no friends, this new end of the world would pass us by. Maybe then we'd all be safe. Maybe Grandpa's only mistake was that in keeping us together he hadn't taken things far enough.

The wind surged, blowing the drifts off the ground and the low-hanging tree branches, whiting out everything around me, erasing it. I thought of Jenny lying there in that dark room, curled around the spot where I had been, a warm place in all that cold. I knew that leaving right then might spare us pain later, but I also knew that I was fooling myself if I thought I could do it. There was this chain that ran from me to her. I didn't know when or how it had come to be, but it was there. I could feel it. I didn't want to imagine what she'd be like in five or ten or twenty years. I wanted to see it. I wanted to be there.

Besides, in the end, who had Grandpa's rules ever saved? Not Mom. Not Dad. Not even himself. If it was true that all paths in our world led to only one place, then why not fill whatever path you chose with the best things you could find?

I wasn't my grandfather. I never would be.

I turned to go back to the casino, but before I took a single step, a dark figure crossed the highway in front of me and moved quickly toward the building, leaning in against the wind. I couldn't make out who it was, but it didn't matter. Jenny was alone in there.

My boots crunched through the snow as I raced back, wishing Grandpa's rifle hadn't been lost in the fire. I gripped the hilt of Dad's knife instead. It would have to do.

The figure, in a black coat with the hood turned up, was at the door when I got there, ready to go in.

"Stop!"

I gripped the knife's handle tight, ready to use it. The figure in black turned to face me and lifted the hood.

"Violet?"

She stepped into the white between us. "Stephen?" she said, moving toward me. "Thank God. Are you okay? Is Jenny? I didn't know they were going to do what they did. When I found out —"

"We're fine."

Violet said nothing for a moment. The snow surged, making her body waver, ghostlike and gray.

"What is it, Violet?"

A plane of snow drifted between us as she looked back in the direction of Settler's Landing.

"He's gone," she said. "I came to tell you he's gone."

"What? Who's gone? Violet, what are you —"

But then I knew.

TWENTY-FIVE

I stepped out onto the Greens' porch hours later. It was late and everyone was asleep. The snow had finally stopped.

I held a lantern I had found down in the Greens' basement. The
land around me glowed a dazzling white. The roads were gone.
The playground had disintegrated into a few ice-covered bars and
odd-shaped mounds of snow. The lines that divided one yard from
the next had been wiped clean.

I descended the steps and started south. The houses to either side
of me were little more than snow-covered cliff faces. Walking through
them was like walking along the bottom of a deep canyon.

It wasn't hard to carry him. As with Grandpa, death had taken Dad
a bit at a time until there was almost nothing left. I passed the entrance
to the town, the wall now just a long ridge, like a curving collarbone,
bleached white in the sun. I crossed the lawn beyond the wall, then
passed through the trees and out again until I came to the great empty
plain on the other side.

The world had disappeared. There was nothing but white as far as I
could see. The casino and the Starbucks were snowy hillocks. Even the
towering billboards to the north had been nearly erased.

I walked out into the nothingness until my legs stopped moving. Then I set the lantern down and eased Dad onto a snowbank. As I did it, the sheet covering his face fell away. The crow black of his hair and beard was startling, lying in the middle of all that white. His mouth was slightly open and his skin was a bluish gray. He looked so small. Shrunken and old. People said that the dead looked like they were only sleeping, but it had never seemed that way to me. To me, there was nothing there at all. An empty house. An abandoned world.

I covered his face with the sheet and picked up the shovel.

Moving the snow aside was easy enough, but when the blade of the shovel hit the ground, it rang like a bell. My palms ached from the vibration. The ground was nearly frozen.

I had changed back into my old clothes before leaving the Greens' so when I pulled off my coat, the icy wind tore through my sweater and patchwork pants. I wedged the shovel into a crack in the ground, then leaned my weight into it, pushing the blade an inch or two farther in to break the icy shell. Once I had done that across the entire breadth of the grave, I was able to dig the shovel in farther and remove the dark soil inches at a time. As I got lower, the dirt became looser. The blade of the shovel scraped across rock as it tore into the soil.

Hours later, my muscles were burning and my chest was heaving. Each time I drew breath, the frigid air tore at my lungs. I couldn't feel my hands or feet. The skin of my ears stung. My body was slick with sweat despite the cold. I stopped digging. Hanging over the shovel's handle, exhausted, I caught my breath and then checked my progress.

I was standing only about two feet deep in the ground. The shovel fell out of my hands. I dropped back into the snow like a rag doll.

The cold reached up into my back, spread throughout my chest, and curled its fingers around my heart.

"Stephen?"

Jenny stood behind me, our blanket wrapped around her shoulders. When I didn't say anything she reached for the shovel, but I yanked it away from her and held it to my chest.

"I have to do this myself."

Jenny stared at me, her hair whipping past her reddened cheeks.

"No you don't."

I ignored her. Using the shovel like a crutch, I got back to my feet. I raised the handle painfully over my head and dug down another foot before faltering again and collapsing into a heap. I forced myself up and began again.

When I was finally done, I sat at the foot of the open grave and pulled Dad to me, wrapping my arms around his thin chest.

I closed my eyes and could see his face as it was, lit from the inside as he held up that first slice of pear in the darkness of a dead plane, then the iron look that came over him when he decided he was going to be a hero for the first time since Mom left us.

I heard his booming laugh and his shuddering sobs as he sat by his father's grave and Mom's and the daughter's he would never know. I felt his chest rise and fall alongside mine, his breath like the dry turning of pages in a book.

All of that had come to this.

Stillness.

A yawning silence.

Like none of those things had ever been.

Jenny helped me lower him down until the white glow of his shroud disappeared in the darkness at the bottom of the grave. He looked like a child, curled up and helpless. Alone. I reached into my back pocket and found the sharp edge of our family photograph. I raised it up into the dim moonlight, tracing the lines of me and Mom and Dad smiling together for one of the last times, before holding it over the grave and dropping it in. It fluttered like a leaf and settled onto his chest.

I stood there for some time, feeling the pull of the grave, like a cold arm wrapping itself around my shoulders and drawing me down with him.

I took up the shovel and filled the hole.

When it was done, I stumbled and fell back onto the ground. A new swirl of snow appeared out of the gray, lightening sky. It seemed like the body of a great white bear tumbling down onto me, its claws out-stretched.

I shut my eyes, and let it have me.

PART THREE

TWENTY-SIX

There was a crash as I fell into one of the gaming tables that littered the casino floor. *How did I get here?* I wondered distantly, then Jenny's hands dug into my shoulder and pulled me up. She threw my arm over her shoulder and pushed me blindly through the dark. My bones ached from the cold. My skin burned. I couldn't stop shivering. I remembered kneeling by the grave in the snow. I told her to leave me with Dad, but she wouldn't listen. I wanted to tell her again, but now I couldn't speak.

Jenny dropped me down on the bed in the back room and covered me up with all the blankets we had, tucking them tight around my body like a cocoon. I lay there in the absolute dark and quiet of the room. The blankets had my arms pinned to my sides. I couldn't move. I couldn't see. It was like being a thousand miles under the ocean with the immense weight of it pressing down on my chest.

But I wasn't afraid. I was relieved. Finally, after all my running, I had arrived at the place I was meant to be, at home, at peace, in the nothingness and the dark and the cold.

The door opened and Jenny was at my side again, leaning over me.

Was it hours later? Days? I didn't know. I couldn't see her, just feel her arms digging under my shoulders and lifting me up.

I groaned, struggling against her touch, trying to keep still. "I'm fine. Leave me alone."

"Stephen, you're freezing to death. Now move!"

Jenny managed to get me up from the bed and out of the room, shoring me up with her shoulder and driving me down a long hallway. I couldn't fight. I faltered along beside her, my legs stiff and awkward as a foal's. We moved deeper into the casino toward a distant light. A fire. Jenny had built it in the center of a tiled atrium. Its smoke twisted upward to the shattered remains of a skylight.

She dropped me within inches of it. Its brilliance made my eyes ache, but I couldn't feel its warmth. It reached out but couldn't touch me. Jenny wrestled me up into a sitting position and arranged the blankets over my shoulders. I tried to push her away, but I was too weak. All I wanted to do was lie down. All I wanted was to sleep, to be in the quiet and alone in that black nothingness, but Jenny wouldn't let me go.

There was a crash somewhere out in the casino, then the sound of shattering glass. Jenny stiffened. Dad's knife appeared in her fist as she crouched beside me like an animal, peering into the dark, listening for more.

"There's no one out there," I said thoughtlessly, my head lolling onto my chest.

"Maybe I was wrong. Maybe Will and them aren't done with us. They could still come."

"They're dead."

Jenny's eyes left the empty dark and fell back on me.

"What? Who's dead?"

I looked up from the tiled floor. Jenny's face, streaked with ash and pockmark burns, was framed in fire.

"Everyone," I said, my voice rising up from the deep in a cold rasp. "Marcus. Violet. Dad. My mom. Even you and me. We thought the Collapse was over but it's not. It just keeps going. It doesn't matter where we go or what we do. We're all dead. All of us. We just don't know it yet."

Jenny said nothing. She eased down beside me, bringing her body alongside mine. She brushed my hair aside with the tips of her fingers. When I flinched away from the warmth of her lips on my cheek, she wrapped her arms tight around me and leaned me in toward the fire, rocking us back and forth.

The heat from the fire pounded against my skin, but it was useless. My body was a gate of iron and I would not let it pass.

All that night, she left my side only to get more wood for the fire or to dart out into the darkness to check on the crashes and groans that seemed to be our constant companions. She was sure that each one was Will or Caleb or some faceless mob with torches in hand, ready to burn us down. But each time it was simply the old building settling into the brunt of winter. Broken glass. Creaking walls.

"We can't stay here," she said.

It had stopped snowing. A thin, watery light began to show through the clouds. The first traces of dawn.

"It isn't safe."

I turned toward the dim outline of the casino's front door. Outside, across the parking lot and through the trees, was the clearing where Dad lay, buried deep underground. There was no cross. No marker. Jenny had pulled me away before I could make one. If we left, I knew I would never be able to find him again.

"You can go," I said.

"I'm not leaving without you."

Somewhere behind us, the roof of the casino groaned under the weight of the snow. I traced my finger along the hills and valleys of the wrinkled blanket piled up in my lap, marking out a meandering path on its folds. *Never the same path twice*, I thought. *That way you're safe. That way no one finds you.* I saw myself on the trail. I saw worn ground and the mall and the neighborhoods, crumbling and covered in vines. I could hear Dad, his shuffling footsteps, his bright babble like water coursing over smooth river rocks. I saw his hands so clearly — long-fingered and strong, a hairline scar running down the index finger of his right hand.

"Steve?"

Jenny laid one hand over mine, blotting out the trail. She used the other to lift my chin up to her, so I couldn't look away, couldn't not see her.

"Maybe there isn't anything better out there, but . . . your dad and your grandpa handed you this life, right? Just like Marcus and Violet handed me mine. This is your name. This is where you live. This is who you are. We never chose any of it. So whose lives are we living? Ours or theirs? Haven't you ever thought about that? Don't you, just once, want to choose something for yourself?"

I pulled my chin out of her hand and looked deep into the darkness of the casino.

"I have," I said.

Jenny stared at me, her eyes wide and hurt, waiting for more, but I said nothing. She let go of my hand.

"I'm sorry about your parents," she said. "But at least they died while they were trying to live. They didn't just sit around waiting to die."

Jenny pushed herself back from me and stood up.

"It's not safe for us here, Stephen. I think you know that. There's an old hospital a few miles west that's still pretty intact. I'm going to leave for there today. I want you to come, but even if you don't, I have to go."

Jenny waited for a response, and when there was none, she walked away from the fire and was gone.

Without Jenny, the immensity of the casino's silence was overwhelming. This was what I wanted, wasn't it? On my own in the dark. I sat there while the fire died out, then stumbled back to our room. Before I drew the curtains shut, I surveyed my little world. I had shelter. I could find food and water easily enough. I had everything I needed.

My eye fell into the corner of the room by the window, to a large white square. I didn't recognize it at first, but I moved closer and saw that it was Jenny's sketch pad. It fell open to the end as I lifted it, to the last picture she had drawn.

It was like a small, soft hand had reached inside of me and pulled the air out of my lungs.

It was the picture Jenny drew our first morning together as I huddled, freezing, under the blankets. All the details of the barn were there: the patched-together plank walls, the early morning sunshine, the rumpled bed. You could almost feel the chill in the air. I was staring up into the rafters and my feet were sticking out of the cover, hanging slightly over the edge of the mattress. I smiled despite myself.

She had made me taller.

I kept coming back to the look on my face. I almost didn't recognize myself. She caught me just as I was waking up, before my worries about Dad and the town had flooded in. I had, not a smile exactly — it was harder to place than that — but more a look of stillness, of thoughtfulness. Of peace. On my face was the look of someone who was exactly where he wanted to be with no thought of the future or the past. Nothing but that moment.

Jenny said that drawing quieted something inside her. I said I had nothing like that, but was I wrong? Wasn't that what being with her did for me?

I thought back to that night out by the snowy highway, wondering if the answer was to walk away and disappear. If being alone might spare us the pain of feeling anything like Dad felt the day Mom's hand slipped from his in the shadow of that amusement park. Maybe if we never built anything, then nothing could ever collapse.

We have to be more than the world would make us.

Mom's words were like a warm breath blowing past my cheek.

The sketch pad fell out of my hands, and I drifted from the room and down the hallway, following the dim morning light toward the exit. I could just barely see Jenny standing outside.

The unbroken snow was dazzling, clean and white. She didn't turn as I stepped through the door and came up beside her. The back of my hand grazed hers. Her fingers fell and intertwined with mine, locking together. I felt a deep sigh in my chest as something settled into place.

"I'm so sorry about your dad," she said.

A chill spread over me again, but I pulled Jenny close. My heart thumped hard in my chest.

"They destroyed their world," Jenny said, looking out over the vast plain of snow. "But this one is ours."

"We should leave," I said. "Today."

We said nothing more for a while. I wished Dad could be there with us. Wished he could leave and come find whatever it was we would find. I wondered if there would always be this empty, aching place inside me where he used to be.

Jenny nudged me with her shoulder. "Come on, then. We've got some packing to do."

She reached for the door, but before we could go in, there was a crunch of snow to our right. Tree branches shook. We jumped back into the doorway and out of sight.

"Probably just a deer," I whispered, but then we saw two figures slide behind the curtain of trees. Once they passed, Jenny motioned me forward. I took her wrist, but she turned back and held up one finger.

Just a second, she mouthed.

I followed as Jenny moved to the corner and we both dropped down low to peer around to the back of the building. Two men emerged from the woods. I could tell immediately that they weren't Will or Caleb or anyone we knew from Settler's Landing. They moved in precise glides, short automatic rifles held ahead of them, communicating with crisp hand signals. They were both wearing some kind of black uniform, their shoulders and waists crisscrossed with pouches of equipment. They looked ex-military to me.

What are they doing here?

The two men circled the building, then disappeared around the other side. Jenny looked at me. I nodded. We moved along the back wall until we saw them climbing the hill toward the highway and Settler's Landing.

"Scouts," I whispered.

"For who? Fort Leonard doesn't have any military."

A buzz of nerves started to rise in my chest. "Come on," I said. "We'll pack up. Go. Like you said, this isn't our —"

Before I could finish, Jenny leapt up from her crouch and ran for the highway.

"Jenny!" I hissed, then scrambled to my feet and went after her.

The scouts were a ways ahead of us by the time we made it to the woods, but we could follow their tracks easily enough. We didn't catch sight of them again until we came out of the trees above Settler's Landing's gates. The men swept down the hill toward them, but instead of passing through, they veered sharply north and into the forest across from us.

"We should see how many of them there are. Maybe they're camped nearby."

"Jenny —"

"If it was just Fort Leonard against Settler's Landing, I'd leave it, but if they've brought in help, we need to tell Marcus and Violet it's not going to be a fair fight. Right?"

I hated the idea but had to admit she was right. I agreed, and we trailed the two scouts from as far back as we could. They followed pretty much the same path Jenny and I had the other night. I thought they were making straight for the Henrys' house, but before they reached it they cut around it and went farther east, disappearing into thick trees.

When their footprints finally petered out, we dropped down onto the snowy ground and crawled up to a fallen tree that lay at the edge of some brush. Voices came from the other side, a mix of languages and accents. We glanced at each other, then peeked over the edge of the tree.

Less than a hundred feet from where we lay was a camp made up of black tents arranged in precise rows. Twenty of them, at least. Men like the two scouts we'd seen milled around, bristling with as many weapons and as much ammunition as they could carry. A fire burned at the center of the camp, and behind it sat a central tent that was flanked by three large dark shapes that sat just outside of the firelight.

Jenny looked at me, but I shrugged, unable to tell what they were. The forest curved around the north edge of the camp, so Jenny and I pulled back from our hiding place and crawled until the three dark shapes became all too clear.

The one closest to us was a flatbed truck. On its back there was an immense metal canister with a hose running from one side of it. A fuel truck, I guessed, meant to service what sat next to it — two hulking black jeeps, their sides and fronts plated with armor and an open back where heavy machine guns were mounted on rotating tripods.

It was like looking at two prehistoric monsters. Both of us stared in awe, speechless at what was looming over Settler's Landing as it quietly slept just a few miles away.

"How could Fort Leonard afford mercenaries?" I whispered. "Aren't they smaller than Settler's Landing?"

Before Jenny could answer, there was a commotion in the camp as the black flap of one of the central tents opened. Two figures walked out and everything inside of me froze.

No. It can't be.

The black man's dreadlocks were longer than the last time I'd seen him, and so was his beard. The white man with the scar seemed, if anything, bigger. There was no doubt who they were though. Their faces were seared into my memory.

Not mercenaries.

Slavers.

The air rushed out of me as I realized exactly what Fort Leonard would have offered them in exchange for ending the war once and for all. They offered them Marcus and Violet and Jackson. They offered them Tuttle and Martin and Derrick and Wendy. They offered them everyone and everything in Settler's Landing.

"Stephen?" Jenny whispered.

She grabbed my arm and pulled me deeper into the forest, away from the camp. Once we couldn't hear them anymore, we eased down the back side of a slope, pressing our backs into the snow.

"We'll tell Marcus," Jenny said. "Warn them. Maybe if they know what's coming —"

I almost laughed. The thought that they had a chance against these people, that they could even risk that, was ridiculous.

"They'll have to go," I said. "All of them. Take what they can and leave."

"Leave Settler's Landing? They won't. Marcus and Violet? They'd die first."

My fists curled in on themselves. She was right. God, what had I started? Were they here because of me too? Had they come looking for me and Dad and found Fort Leonard instead?

We sat there, a moat of empty space between us. Jenny chewed on her thumbnail, staring at the ground. We both knew what was coming.

I had seen it in the belly of that plane and she had seen it in a mass of men with their guns and their wild, hungry looks.

"It's not our fault," Jenny said. "What we did was stupid, but it was Caleb who went to Fort Leonard. Not us. *He* started this."

I murmured something in agreement, but I didn't believe it and I knew Jenny didn't either.

A light snow began to fall again, whipping through the trees and tapping against our shoulders. A laugh, loud and throaty, rose from the slave traders' camp. It was like the grunting of an animal ready to hunt.

I took Jenny's hand and we fled through the woods.

Violet and Marcus were at the kitchen table when we arrived. Violet was at one end, knitting distractedly, while Marcus leaned grimly over a mug of tea.

"What is it?" Violet asked.

Before I could speak, Jackson came thundering down the stairs. I felt a flash of happiness to see him again but as soon as he saw me and Jenny, he stopped where he was, grasping the rail and eyeing us sharply.

"What are they doing here?"

The way he spat it out, I knew instantly that Marcus told him everything about our raid on the Henrys'. How we had started all of this. My mouth went dry. I felt sick. Ashamed.

"Come sit down, Jackson," Violet said. "Stephen and Jenny say they have something to tell us."

Jackson crept down the stairs, then took a seat at the far end of the kitchen table. He didn't look at me and I found I couldn't look at any of them. How could I? I'd abandoned Jackson, stolen from Violet, and betrayed Marcus and everyone else in the town.

"Well, Stephen?" Violet said.

They all sat there watching us. Waiting. I clasped Jenny's hand under the table and told them about the slavers that Fort Leonard had hired. The jeeps. The weapons. That they were the same ones my Dad and I had fought. Everything.

When I was done, Marcus rubbed his hand over the thick collection of stubble on his chin.

"Slavers," Marcus said carefully. "You're sure?"

I nodded. "I'm sure."

Marcus looked across the table at Violet, but she stared down into her lap, all the color drained from her face.

"I know you don't want to leave," I said. "But you don't know what these people will do. They —"

"They won't do anything," Jenny interrupted.

I turned to where Jenny sat beside me.

"What do you mean? Of course they —"

But Jenny wasn't looking at me. She was focused on her parents. Her parents, who wouldn't meet her gaze.

"Will they?" Jenny asked, holding the words out like bait.

Marcus and Violet said nothing. Jackson didn't move.

"I don't . . ."

And then I got it. I saw what Jenny saw.

Ever since the night of our raid on the Henrys', they should have been expecting the forces of Fort Leonard to arrive at any moment. But if they did, then why was Violet sitting at the table knitting? Shouldn't she have been preparing for the coming fight? Shouldn't Marcus's rifle be close at hand instead of sitting in its rack on the wall?

And when I told them that a small army of slave traders was bearing down on them, they didn't seem scared. They didn't pack up. They didn't flee town.

Most of all, they didn't seem surprised.

I felt something like a barbed hook sinking into my gut and in that instant I knew.

Fort Leonard didn't hire the slavers.

They did.

TWENTY-SEVEN

"Caleb told us they were mercenaries," Marcus said, looking down into his tea. "Ex-soldiers. I don't know where he found them. He said they'd run the people at Fort Leonard off so they wouldn't come back. That's all. He said no one would get hurt."

"What are you supposed to do for them?" Jenny asked.

"They want to expand west. Caleb said we'd be like a way station. Nothing more. They'd store fuel here, food. He didn't tell us they were slavers, I swear."

"When does it happen?"

"Tonight. Sundown. We're supposed to meet them at the gates and then we all go together."

"We have to talk to Caleb," Violet said. "Now."

Marcus looked up at her. "And say what? You don't think Caleb and his friends know what these people are already?"

"Then we talk to everyone else. Sam, Tuttle — we'll have a vote."

"You think if we have a vote and we actually win, they'll just leave?"

We all sat there, still as statues as it sunk in. Slavers were no different from starving animals. Deny them Fort Leonard and they'd eat Settler's Landing just as happily.

"Then what?" Violet asked.

Marcus turned to face the swirl of white outside. It was mounting steadily on the porch and bending the trees until their branches hung down miserably, nearly ready to snap.

"We did well this year, but you know the winters as well as I do, Vi. We'll lose at least ten people from the cold and lack of food alone. If we have to deal with Fort Leonard picking away at us too, we could be done for. Our home. All of us. Gone."

"What are you saying? We let this happen? Marcus —"

"I'm saying we don't have a choice, Vi."

"We do," Violet said. "We have a choice about what we become, Marcus. Maybe it's the only thing we *do* have a choice about."

"Do you want to be out there again? Us and not them? Is that what you want?"

"How many times have we come close to doing the right thing," Violet asked, "and then stopped because we were afraid? This. Sean and Mary Krychek —"

"Violet."

"— that girl of theirs, just nine years old?"

"We did the best we could for them."

"We stood up for them for an hour before giving them an old blanket and a day's worth of bread and sending them on their way! Because we were afraid!"

Violet was red with anger and shame, leaning up out of her chair, her nails digging into the table. Marcus had no answer for her.

The wind howled and the snow mixed with hail that sounded sharp and metallic, like fingers tapping on a tin roof.

"You remember that day we played Go Fish, Jenny?"

Everyone turned to Jackson. His back was to us, caught in the half-gloom at the edge of the kitchen, looking out past the marble-topped counter to the storm outside.

"Yeah," Jenny said. "I do."

"Everyone in Fort Leonard is just waking up," Jackson said, almost to himself, the words tumbling out. "They're talking. Starting fires for breakfast. Wishing it wasn't snowing. But then these people, us, will appear and some of them won't live through the day. Some of them have maybe a few hours left until they're gone, or their families are gone and they're alone. And they have no idea it's coming. They think it's just another day."

Jackson's voice hitched in his throat. A redness crept into his cheeks like leaves of flame.

"Jack," Marcus urged. "Listen to me. I don't like it either, but it's us or it's them. It's —"

Jackson turned from the window and faced Marcus head-on, searching his face. Marcus deflated. He dropped his head, looking down at his hands. They seemed so small now, framed against the hardness of the table.

Violet moved over to Jackson, wrapping her arms tight around him from behind.

"I'm afraid too," Violet said to Marcus. "But if fear's all we've got, then we're building this world on the same rotten foundation as the last one. What good are we doing Jackson or Jenny or Stephen? What good are we doing anyone?"

Marcus turned and regarded each of us one by one, like we were a jury deciding his fate, before struggling up out of his chair and gathering his rifle and his coat.

I stood up at the table. "No," I said, urgently. "You can't fight them. If you try to be a hero —"

"Caleb lied to us," Marcus said. "And he did it so he could turn this place into something none of us want it to be. This is our home. If this isn't worth fighting for, then what is?"

Jackson left his mother and crossed the room to stand with Marcus. Together they went out into the front room. A moment later, the door shut with a deep *boom* that shuddered through the house.

No one moved for a time. The wind moaned. The finger-tap hail pattered on and on.

Violet went without another word to her cabinet. She lit candles and then opened each drawer one by one, taking inventory with crisp practiced motions, preparing for whatever was to come.

Beside me, Jenny sat with her chin resting on her fists, absorbed in the whirl of white. I pushed away from the table and went out the front door.

A rush of wind and snow blew toward me as I stepped outside and dropped down onto the front steps. Across the street, Marcus and Jackson moved from one house to the other. They'd disappear inside for a time, and when they came out they'd be joined by one or two others and they'd all move on, snaking their way through the town.

With their dark coats cutting through the snow, they reminded me of an army of black ants gathering to make a valiant stand against a farmer's boot.

Behind me, the front door opened and closed. Jenny descended the steps and went to stand beyond the porch's roof, looking from house to house, taking it all in.

"You're staying," I said. "Aren't you?"

Jenny lifted her chin, examining the cottony sky. "I thought I could leave," she said. "I thought it'd be easy. But I can't. Not if they don't."

Everything in me ached. Of course Jenny would stay. She'd join with whoever Marcus could raise to fight Caleb and the slavers, and they'd all suffer.

And what could I do? Only one thing.

"I should get our things," I said, looking down at the brick steps beneath my feet. "From the casino. Before anything starts."

"Want me to come?"

I turned back to face her. Jenny stood on the porch with her hands jammed in the pockets of her coat, her hair a cloud of black. She was looking over my head, scanning the neighborhood, her eyes focused to a knife's edge. There was no stopping her.

"It's okay," I said. "I'll do it myself."

Jenny darted in and kissed my cheek. "Hurry up. It'd be a shame if the cold killed you before the slavers had a chance."

I nodded and Jenny threw open the front door and went inside. I stood there a moment looking at the blank face of the door, listening to the falling snow, before I crossed the Greens' front yard and went out into the street.

The walls to either side of the Settler's Landing gates had never seemed more like two gravestones as I passed them and went into the forest. Looking out over the crumbling highway and the casino, everything seemed so far away. Jenny. Jackson. All of my friends. I wished the chain that bound me to them could be cut, but it was there, strong as ever.

I bypassed the casino and trekked some miles until I found the clearing where I'd buried Dad. In the center there was a swell in the blanket of white. My hands stung as I knelt in front of it and scooped the piles of snow away until I reached the loose dirt at the top of the grave. I pressed my palms deep into it. My breath dropped to a whisper. A yawning emptiness opened inside me.

I'm here, I thought. *I'm right here.*

I used Dad's knife to cut a thick branch down from one of the surrounding trees, stripped it of its bark, and flattened one side. I held it in my lap and carved the letters of his name before plunging it deep into the ground at the head of his grave. When I was done, I traced my fingers over its surface.

STEPHEN R. QUINN.

I thought of Grandpa lying out alone in the woods so far away. If we had left a marker for him, it would have said the exact same thing.

And soon so would mine.

I started to speak, to say good-bye, but it was like my mouth was stuffed with dead leaves and sand.

The wind rose, carrying the scent of pine and earth, and for a second I felt Jenny's lips, soft and warm, against my cheek. She lingered there, her forehead at my temple, her breath on my neck. I had to shake her ghost away.

I drew my knife and tested its dark edge with my thumb. Though its surface was pitted and scarred and worn with age, it was still sharp. It killed me to lie to Jenny, but I knew that what I had to do, I had to do alone.

TWENTY-EIGHT

I slipped into the trees as quietly as I could, staying low and in the shadows. I had to stay hidden for as long as possible.

The snow had stopped and the day had grown warmer, leaving slippery patches of ice and snow and mud. As I drew closer to the slavers' camp, I caught metallic clanking noises and snatches of voices, faint at first. Despite the cold, sweat was dripping off my forehead. When I slid Dad's knife from its sheath, my palms were slick on the handle. A heavy thump shuddered through my chest.

I closed my eyes and was once again cowering in the back of that plane, choked with the musty smell of dank water and the tangles of weeds and dirt all around us.

I wiped my hands off on my jeans and stood up, surveying the last stretch of woods between me and the slave traders' camp. I gripped the blade tight and began to step over a fallen tree, but a pair of hands grabbed me from behind and yanked me backward. I struggled to get away but my knees hit a stump and I toppled over it. The knife shot out from my hand. I thought of Jenny and the Greens. I couldn't lose like this, not when I was so close. I tried to get myself up again, but before I could, my attacker vaulted over and pinned me down. A face framed with long wisps of black hair darted down toward mine.

"Jenny?"

She put her fingers to her lips, then dragged me away, farther from the slavers' camp. We stopped on the other side of a fallen tree and she dropped down in front of me.

"What are you doing here?" I hissed.

"What am I doing here? Following you, that's what I'm doing. Man, I've known you for, like, a week and I can already see right through you. 'Going to get our things from the casino.' Yeah, right. Why didn't you tell me you had a plan?"

"There is no plan," I said, picking Dad's knife up out of the snow. "Go back to town."

"Oh sure. I'll let you waltz into camp and stab their two psycho leaders on your own. I'm sure that'll work out just great. Are you insane? This was your plan? Why didn't you tell me?"

"'Cause I didn't want you to follow me! Look, just go home. I don't want you involved in this. This isn't your problem. Let me —"

"That isn't how this works, Stephen."

"How what works?"

Jenny stared at me.

"Us," she said. "If you're going to do something stupid, then so am I."

My hands went weak on the handle of the knife. "Jenny —"

"Marcus gathered about forty others," Jenny said in a hush. "They're meeting Caleb and the slavers at the gates at sunset. If they can't call it off, they'll fight. I figure the best we can do is slow them down, hobble them a little to give Marcus a chance. Without those jeeps, things would be a little more even. Right?"

I wanted to argue but she was that hurricane again, ready to tear through whatever was in her way. How do you fight a force of nature?

"Right," I said. "But how —"

An explosion of light came from the direction of the camp, piercing the gloom with razor-thin fingers. Jenny and I fell flat in the snow. We glanced at each other, then Jenny crept forward before I could stop her. I scrambled along behind, and together we peeked over the edge of the fallen tree.

The jeeps' headlights washed over the camp, throwing the shadows of the slavers onto the trees. Their engines roared. The men were making final preparations, fueling the jeeps, strapping on their gear, and checking their weapons.

There were at least twenty of them. With just the two of us and practically no weapons, I didn't see any option for us that didn't look like suicide. I was about to tell Jenny it was impossible, but before I could, she nodded out to our left where a lone backpack sat by the side of a tent.

At first I didn't see why, but then I looked closer. Hanging from the side of the pack was a string of black baseball-size orbs with pins sticking out of them. Grenades. One of the men must have set them aside, meaning to grab them on the way out. I looked across the camp. The pack was a good ten feet from where the slavers were gathering for their instructions, but at least forty feet from where Jenny and I were.

"We'll never get to them before they get us."

Jenny was silent, chewing on it. She kept her eyes fixed on the camp. The man with the scar climbed into the driver's side of one of the jeeps just as it was finished being fueled.

"This isn't going to work," I said. "We should just —"

Jenny pulled off her heavy coat, revealing her old Red Army jacket beneath. She started buttoning it up.

"What are you — ?"

"I'm taking care of the first part." Jenny pulled her hair back tight and secured it with a leather thong she took from her pocket. "Second part's on you."

"Jenn —"

Before I could finish, Jenny kissed me quick, stepped out from behind the tree, and walked right into the middle of the slavers' camp.

TWENTY-NINE

My heart seized. The slavers saw her immediately and raised their weapons, but for a strange moment no one fired. It was as if Jenny's sudden appearance was so unexpected that they were all trying to make sure they weren't dreaming. Jenny stood ramrod straight, her arms clasped crisply behind her, a scowl on her face.

With her hair back and her army jacket, she looked like the picture of a grim and fearless Chinese soldier.

"*Ching-ma!*" she shouted. "*Cho wen dow! Cho wen dow. Ching-ma!*"

As the men looked, puzzled, from one to the other, I got up and started moving to our left. Jenny kept shouting in her nonsense Chinese, but the distraction wouldn't last long. I had ten seconds, tops, before the men put it together that she was not being backed up by an entire Chinese regiment and then started shooting.

The man with the scar was starting up his jeep while the man with the dreadlocks moved off toward the one parked on the opposite side of the fuel truck.

"*Ching mow don! Kai! Kai!*" Jenny called forth her imaginary soldiers, then took off into the trees. There was a split second of confusion before shots rang out as about half the men chased after her. Leaving her on her own felt like a knife twisting in my gut, but I had to stay focused.

I leapt into the camp, running as hard as I could to the grenades. Out of the corner of my eye I saw the dreadlocked man yanking the steering wheel hard, trying to get his jeep moving. Smart. Not even a little bit interested in Jenny's distraction. I pushed through the burn in my legs and drove toward the bag, skidding to a stop and grabbing it before taking off again the way I had come.

"Hey! You! Stop!"

There was a sharp *crack*, then a bullet tore past my shoulder and cut into the branches next to me. I pumped my arms, running hard until I was even with the fuel truck and stopped. I took a grenade and yanked out the pin.

I pivoted to the camp. The dreadlocked man had the jeep turned around now and was only seconds from getting away with it.

I thought of John Carter pitching as I wound up and threw the grenade at the side of the fuel truck.

The boom of the explosion was deafening. A yellow flash blinded me as the shock wave tore through the trees and knocked me to the ground. I lay there, arms over my head, as three more explosions rang out one after another. Deep, hollow booms. After that, there was a moment of silence when everything hung, suspended, like the world was holding its breath and waiting. Then all at once everything came crashing back. There were shouts and cries and the sound of burning that seemed to be everywhere at once.

The camp was in chaos. The air was thick with black smoke that smelled sickeningly of chemicals and burned my throat and eyes. The men who hadn't chased after Jenny were battling the flames that had erupted with the explosions. One main fire at the eastern edge of the camp was out of control. I could just make out a dark skeleton of twisted metal deep in the yellow flames. One of the two jeeps burned next to it.

The other was gone.

"Stephen!" Jenny was standing behind the first rank of trees. "We have to get out of here," she cried. "Now!"

I ran toward her. The oily smoke had already seeped into the woods, mixing with shafts of moonlight and the hellish glow of the fire, turning the forest into a confused maze. I had no idea if we were even headed in the right direction, but Jenny pushed on.

"Hey! Hey, you over there! Stop!"

A string of shots crackled behind us. We dodged to our right, following a sharp ridgeline. More gunfire came from behind us. Men shouted and we ran flat out, as fast as we could, sometimes missing trees by just inches.

"This way," Jenny said. We ran for a mile or more, turning back for Settler's Landing only when we were sure we had lost our pursuers. We came out of the trees at the crest of the hill that led into town. A thick haze of black smoke filled the air and dirtied the snow. The slavers had beaten us there. Everything reeked of burning wood and gunfire.

"God," Jenny breathed.

I took her hand and we moved on, past the front gates and down the road into town. The first two houses we came to were on fire. Orange flames poured out of the smashed windows, throwing awful jerking shadows onto the dark road and the woods. We passed a green house with an American flag just as its roof collapsed with a moan.

"Stephen, what if . . . ?"

I nodded down the road, toward the distant sound of gunfire. "I think they all pulled back that way. Everyone probably left their houses before the soldiers even got here. Those houses are empty."

I was amazed by how sure my voice sounded, given that I had no idea if what I said was true. I prayed it was. We leapt over tire-shaped scars in the grass and past the swing sets and slide that were lying smashed in the mud.

We followed the sounds of gunfire down the road, turning off to the left and down a short hill. I suddenly realized where they were leading us. The school. We slowed as we got close, staying low, finally taking cover behind the brick corner of the building. We flattened our backs to the wall. It was hard to make anything out in the fog of gun smoke, but I saw one group across the playground by the swing sets. It seemed to be a row of people on their backs and someone who moved quickly among them. In the lulls between the gunshots I could hear steady moans coming from them. Beyond them, lying in a rough line behind the crest of the hill that led up to the baseball field, were thirty or more townspeople with rifles, taking the only cover available. The slavers' men must have been just over the hill.

"Stay here," I said to Jenny as I started around the edge of the wall. "I'm going to go see if I can help."

"Did you just meet me?"

"Jenny, if it wasn't for me, this wouldn't —"

She darted out into the darkness.

Right. Should have known. I shot out from behind the school as a volley of gunfire erupted from the crest of the hill, lighting the playground in flashes of yellow and orange. I ducked my head and ran, passing within feet of the swing sets.

A voice called out from my left. "Stephen, over here!"

It was Violet, kneeling down among a group of ten or more people.

"Violet, I have to get to —"

"Later." She pushed a flashlight into my hand and pulled me down next to her. "Shine that here."

I looked up the hill, searching for Jenny.

"Now, Stephen!"

I flicked the light on, shining it down onto someone on the ground. As soon as I did, my hand shook.

All I saw was blood, shockingly red against the white of the snow.

"Steady," Violet said.

I didn't know the man on the ground in front of me. He had been shot as many as three times. There was so much blood it was hard to tell where. He was unconscious. Violet leaned over him, probing a wound on his shoulder with a small pair of pliers until she pulled out a big piece of shrapnel. As soon as she did, blood welled up in the gash and coursed down his arm. I was sure I was going to be sick. Violet grabbed a towel off the ground next to her and pressed it deep into the man's shoulder. My stomach turned again as the towel grew damp with red. I turned my head away. Others were laid out to Violet's left, a line of wounded men, women, even kids my age. Some unconscious, some twisting and moaning.

"The soldiers didn't expect us to fight. Neither did Caleb and his people. His family and a few others joined with the slavers. We let them chase us back here to get away from the houses and then we turned on them."

I fumbled for a roll of bandage on the ground and handed it to her, still holding the flashlight on the figure in front of me. I got a better look at him. He was young, maybe even my age, wearing a dark T-shirt and jeans. He had fine features and his hair, where not matted and red with blood, was golden and flopped down over one eye.

Something inside of me went cold.

It was Will Henry.

"But . . . he's with them," I said. "With Caleb and the slavers. He — "

Violet gritted her teeth and yanked a bandage tight. "He's dying, Stephen. It doesn't matter what side he's on."

"Is he really going to . . ." I couldn't finish. My throat had closed up.

"I don't know," Violet said. She wiped her hands on her jeans, then moved down the line. "I've got it from here." She took the flashlight from my hand. Another volley of gunfire roared behind us and we ducked instinctively.

As Violet moved along the line of wounded, I wiped a splash of blood off Will's cheek with the edge of my sleeve. For an awful moment I thought I would never be able to leave that spot. There was a time I probably would have claimed that I wanted Will Henry dead, but now, seeing him lying there pale and covered in blood, all I felt was emptiness, waste, and stupidity.

I pushed myself off the ground and ran up the hill, anger crashing through me. When I got to the crest I dropped down into the grass and peered over the edge. Out across the field, near second base, was the black shadow of the remaining jeep. A line of low swells in the grass stretched to the right and left of it. The soldiers and Caleb's people, I suspected, dug into shallow pits.

Jackson was lying to my left, a rifle in his hands. Marcus and Sam were on the other side, their eyes steady on their rifle sights. There was another barrage and we all ducked our heads. Bullets whistled past inches from us.

"Where's Jenny?" I asked.

"She said she was going back to town to help look after the little ones," Marcus said.

Right, I thought, looking all around trying to find some trace of her, but seeing nothing.

A roar of machine-gun fire rose from up ahead and was answered with shots from the line to either side of me. The bullets slammed into the ground between the two sides, kicking up a fog of snow but doing no damage.

My mind raced. When I was little, Grandpa would sit me down almost weekly for one of his endless lectures on military tactics. I'd humored him, barely paying attention, but I struggled now to bring some of it back. Marcus had numbers, but the slavers were so well armed it more than evened things out. I scanned the snowfield and surrounding trees ahead, looking for a way out. Suddenly something fell into place.

"You're pinned down," I said. I could almost hear Grandpa's voice in my head. "You need a smaller group to go out into the trees, around to their flank, and distract them so the main force can move in."

"I can't spare anyone to —"

"Don't worry about it," I said. "When the flanking group attacks, the soldiers will be distracted. That's when the rest of the line has to get up and rush them. It's the only way."

"Wait, where are you going?" Marcus yelled. "Stephen!"

But I was already on my way, hurtling down their line toward the woods, staying as low as I could. There was no time to worry about where Jenny had gone. It was best we were apart, given what I had planned.

As soon as the soldiers noticed my movement, they let go with a hail of bullets that Marcus and the others quickly answered. The mud and snow made it tough going, but I made it into the trees and out of sight. I thought I was home free until I heard someone running after me. I turned and there was Jackson, his rifle slung across his chest.

"Jackson, go back!"

He ignored me and kept coming. I ran as fast as I could, putting some distance between us, but I could still hear him behind me, his footfalls mixing in with the gunfire and shouting. There was no time to try to turn him back. I prayed that I'd either lose him or, when he saw what I was planning to do, he'd turn back on his own.

I ran until I was sure I'd made it as far as the soldiers' line out in the field, then jogged to my right. My heart sank when I saw who was waiting there.

"What are you —"

Jenny put her finger to her lips, then motioned me over next to her.

There were only a few thin ranks of trees between us and where the soldiers lay. It had gone quiet out in the field. The jeep was maybe fifty yards away, surrounded by about twenty men arranged in a half circle. One man stood at the back of the truck behind an armor plate, operating the swiveling machine gun and shouting orders. I could tell from the hulking outline that it was the man with the scar.

The underbrush behind us crunched. Someone coming. I slipped my knife out of its sheath and turned, but when the trees parted it was Jackson, rifle in hand.

"Oh great," Jenny whispered. "The cavalry's here."

"What are you two — ?"

We both shushed him and motioned for him to get down.

"What are you doing here?" Jackson said, pulling close to us.

"Up and at 'em," Jenny said. "You in?"

"No," I said sharply, then dropped my voice down to a whisper. "We're not doing it. We're going back and joining Marcus's line."

"That's stupid, and you know it," Jenny snapped.

"It's not."

"Then what did you even come here for? God, Stephen," she said. "These people have more guns and more ammunition. They can just wait us out. I mean, think about it — the only reason they're firing right now is so Marcus and them will waste ammo shooting back. Right? Am I right?"

What could I say? Of course she was. From the other side came the rustling of soldiers adjusting in their places and the metallic clinking of reloading from both sides. It was about to start again.

"Okay, then," Jenny said. "How about it, Jackie boy? You up for some mischief?"

Jackson nodded. He looked terrified, but he was serious. He was going to do it. They both were. It was pointless. I knew we wouldn't get ten feet before that machine gun swiveled our way and chopped us down. I peered into the brush I had come through, my mind scrambling for another idea, some alternative. If I'd been alone, I would've been running right out into the field, no matter what my chances were. Seeing Will had settled that. But now Jenny and Jackson would be right there with me, and they'd be cut down as fast as I'd be.

Jenny hopped up off the ground. Jackson slung his rifle over his shoulder.

"You coming, Steve?" Jenny asked.

I had no choice. If they were going, so was I. Whatever was going to happen to Jenny and Jackson, I wanted to happen to me too. As I pulled myself up off the ground, something about the brush surrounding us made me stop short.

Mischief.

"What's on the other side of those trees?"

"The Henry house," Jackson said. "Why?"

My mind raced. I turned back to the soldiers arrayed along the ground.

"Steve?"

I felt what I always imagined Dad and Grandpa felt in times like these, a moment when all the twisting confusion and uncertainty collapsed into a simple straight path.

A moment of being sure.

"Come on," I said, pushing between the two of them and up the trail. "Follow me."

THIRTY

I led the two of them at a run through the woods.

"Where are we going?" Jackson asked from behind me, more insistent now that it was the third time he'd asked without me answering. I ducked beneath a low-hanging branch and took the last leg at a sprint. The rocky ground gave way to the snow and grass that surrounded the house, and I had to stop, unsure where to go next. Luckily, as soon as we made it to the yard, Jenny knew exactly what we were doing.

"Stephen, you're a genius," she said. "Come on, it's this way."

She took off. I started to follow her, but Jackson grabbed my coat and jerked me back.

"What are we doing here?"

"There's no time to explain," I said, but he wasn't backing off. The mix of fear and anger in his eyes was electric.

"Why should I trust you?" he asked through gritted teeth. "After what you and Jenny did — you just left. You didn't even say anything. I thought we were friends."

"We are."

"Then why —"

"I was trying to protect you!"

"Well, I don't need your protection!"

"Look, this whole thing was my fault. I know that, but I need your help to fix it. I'm sorry I left. I am. I didn't know what else to do."

Jackson didn't relent. He held me there, sure that I was lying; sure that it was a trap. The distrust in his eyes bored through me. Some part of me that was still Grandpa's wanted to push him away and finish things with Jenny, but I held my ground.

"It's not going to be like before," I said. "We're not going to let them have this place, Jackson. And we're not going to run. I swear."

Jackson fixed me hard with his eyes, looking deep for the lie. A clatter of gunfire rose behind us, followed by three deep booms that lit up the sky in orange flashes. Jackson pushed me aside and ran after Jenny. Praying I was right, I followed.

We found Jenny at the northern edge of the Henrys' big house, kneeling down and peering out around a corner of the wall. In the darkness all we could see was the sharp outline of two paddocks and the wall of trees that separated them from the Henrys' pigs and sheep. Inside the pens, the horses and cows, anxious after the night of gunfire, were a confusion of restless shadows, snorting and attacking the ground with their hooves. The sound of it, angry and wild, made a piece of my heart lodge firmly in my throat.

Jenny nudged Jackson with her shoulder. "Whatcha think, Jackie boy?"

Jackson's forehead furrowed as he put it together. "Will it work?"

"Did last time," I said, earning a glare from Jackson and Jenny. "What? It did."

Jackson stared into the darkness, his hands fidgeting and seizing into fists, relaxing, then doing it again.

"We can do this," I said quietly, just to him, hoping it was true.

Jackson turned to me and something seemed to click inside him. He stood up and swept the rifle off his shoulder. Without another word, he tore out into the open.

Jenny and I followed him, running out across the Henrys' yard, slowing as we came to the pens. Closer up, I could see how panicked the animals really were. The horses paced and bucked fitfully in their small area, thousands of pounds of muscles and fear, the whites of their eyes flashing in the low moonlight. Near Jenny, the group of twenty or more cows lowed and snorted and dug their hooves into the ground, swinging their horns wildly around them. My stomach twisted with nerves as I set my hand on the flimsy latch that held the wooden gate closed. Whenever one of the horses so much as touched a rail the whole thing shook. Jenny looked up at me. I took a deep breath and nodded.

"Okay!" Jenny called out. "Now!"

Four shots from Jackson's rifle exploded into the air across from us. The animals reared up and crashed into one another, filling the air with their high-pitched squeals. When they started moving, the ground beneath us shook. Jenny and I yanked the gates open, scrambling to get out of the way as the animals came boiling out as a single mass, like water exploding from a burst dam. They trampled through the mud and snow past the house, headed for the trees, throwing up a haze of debris all around them, their dark bodies shooting through it. I pressed my back against the wooden gate until I saw a flash of Jackson through the dust. He was moving south, firing his rifle into the air, herding them along.

I left the pen after the last horse had cleared it and followed along behind. I didn't see Jenny anywhere — the cloud of mud and smoke was too thick and the roar of the animals was deafening. I was swept away with it, running, stumbling, barely able to see the ground beneath my feet, my mouth and nose clogging with dust. I thought I heard someone calling my name, thought I saw someone up ahead, but then it would all disappear in the gray churn and all I could do was run and hope I didn't fall.

It was worse when we moved out of the field and into the woods. There, the rumble and blare of the stampede were enclosed in the trees and focused, like an avalanche finding its course. The animal surge tore apart everything in its path: brush and leaves, exposed roots and saplings. All of it was shredded and sucked into the deluge, leaving a barren strip of land in its wake.

The herd spread out as it poured into the field. When the firing and screams began, I knew they had found their mark. Out in the open now, I could see the animals breaking around the body of the jeep. Most of the soldiers had heard them coming and fled, but as I ran I passed the few who hadn't, lying beaten and bruised on the ground, the conscious ones gasping for air as though they'd nearly been drowned.

I didn't know if Marcus and his people were taking the opportunity to attack or not — there was too much confusion to be sure — but up ahead I did see the one thing that mattered.

Somehow the man with the scar had managed to hold his place on the machine gun at the back of the jeep. He was no fool either. He knew what was happening and wasn't paying the slightest attention to the stampede around him. He was aiming squarely ahead, fully prepared for Marcus and his people to attack.

I ran toward him as he leaned into the gun and a tongue of orange flame roared out of it. Taking three quick strides, I leapt up to the lip of the jeep's bed. My foot hit the edge of it and I pitched forward, piling into him. He jerked around and, not missing a beat, dropped his fist like a hammer. The breath shot out of me. I gasped but somehow managed to hold on to him. He struggled, squirming and punching, until his feet hit a pile of shell casings that littered the floor of the jeep and he went down. I fell on top of him, my legs landing on either side of his chest. He looked up at me and a sudden burst of recognition shot through him.

"You," he growled.

Before he could say anything more, I braced my forearm on his throat and pressed down with all my weight.

I stared down at his white face, craggy and pitted and hard as Grandpa's. His teeth were bared, his eyes burning but empty. I saw him coming at us in the plane, drunken and full of hate. For so long I had blamed Dad for what had happened. But I knew right then, leaning over that monster, that it was this man's fault, everything was. All Dad had been trying to do was be a better man than him.

I grabbed my wrist and leaned in, pressing down onto his throat. His fists slammed into my sides but I barely felt them. I wasn't going to miss my chance. He gasped and his eyes widened, but he was far from giving up. He struggled even harder, his balled-up fists beating at my ribs, then grabbing at my shoulders. His hands went white, trying to tear me off. His left hand made it to my throat, his fingers clamping down as his right braced against my chest.

I had to let go of him to pull his hand from around my neck. As I thrashed, his other hand closed around my throat as well. He pushed me over onto my side, then rolled on top of me, both hands on my throat.

"Stupid kid," he said as he squeezed. "You may have helped that woman and her brat, but looking for you and your dad led us right here where we made some nice new friends. I should thank you."

I threw my fists into him, but they bounced uselessly off his thick shoulders. I gasped for air as he put me down on my back and leaned over me, squeezing his big hands tighter and tighter.

Gunfire crackled around me as the world tripped into darkness, collapsing until there was just his face, twisted into a snarl or a smile — I couldn't tell which — hanging over me like an awful moon.

The shouting and gunshots faded, receding farther and farther away. As darkness seeped in, I saw Mom and Dad. He had his arm around her, drawing her in close to his side. They were standing in a sun-drenched field against a blue sky, smiling, skin bronze and shining. Mom was in her red and gold dress, her hair blowing in the breeze.

Mom's hand grazed my cheek, then took my shoulders and brought me in between her and Dad so I could feel the warmth of their bodies and the steady rhythm of their breath, in and out, in and out, all around me.

I looked up and saw the flash of her smile like a winking star.

Then there was a *crack*, like thunder, and everything went black.

THIRTY-ONE

I was being dragged across the ground by my wrists, my arms thrown over my head, aching badly. *Shackles. I'm in shackles.* Rocks and shell casings scraped my back, and when I tried to breathe, the air was thick with smoke and my throat was wrecked. My head pounded.

I was alive. How? I opened my eyes, but they stung from the smoke. All I could see were hazy blooms of light in the sky. Orange and yellow and then a smear of bloody red. I wrenched my head back, hoping to see who had me, but I couldn't see any farther than my own wrists and the pair of hands that were clamped around them. Not shackles. Hands. Pulling me. But to where? I writhed, trying to free myself, but I was too weak.

"Who are you?" I croaked. My throat was ragged, dry, and swollen like it was full of thorns. "Where are you taking me? Where's Jenny?"

A canopy of trees closed over us and whoever was pulling me dropped my hands and stalked a few feet away. I tried to sit up, but my back screamed in pain, so I lay there catching my breath, trying to ready myself for whatever was next. The fighting was a distant series of thumps and cries somewhere out on the field.

A shadow fell over me and I cringed, attempting to get my hands over my face to protect myself. But all that came was a cool rush of water sweeping down over my forehead and across my eyes, wiping away the grime and the burning. I opened my mouth to let the water rush down my throat. Once I drank all I could, I opened my eyes again.

Sitting behind me, a canteen in his hand, was Jackson. He wasn't looking at me. His arm was wrapped in a bandage that was soaked through with blood. There was a clatter of gunfire way out in the field and then the yellow flash of an explosion that lit up his dirty face.

"You okay?" I asked.

Jackson nodded.

"Where's Jenny?"

"With Dad and the others. They're chasing the last of them out now."

I urged myself up to my elbows painfully. A low fog hung over everything, and a column of smoke billowed into the sky from the corner of the school's roof that was visible.

What had once been a baseball field was pitted and torn. A few animals stood here and there, lost. Some lay dead on the ground. The fighting had moved east into the woods. The jeep sat in the middle of the field.

"What happened to . . ."

And then I saw him. Just behind the jeep lay the man with the scar. He was facedown in the mud, his arms thrown over his head. The snow around him was stained a deep red.

I turned to Jackson. His rifle lay on the ground next to him. He stared across the field at the man, looking hundreds of miles away.

Jackson shuddered, then dropped his head into his hands, his chest heaving as he sobbed.

I dragged myself closer and put my hand on his shoulder. I wanted to say thank you. I wanted to say I was sorry. I wanted to say a lot of things, but right then it seemed best to say nothing at all, so I sat there with him until his breathing slowed, thinking how the end of the world had made so many of us unrecognizable, even to ourselves.

Soon, Jenny came running across the field and dropped down beside us. Her clothes were torn and dirty and there was a smear of blood on her forehead, but I couldn't tell if it was hers or someone else's.

"Are you —"

She lunged across me and grabbed Jackson into a hug. He seemed surprised at first, but then his hands tightened around her back, grasping her to him.

"Mom and Dad are all right," Jenny told him breathlessly after they parted. "After the man with the dreadlocks ran, the rest started to fold. There are a few stragglers, but we're pushing them back."

"How many of our people —"

"Don't worry about that now. We can —"

"How many?" I insisted.

Jenny looked at her brother, then at me. A tattoo of rifle shots crackled through the air, followed by the boom of explosions like a waning thunderstorm.

"Twenty," she said. "Maybe more."

"Will?"

Jenny turned to track a low rumble that rose in the east.

"He's dead."

It was like the deep toll of a bell, leaving us silent, kneeling together under that stand of trees.

248

We all turned as some kind of commotion broke out down the hill on the way to town. The few adults who remained were racing up the road past the school, shouting back and forth to one another.

"What's going on?"

Jenny helped me and Jackson up, and together we trotted across the field and down the road. We reached town just behind the gathering group of people. They were all hurrying into the park, but the three of us froze where we were.

Sam's house was a wall of fire. Three houses down the road from it were smoking, their windows lit a livid orange from inside. Trees were burning like torches and spreading the fire from house to house. The slavers may have gone but we had a new problem now.

Settler's Landing was in flames.

THIRTY-TWO

Jenny pulled at my hand and we all raced into the crowd that was gathering in the park between Sam's house and the Greens'. Others flooded in behind us, returning from the fight only to find their homes close to destruction.

Tuttle stood at the center of the crowd shouting instructions I couldn't make out over the roar of the fires and panicked voices. Buckets were passed out and people began filling them with snow and rushing off to the houses that hadn't caught yet. Another group took axes and ran to the stands of trees between houses, hoping to fell them and create firebreaks.

It seemed hopeless. The air was thick with smoke and the smell of burning. There was screaming as the crowd surged and pushed. Tuttle tried to keep people organized, but his voice was getting more and more drowned out.

Someone forced a bucket into my hand and I was pushed on by the crowd, Jenny beside me.

"We're going to the school," she shouted into my ear. To her right were Jackson and Derrick and some others.

"They sent the little ones there," Derrick said. "Thought they'd be safe there during the fight. We think some of them are still there now!"

I remembered the plume of smoke I'd seen rising from the school roof and broke into a run. There were about twenty of us, some with axes and some with buckets. We tore down the hill and across the parking lot to the school.

It was better off than many of the houses, but smoke was seeping out of the cracks of doorways and some of the windows were lit up with flames. Derrick led a group to a snowbank nearby where they began to fill their buckets.

"Where are they?" I asked Derrick. "The kids?"

"Toward the back, I think."

I dropped the bucket and once Jenny, Jackson, and I made it to the school's front doors, I slammed my shoulder into them. The doors gave with a screech and a wave of heat. It was worse inside than it looked. Jenny motioned some of Derrick's team into the doorway and they began tossing loads of snow onto the walls to try to keep the fire from growing. There was a hiss and gasps of steam as some of the flames were squelched.

"Stay low," Jenny called.

The three of us covered our mouths and noses and ducked down, crawling along the floor where the air was clearer. We checked all of the small classrooms we passed, but each was empty except for overturned desks and chairs. The smoke was already massing in my throat and burning my eyes. We had to find them fast.

The three of us finally reached the main classroom at the end of the hall and tumbled through the doors, coughing. The air inside was clearer, but still just as hot. I doubled over and sucked in a painful breath. At first the room seemed empty, but then I saw a leg poking out from behind Tuttle's big desk.

"There!"

We found ten of the little ones cowering behind the desk, all of them stained with soot and looking terrified. Jenny dropped to her knees by their side.

"It's going to be okay, guys," she said calmly. "Just come with us and we'll get you out of here."

The kids shied away at first, like scared animals, but she was finally able to pull them to their feet and lead them back to the doors. I paused by the desk as she went. Jenny turned back.

"Take them out of here," I shouted.

"What are you going to do?" Jenny asked.

I turned toward the far wall of wooden shelves. Each level was stacked with row after row of books. Science. Government. The arts. Everything.

"Are you crazy? We don't have time, this place is coming down!"

Over her shoulder I could just see Jackson leading the kids into the smoky hallway.

"Then go! Help Jackson with the kids!"

I knew Jenny would keep protesting, so I turned from her and ran for the bookshelf, weaving through the lines of desks and pulling books off as fast as I could, filling my arms with them. I reached for a copy of *To Kill a Mockingbird*, but Jenny got it first.

"One more stupid thing I have to do because of you," she said with a sooty smile as she yanked down a score of books.

Our arms were full when there was another moan from behind us. The far wall of the classroom was blackening and about to go. Soon the whole place would be on fire.

"Think we're out of time, pal. Let's get out of here!"

Just as we turned to the doors, a curtain of flame appeared, blocking our way. The wall alongside it had begun to smolder too. Smoke was now seeping into the room.

We both stood there, our arms weighed down with books, looking for some way out. The walls around us groaned. Tinder deep inside them crackled and popped. We were trapped.

"Well, Stephen? Any more bright ideas?"

I looked all around the room. I had nothing. The only doors out were blocked and the fire was only growing stronger and hotter. The books felt like lead in my arms. How could I have been so stupid? We were going to die for these? As the smoke grew thicker all I could think of was the whole town wiped away, little more than a smudge of ash in the woods. All they had done, all they had built, would be lost, forgotten.

"We have to just run for it," Jenny said. "Drop the books and jump through the fire. It's the only way."

It was insane. The fire had grown too big, feeding off the old wood. "Jenny, no. We can't —"

"Just do it!"

Jenny dropped the load in her arms, but then someone screamed my name from behind us. I turned to see Jackson leaning through the open window high up on the back wall.

"Come on," he shouted. "This way!"

I looked up at the window. It was narrow and set a good fifteen feet high. We'd never make it. I spun around the room, hunting for a solution, but all I saw were desks and chairs and . . . something snapped. I had it.

"The desks!" I shouted to Jenny. "Come on."

Jenny started grabbing desks out of their neat rows and dragging them over to the window. There, we stacked desk upon desk until we made a ladder leading up to the window. Jackson knelt at the window's edge and held out his hand. I pushed Jenny up first. When she reached the top she turned and held her hand out for me, but instead of starting the climb I reached back and gathered the stacks of books.

"Come on!" Jenny urged.

"Hey, remember how I promised Tuttle I'd bring about the new golden age?"

"Stephen!"

"I'm not moving until you take them!"

Jenny grimaced but held out her hands as I dug into the piles and handed up as many as I could. She passed them off to Jackson, then dove through the window and reached down for my hand.

"Okay, now you!"

The desks were shakier than I'd thought. The thin metal legs quivered as I climbed. I could feel the heat of the fire singeing my back, growing by the second. I made it up one desk, then two, but as I reached for the third, there was another collapse behind me and I felt the bottom desk shift and falter.

"Jump!"

My legs shook. There was a crash as the desks tumbled beneath me and then I was falling, my arms pinwheeling as the hands of gravity pulled me backward, down into the smoke. There was a strange moment as Jenny's face seemed to rush away from me and everything else slowed down. I felt weightless and weak and I knew there was nothing I could do. I would fall and the smoke would swallow me whole, but at least Jenny and Jackson and the kids would be safe. I closed my eyes, accepting it, but then I jerked to a stop.

I opened my eyes and there was Jenny leaning halfway out of the window, her hand locked onto my wrist.

"Gotcha," she said, and then other hands appeared, latching on to me and dragging me up toward the window. As I got closer, Jackson took hold of my sleeve. I grabbed on to them, pushed against the wall with my feet, and climbed, the fire licking at my heels.

When I made it to the window more hands reached out: Derrick's, Martin's, Carrie's, and others'. I felt the cold, fresh air rush into my lungs and I bent over, coughing, then fell onto my side. Behind my friends were the ring of little ones and a stack of books mostly untouched by the fire.

I had only a moment to rest before Jenny lifted me up and we all stumbled away from the building and out to the battlefield. Once we were far enough away, we stopped and turned back to the school.

Flames had consumed most of the west wall and were spreading around to the front. Soon the roof groaned and fell in. When it did, the fire surged, lighting up the gray sky and filling it with columns of smoke. It seemed as though only minutes passed before there was nothing but piles of burning wood and scattered bricks.

I remembered sitting inside that first day, desperate to flee, feeling alien and alone amid all those kids who seemed nothing like me. I looked around at the group of us now. Everyone was streaked with ash and peppered with burns and trails of blood, our clothes torn into ruins. Carrie was leaning into John Carter's shoulder while Derrick and Martin sat on a snowbank on either side of Wendy, helping her wash the ash out of her eyes. Jenny's hand fell into mine.

Standing there as the school burned, that group of us drew together into a tight little band that felt solid as iron. The houses could burn and the school could fall, but maybe together we'd survive.

"Look," someone said.

We turned toward the field just as a group of people emerged from the trees opposite us, maybe forty in all.

"Are they ours?" Derrick asked.

"All of our people went back to fight the fires," Jenny said.

The group moved slowly, weaving their way past the bodies and the wreckage of the jeep. They definitely weren't slavers, but as they got closer I made out the thin silhouettes of rifles in their hands.

Whoever they were, we still weren't done for the day.

THIRTY-THREE

Jenny, Jackson, and I moved the younger kids back into the woods with Derrick and the others.

"Should we go get Mom and Dad?" Jackson asked.

Jenny shook her head. "There's too much to do down there. Looks like it's just us."

The three of us made our way through the carnage, our boots sliding on the muddy and blood-soaked snow. As soon as the others saw us coming, they unslung their rifles and lifted them. The three of us slowed.

"Just stay calm," I whispered. "Don't make any sudden moves and keep your hands where they can see them."

It was a ragged group, a mix of old and young. They weren't clothed or fed as well as those in Settler's Landing, but we couldn't mistake that for weakness. Some looked just as scared as I imagined Jenny and Jackson and I did, but some also looked hard and ready for whatever might happen. They would use their weapons, no doubt about it.

This looked especially true of the one I took for their leader. He was a tall, rail-thin man with a scraggly black-and-white beard and a patch over one eye. He had a chrome revolver attached to his hip but was so calm he hadn't even drawn it yet, just moved across the field with his hand resting on the pistol's grip.

We kept our approach slow and easy until there was only about ten feet separating us. Everything around us stank of blood and fire. Jenny and Jackson and I stopped where we were; the man with the patch lifted one hand, and his people stopped too. Gun barrels dipped slightly but did not drop.

No one said anything for a moment as we took a measure of one another. I looked back over my shoulder. No one in sight. Everyone was still in town fighting the fires. A shot of nerves quaked through me. I'd have given anything for Marcus and the others to appear, but we were on our own.

I took a step forward. My mouth felt full of cotton. My hands shook.

"You're from Fort Leonard," I said.

The man nodded slowly. "Looks like you all had a bit of trouble here."

"Yes sir."

The man appraised the field around us and spit on the ground. "Slavers. We passed a bunch of them retreating on the way over. No coincidence they were here, I guess."

"No sir."

"You all hired them to take care of us."

I looked over at Jenny and Jackson. I could tell both of them were scared, but they were putting on stony faces. I felt their strength bleed into me, straightening my spine, making me even more sure of what I had to do.

"Yes sir," I said. "We did."

"Guess it didn't go as planned."

"Some of us thought the folks who hired them shouldn't be running things anymore," Jenny said from beside me. "When we told them and the slavers to take off, they went after us."

"You think I'm going to thank you for deciding *not* to turn all of me and mine into slaves?"

"No sir," Jenny said.

It went quiet again and I had to fight to keep still. This wasn't going right. *What were we thinking, coming up here?*

"Stephen, Jenny, Jackson — step away from there!"

The three of us whipped around to see Marcus and Sam and about ten others appear on the field behind us. Each of them had a gun trained on the people from Fort Leonard, who in turn raised theirs with a metallic clatter. The man with the patch had his gun out now and was pointing it right in Marcus's face. The chrome hammer was drawn all the way back.

"Stephen," Marcus said slowly, "take Jenny and Jackson and move out of the way."

I swallowed hard. "They're not here to fight," I said.

"Stephen."

I turned to the man with the patch. "Are you?"

The man tightened his grip on the revolver.

"They killed two friends of ours. We will fight if we need to, son."

"Tell them it was an accident," Jenny pleaded.

"Just get out of the way!"

I turned away from Marcus and back to Fort Leonard's leader.

"It was my fault," I said. "Okay? It was a dumb prank. I made everyone here think your people were attacking us and that's why they sent the group that shot your friends. So if you want to shoot someone, then shoot me, but we're telling you the truth. The ones who sent the people who killed your friends, the ones who hired the slavers, are not in charge anymore. I swear they're not."

The man with the patch considered this as we all held our breath.

"Look," I said, as steady as I could, "the people who came before us nearly destroyed the whole world, but that was yesterday. This is today, and today we've got a choice, right?"

The group from Fort Leonard gripped the stocks of their guns like they were trying to keep their heads above water. If the wind blew wrong, they'd fire. And if they did, Marcus and his people would too.

"Marcus," I said, "have everybody put their guns down."

"Them first," Marcus said. "We're not —"

"Just do it," Jackson commanded, turning around to face his father. "You've come this far. Just go one step further."

Marcus gripped the rifle to his shoulder, sweat cutting channels through the soot on his face.

Jenny took a step toward him. "Please, Dad," she said, and reached out to lay her palm over his rifle's sight.

Painfully slow, Marcus lowered the barrel of his rifle, keeping his eyes on the people from Fort Leonard the entire time, looking for any hint they were about to take advantage. When they didn't, he lowered his gun all the way and then motioned for Sam and the others to do the same.

Jenny turned to the man with the patch. "Now you."

The man looked back at his people and gave a slight nod. All around us gun barrels wilted and fell until we stood there, two divided fronts without a war to fight.

Marcus took a tentative step forward and held out his hand.

"Marcus Green," he said.

The man holstered his revolver, then lifted his own hand to take Marcus's.

"Stan Allison."

The two stood silently for a moment. Marcus looked back over his shoulder at the smoke rising above the trees.

"If you all could spare it," he said, "we could really use some help."

Stan nodded, then waved his people forward. Marcus and Sam and the others from Settler's Landing led the way, but soon the people from Fort Leonard had caught up. They all mixed together, one side indistinguishable from the other as they marched toward the fires.

We watched them go, then Jenny took my hand and Jackson's, and once we gathered up the little ones, we followed them back to town, all of us hoping there would be something left.

EPILOGUE

It was a Saturday, but there I was anyway, sitting at the edge of Tuttle's new desk, a copy of *Charlie and the Chocolate Factory* in my hand, facing a crowd of kids who were looking up at me expectantly.

"Who wants to read the next chapter?"

Everyone's hand shot up, everyone's except Claudia's, of course. She was a small girl with long blond hair and freckles. She almost never spoke in class and seemed paralyzed by shyness. Tuttle said that sometimes you have to force them to do what they need to do.

"Claud? How about you read some to us?"

The little girl shook her head vehemently. I left the edge of the desk and sat down on the dirt floor beside her, slipping the book into her lap and leaning in close to her ear.

"How about you just read it to me?"

Claudia's blue eyes shone as she sucked back the fear.

"It's okay," I said, nudging her shoulder with mine. "Go ahead."

Claudia lifted the book up off her lap. Her first words came out in a halting trickle. There were snickers and I threw out some hard glares to silence them. She stumbled over the next three words, then let the book fall into her lap.

"Claud . . ."

The book fell to the floor and she ran out — crying, I was sure. Great.

"Eddie, can you pick it up?"

Eddie, the oldest in the bunch, nodded, and I went off to find Claudia. I left the log cabin schoolhouse we had built on the site of the old school and walked out into the grassy field. It amazed me that, even months later, I could still smell the smoke.

I had been doing the little ones' Saturday classes for the last month or so while Tuttle healed from his broken arm and smoke inhalation. He did the weekday classes himself, gasping and wheezing, but he said the weekends were too much. I was hesitant at first, but once I got into it, I found that there was something strangely comforting about being in the new school and, despite what Jackson and the others thought, the little ones were actually kind of fun.

I found Claudia out under the big sycamore tree at the top of the hill, her chin in her hands. Across from her, a crew of twenty or so people raised the roof on one of what was going to be a few new cabins behind the school. Claudia was lying on her stomach, staring not at the construction but at what lay beside it.

Twenty-three wooden crosses.

They were set out in neat rows in the grass, most of them surrounded by bouquets of wildflowers, cards, or keepsakes of the person who lay beneath them. Twenty had died that night, along with three injured who followed soon after. Claudia's dad was there. Her brother too. Her mother had died years before.

"Hey," I said, landing nearby.

"Hey," Claudia said, pulling at the grass and tossing it aside.

"You okay?"

The little girl nodded, her pigtails swinging. "I don't know why we have to come here on Saturday too."

"Makes you one day smarter."

"My mom told me when she was little they had Saturdays and Sundays off."

"It's a brave new world."

"What does that mean?"

I picked a strand of grass and twirled it around my finger. "I don't know," I admitted. "Something Tuttle says."

"Are you gonna teach us when Mr. Tuttle dies?"

"Jeez, Claud."

"Well?"

"I'm pretty sure Mr. Tuttle will live forever. Like a vampire."

Claudia laughed, and I figured this was my chance. I reached around to my back pocket and threw my own copy of *Charlie and the Chocolate Factory* down in front of her. She leaned back from it like it was diseased.

"I think you'll like it," I said.

"But . . . why?" Claudia asked, looking out at the graves. "I mean, it's not even real."

I searched for something Tuttle might have said then, but found nothing. I looked from the graveyard up to the roof as it was carefully nailed into place by a work crew that was half Settler's Landing and half Fort Leonard, distinctions that were fading more and more by the day.

"I don't know," I said. "I guess . . . maybe it makes you realize that other worlds are possible."

Claudia considered that and, even if she didn't seem totally convinced, she opened the book to the first page and began to read. It came slowly at first, like the words were nettled things too large for her

264

mouth, but gradually they tripped out more and more easily. She read as the workers muscled up the roof and the wind blew the smells of sawdust across the grass.

Other worlds.

I hoped it was true. That the leap of faith we all took was a beginning and not just a blip, soon to be wiped away like so much had been wiped away before. Like Mom and Grandpa and Dad. As much as things had changed, I still heard their voices and felt their hands guiding me, though their grip seemed looser each day.

Another family had already stepped forward to take Claudia in, just like the Greens had done for me. In time I hoped she would feel at home and the world would move on for her, leaving everything else safely behind.

By the time Claudia reached the second chapter, I could tell she had forgotten I was there. The words moved from the page and out of her mouth, like a mill wheel dipping into the water, lifting it up and casting it down again in a glittering shower. After a while, the workers took a break, moving off into the shade of the trees and swatting the sawdust off themselves. Even when the rest of the kids broke free from the school and poured into the yard in a riot of shrieked laughter, Claudia didn't move.

Her words rose up into the air, up beyond the trees and into the sky.

I walked into town, past the scars from the fight with the slavers. The fires had spread quickly and destroyed more than half of the houses in town. The ones that couldn't be saved were torn down and replaced by what were little more than rough log cabins, neat and warm but small.

They were integrated with the houses that still stood, giving the neighborhood an odd mixed look of past and future. Though sometimes it was hard to tell which was which.

I headed out through the front gates and crossed the forest to the highway. Once I got to Dad's grave, I knelt down beside it and carefully cleaned away the week's accumulation of leaves and twigs and discarded acorns. The wood marker that sat at the head of the swell in the grass looked old and dry, the letters in his name already fading. I'd need to replace it soon. I used to come every day, but soon the demands of school and of a town that needed to be rebuilt kept me back.

Once I was done cleaning the grave I stayed there for a time and then leaned over the grass, pressing my hands deep into its waxy depths.

"Hey."

I jerked my hands back and turned around to find Jenny standing over me, in a T-shirt and jean jacket. The bill of Violet's old baseball cap was pulled down low over her eyes. Back near the tree line, her horse, Wind, was tied up and munching on grass. His sandy flanks glistened in the sun.

"You must have ridden him far."

"Farthest yet," Jenny said, pulling off her rawhide gloves and stuffing them in her belt before flopping on the ground next to me. "I swear I could see the Rockies."

"You could not."

"Well . . . it was something."

"Any trouble?"

"Oh yeah," she said. "Always."

"You didn't have to shoot anyone, did you?"

Jenny pulled off her cap and leaned on her elbows in the grass. The sunlight hit her face like a splash of cool water. "Not today, Steve-O. Not today."

Jenny closed her eyes and lay down next to me, her chest rising and falling gently, a glisten of sweat like a mist of diamonds on her forehead.

As soon as things calmed down, Jenny had set about tearing apart the Starbucks down the highway and hauling it in pieces back to town. It had taken her weeks, but when it was done, she'd been able to trade it all for Wind and a rifle of her own. From that day on, she'd throw herself onto her horse and disappear, always heading west, always pushing a little farther each time, stretching the boundaries of her world like a rubber band.

Every time she came back, we would stay up late and she would tell me stories of the things she had seen, so excited you would have thought she'd uncovered a field of gold when it was no more than a new tract of houses, or an abandoned car rusting in the woods.

"You should have seen it," Jenny murmured into the air above us. "Animals everywhere. *Everywhere*. I saw elk and mountain lions and beavers. I even found this whole herd of buffalo. Hundreds of them. Thousands maybe. I ran Wind right through them. It felt like flying."

Her eyes were distant, locked on the cloudless blue, glazed with joy at remembering.

"Is today the day?" I asked . . . and immediately regretted it. Jenny's eyebrows drew together, making a gloomy little wrinkle. She checked on Wind over her shoulder.

"I think so," she said. "Maybe. I don't know."

I turned on my side to face her. I had said it a hundred times before and I'd say it a hundred times again. "It's still dangerous out there."

"I know that."

"Dealing with the slavers wasn't magic. There are others — the army and a thousand other —"

"I know, Stephen."

Jenny turned onto her stomach. I plucked a blade of grass and settled it between my teeth. We had had this fight before. I knew when it was over.

"So, how's shaping the minds of the next generation going?"

"I'm just helping out."

"Then what?" Jenny asked. I could feel her staring at me. "Have you thought about it anymore?"

Jenny laid her head on my chest. Her breath went in and out, reminding me of a swing arcing up toward the sky and then falling again, over and over.

"Okay," she said, and after a long while she drifted off.

I lay there, the heat of Jenny's body beside me, the far-off smell of sawdust floating through the air.

Behind us, Wind shook his mane and stamped his foot into the grass, eager to be on his way.

"You ready, tough guy?"

When I opened my eyes, Jenny was adjusting Wind's saddle and harness. Her rifle sat in a handmade leather case along his side. She pulled it out, checked it over, and replaced it. Then she drew on her gloves and cap and mounted Wind in one smooth, liquid motion.

Jenny guided Wind over to me. I pulled myself up onto the back of the horse between her and her rolled-up gear. Jenny turned Wind around and we trotted off toward Settler's Landing, racing him when we reached the main road, his hooves making a machine-gun rattle against the asphalt.

We came to a halt out in front of the Greens' just as Jackson stepped down off a ladder that led up to the house's gutters. "Hey, cowgirl!"

Jenny slid down off Wind's back. "Hey, Jackie boy! What's happening?"

"I'm a gutter slave today," he said, wiping the muck of wet leaves from his hands before giving her a quick hug.

"Mom and Dad inside?"

"Yep." Jackson pulled the ladder off the house and carted it around back. After Jenny got Wind tied up in the park across the street, we went inside to the smell of baking bread.

"Hey, you two!" Violet called out from the kitchen as we came in.

Marcus was coming down the stairs and grabbed Jenny as soon as he saw her.

"Whew! Somebody smells like a horse."

"Yeah, I gave up on trying to make it go away."

"Well, sit down," Violet said. "We'll have lunch ready in a minute."

"So what's out there these days?" Marcus asked once we'd all sat down and passed plates of food from hand to hand.

"It's mostly quiet," Jenny said, handing me a bowl of potatoes. "I hear about more towns going up though. Little ones, but it won't be long until it gets crowded around here."

"Are you talking to people?" Violet asked, trying to sound casual but under the table she was probably twisting a napkin into tight knots.

"Only if they look friendly, Mom."

"And if they don't?"

"I shoot them on sight." Jenny grinned, but then pulled it back when Violet didn't so much as crack a smile. "If I see more than a couple people together, I run and hide. I've gotten pretty good at it. It's fine. I promise."

We ate lunch while Marcus quizzed Jenny about how many people she had seen, what kinds of animals and plants, any sign of a government. Then we lingered there, drinking glasses of sweet tea that Violet made from an herb she'd discovered growing wild in the woods. It was my favorite time, everyone sitting there with the afternoon sun streaming in from the porch window, yellow as a dandelion, voices mixed with the bright clinking of forks and knives on plates.

The months after the fight hadn't been easy, even for us. It had taken time to mesh back together again. But, like everything, it couldn't last. I knew that as soon as Jenny slid her plate out in front of her.

"I'm going to go past the mountains."

The silence was like a granite wall. Violet looked over at Marcus. He swallowed and set his fork down neatly next to his plate. "To do what?"

"To see what's there."

"It's not a vacation," Marcus said.

Jenny leaned across the table on her elbows. "Look, you need a scout —"

"Why does it have to be you?" Jackson asked. He was sitting across from Jenny, his fork still in his hand, his fingers white around its metal body. He was trying to cover it, but I could hear what was in his voice. Something welled up in Jenny's eyes, but she pulled it back.

"Because I want to," she said. "And because there's no one who will be better at it than me. We can't sit here with our heads down and hope everything's going to be okay. The slaver, the one with the dreadlocks, is still alive, and there are more like him. You need to know if there's danger out there, or people like us we can join forces with."

Marcus and Violet exchanged a look and entwined hands.

"You know it's true."

Violet pulled in a shaky breath. "You weren't meant for one place," she said. "I know that, but . . . we just got you back."

Jenny set her hand on top of Violet's, and along with Marcus they held on to it.

"I'll come back," Jenny said. "I'll always come back. This is my home."

There was more talk, but the sound of it dropped away for me. I dug my thumbnail into the soft wood at the edge of the table and wondered if it was true, if she really would come back or if there would be a time when that rubber band stretched as far as it could go and would snap, releasing her into the world, never to return. The thought of that was more than I could stand.

"I'm going too."

I didn't even know I'd said it out loud until the talk at the table went silent. When I looked up, everyone was staring at me.

"Stephen . . ." Violet began.

"I've thought about it a lot, and it's what I want to do."

Violet glanced at Jenny, who dropped her hand onto mine, squeezing my palm under the table.

"Well . . ." Violet said after a long pause. "I guess we better get both of you packed up, then."

Violet pushed away from the table to gather things for Jenny, and I went up to my room, Jenny's old one, and packed my things. Soon

Jackson drifted into the doorway. I folded a shirt and a sweater that Violet had knitted for me and placed them down in the bottom of my bag.

"You're really going?" Jackson asked.

I picked up the rest of my clothes and tucked them in the bag. "I'll be back," I said. "We'll be back."

"What books do you want to take with you?"

"Those are yours."

"Yeah. I know. It's just . . ."

I pulled my tent out of the closet and started folding it up. "What?"

Jackson leaned against the edge of the door and crossed his arms, his eyes on the messy carpet at my feet. "Nothing," he said, and disappeared back into his room.

I got the tent into its pack and lashed it to the outside of my backpack, then went back through the closet, looking for anything I'd missed. The bat and glove that Jackson and Derrick had given me as a present at the start of the season sat in the corner. I ran my fingertip down the face of the bat, dipping in and out of its dents. The well-seasoned leather of the glove smelled spicy and sharp. I left them there at the back of the closet.

I was about to close my pack when Jackson reappeared with a stack of paperbacks in his hand.

"Take them," Jackson said. "If you don't, you'll have to spend all your time talking to Jenny. I've read them all. That Piers Anthony is really good. And the Peter Straub."

"Thanks," I said, stuffing my bag with the books. "You guys have a good game today."

Jackson studied me with that penetrating look of his, the same one I had seen for the first time as he'd struggled along behind the wagon that brought me here. He'd changed so much since then, and I was sure he would change more. I wondered how long it would be until Jenny and I would be back this way and who he would be then. I wondered if I'd even recognize him. If I'd recognize any of them. Or if they'd recognize me.

Jackson ran his fingers down the door frame. "Yeah. We'll try," he said quietly. Then his shoes whispered down the carpeted hallway and he descended the stairs, leaving me there alone.

I took my bag's straps in my hands, but it felt like it was full of bricks. I couldn't move. I stood listening to the hollow silence of the house until Violet's voice drifted up the stairs.

"Stephen?"

"Coming," I called weakly, but it was a struggle to lift the pack up off the ground and place it on my shoulders, a struggle just to reach the door. I stopped in the doorway and ran my hand down the smooth wood alongside it. Marcus had covered over the spot where Jenny had caved in the wall months ago. All that was left now was a small depression in the plaster.

The house was empty by the time I got downstairs. I moved through the silent place like it was a museum, remembering the strangeness of it all when I'd first come there: the smell of the food, the sounds of people talking.

I made it through the kitchen and the front room to find everyone waiting outside, gathered around Wind and finishing their good-byes. I threw my pack down at the horse's feet and hugged Violet and Marcus. Sam appeared from his house and shook my hand. I didn't know what to say. Violet squeezed my arm, then hugged me tight again. Her eyes began to glitter with tears that she sniffed back. Marcus gave me a firm handshake before laying his arm over Violet's shoulder and walking her across the park along with Sam.

Jackson hugged Jenny again. "Be careful."

"I will."

"Come back, okay?"

"I will," Jenny said. "I promise."

Jackson didn't move away or take his hands from her shoulders.

"Yo! Jackson! Quinn! Time's wasting! Let's go!"

Derrick and Martin and Carrie were crossing the park, heading toward the road that led to school and the baseball field. Martin was throwing the ball up high into the air and racing to get under it. There was a snap as it fell into his glove.

Jackson's hand slipped off Jenny's arm and he glanced at me one last time.

"See ya," he said, then ran off and joined his friends, disappearing down the road with them and a wave of others who followed.

"You ready?"

Jenny was standing with Wind's reins in her gloved hand. I nodded and lifted my pack up off the ground to load it onto Wind with Jenny's equipment, her tent and rifle and provisions. I stopped when Jenny's hand fell on my arm, holding it down.

"What?"

Jenny looked at me evenly. "Go," she said.

"What are you talking — ?"

Jenny nodded over my shoulder. A stream of kids stormed out of their houses and surged down the road toward the school to join Jackson and the others. Claudia trailed the group, tossing *Charlie and the Chocolate Factory* into the air and catching it over and over. I couldn't lie — I felt a pull toward them. But then, behind them, came Sam and Tuttle and Mr. Allison, who still looked fearsome with his scraggly hair and eye patch.

"They're talking about building a church," I said, watching them go. "Forming a government. Mr. Allison even thinks he can get some of the electricity back up. It's just like you said. They're going to start the whole thing all over again. Take us right back where we started."

"Then maybe they need someone to keep an eye on them."

"Jenny —"

She pulled me close. "Look," she said. "Forget the future. Forget them. Forget me. You spent your whole life following somebody else. This is your world now. What do *you* want?"

My heart thumped. Jenny placed her palm in the center of my chest, covering it. Everything that had happened to us spun through my head.

After the storm and the deaths and the fires and the guns: What did I want? I closed my eyes, desperate to hear Grandpa's voice, or Dad's, or Mom's, but there was nothing.

There was just me.

"I want a home," I said.

I don't think I knew it was true until right then, but it was. Jenny leaned in and set her lips lightly on mine. The sweet, spicy smell of her mixed with the clean wood of the town surrounded me.

"This is your home," Jenny murmured into the small space between us. "You fought for it. Don't be afraid to take it."

My breath caught in my throat. I thought I could stay right there with her forever, but I knew that she had a path and so did I. After so long, mine had led me here and hers led . . . out there.

I kissed her and stepped away. Wind jerked and snorted as Jenny glided up onto his back, and the muscles in her arms stood out as she tried to hold him still. He was as ready as she was.

"Hold the fort down while I'm gone. Okay, Stephen? Don't let them do anything too stupid."

I nodded. A stone, thick as a fist, was resting in my throat.

Jenny twisted around in her saddle and took a last look around the town, the houses, the park, the road.

"My God," she breathed, then gave the reins a quick shake. Wind exploded out across the park and up the road. Jenny paused at the top of the hill and raised her hand high in the air and then there was a great joyous *whoop* and that was it.

She was gone, but she'd be back. I believed. I hoped.

I turned to face the park. The neighborhood had gone soundless and empty, like a ball suspended, weightless, in midair. I could have believed that there was no one else around me for miles until a voice snapped through it all.

"Yo! Stephen! Let's go! We've got work to do!"

Derrick had come back to the head of the road to school and was standing there with his arms out, a ball cap arranged messily on his head.

I started walking, slow at first, then faster, following what felt like a string fastened to my chest, yanking me forward.

Derrick broke into a run, so I was alone when I reached the field. An excited chatter overflowed the small wooden risers that had been built earlier that month. I let my hand slide across the wood of the stand as I passed. It had been planed smooth and smelled powdery and clean. Everyone was there: the Greens, Sam, Claudia with the book balanced on her knees, Tuttle with a stack of papers to grade.

I dropped my bag near the stands. Violet nudged Marcus and shot me a wink. Jackson was off in the outfield having a catch with Martin. They stopped when they saw me. Jackson was still for a moment, unsure, then he raised his arm and waved, a broad smile on his face. I waved back and trotted out onto the field.

"Let's do this, people!" Derrick shouted as we all converged on home plate, pushed forward by the cheers from the seats behind us. We formed into a tight knot together, Jackson on one side of me and Martin on the other. Carrie and Wendy and John Carter stood opposite. "Now, I need everybody to keep in mind that Stephen has decided to join us today, so we'll all have to up our game to compensate for how much he sucks."

Martin popped Derrick on the back of the head. "Jeez, Derrick, shut up already and let's get going!"

As the group broke up and everyone moved to their places, I looked past them, out toward where the forest shrouded the Henry house in green and shadow.

After the fight with the slavers, a trial was organized with a judgment of banishment seeming all but sure for the Henry family. Sure, that is, until Marcus stood up and, to everyone's amazement, spoke on their behalf. He said it would be too easy to send them out into the world like some gang of unruly children, only to become someone else's problem. It was Settler's Landing's responsibility, Marcus said, to make sure nothing like this ever happened again.

And so they were stripped of any power they had and were made to work and contribute like anyone else. So far it had worked, but like many of the wounded from that night, I wondered what would happen when Caleb finally recovered. Would Settler's Landing's mercy and Will's death really make him a different person, or would he still hear dark voices as I had once heard Grandpa's?

"Hey, man, you ready?"

Jackson was at the end of our team's line, holding a bat out to me.

"You're up," he said.

Maybe Jenny was right, I thought. Maybe they really did need someone to keep an eye on them.

But there would be time for that.

The bat seemed to vibrate in my hands as I took it and stepped up to the plate. John Carter checked the bases, then wound up and set the ball tumbling through the air. When it was time, I unfolded my arms in a smooth arc. There was a *crack* as the ball sailed out into the air over everyone's heads, streaking past the houses and across the wide emerald field. A roar went up from the stands and from my friends massed behind me.

The outfielders scrambled for the ball as I dropped the bat and ran, tagging first and second easily. As I strained past third, Jackson yelled for me to stop, but I just threw my arms into the air, laughed, and dove toward home.

ACKNOWLEDGMENTS

So many folks to thank. Up first, thanks to my wonderful family, Lara, Wyatt, and especially Mom and Dad, for insisting I read as a kid (even if it was just Batman comics) and for supporting me through all the twists and turns of my life. Also, to Mom and Dad for acting as, respectively, Official Medical Adviser and Official Agriculture and Animal Husbandry Adviser on this book. Thanks also to Patty, David, Bryan, and Amanda Sauer for all their support.

Thanks to my agent, the delightful Sara Crowe, who made me see I was thinking too small. To David Levithan, Cassandra Pelham, and everyone at Scholastic for their belief in the book, their enthusiasm, and most of all for making this thing so much better. For early encouragement and much needed criticism a big thank-you to Deborah Halverson, Ken Weitzman, and Ryan Palmer. For constant support, inspired silliness, and being a living link to my own days as a teen, thanks to Dave Denson, Ken Fortino, and Chris Ham. And to all the fine folks at the Society of Children's Book Writers & Illustrators who supported the writing of this book early on with a Work-in-Progress grant.

Lastly, thanks to Gretchen because, for me, it's turtles all the way down.

ABOUT THE AUTHOR

Jeff Hirsch graduated from the University of California, San Diego, with an MFA in Dramatic Writing, and *The Eleventh Plague* is his debut novel. He lives in Astoria, New York, with his wife. Visit him online at www.jeff-hirsch.com.